AN ACT OF
BETRAYAL

AN ACT OF BETRAYAL

America's Involvement In the Bay Of Pigs

R. J. Schuster

A Novel

Tri-Star Books

Library of Congress Catalogue Number: 96-90782

ISBN 1-889987-01-8

Copyright 1997, R. J. Schuster

Cover Designed by Patrick Foster

Printed in USA

Second Printing 1999

Tri-Star Books
***

This book is dedicated to the heroic members of the Cuban Brigade.

I would be remiss not to acknowledge the contributions of my wife and lifetime companion to this work. Her assistance with the research was invaluable, but more importantly, her encouragement when I became frustrated and her prodding when I became discouraged is what ultimately made this novel possible.

The Monroe Doctrine

The American continents are henceforth not to be considered as subjects for future colonization by any European powers. We owe it, therefore, to candor, and to amicable relations existing between the United States and those powers to declare that we should consider any attempt on their part to extend their system to any portion of this hemisphere as dangerous to our peace and security.

James Monroe in his annual message to Congress, December 2, 1823

CHAPTER 1

August, 1968

It was 4:55 a.m. Mike Canfield awoke from his sleep and reached over to turn off the alarm. Slipping quietly out of bed, he glanced over at his wife, Jen, sleeping by his side. The first light of the day, filtering through the window, played across her face. In the dim light, Mike could faintly make out the curves of her naked body underneath the sheets.

Little did he realize it at the time, but before this day was over a chain of events would be set into motion that would forever destroy his faith and his naive belief in the infallibility of the system.

Making his way to the bathroom, he closed the door and turned on the shower. As the warm water ran down over his body, he thought about Jen, and how she seemed to grow more beautiful with each passing year. Some wives had a difficult time handling Navy life with all the uncertainties and special demands it placed on a marriage. Jen, by contrast, seemed to thrive on the challenges provided by the constant moves and separations.

Stepping out of the shower, Mike dried off and wrapped a towel around his waist. When he returned to the bedroom to dress, Jen's eyes fluttered open. "Morning," she said sleepily, propping herself up on her elbow, allowing the sheet to slip down, revealing her smooth, firm breasts. By now, she was wide awake. As he dropped the towel to put on his shorts, her eyes moved downward, taking in his lean, hard body. "Not too bad for a forty-year-old man," she said teasingly.

"Stop it, Jen. Don't go saying things like that," Mike replied, reading her mind. "I have a mountain of work at the office, and a meeting with the admiral at 0900."

"I guess, I'll just have to wait then," she said, putting out her lower lip, pretending to pout.

Mike decided it was time to change the subject. Buttoning up his shirt, he asked, "How about helping me pick out a tie to go along with this suit?"

When he had received orders to Washington, he had looked forward to being able to wear civilian clothes to work, but now he was not so sure. Wearing a uniform at least eliminated the decision as to what to put on each day.

"How about the blue-and-white-striped one?" Jen suggested. "It goes well with the dark blue in your suit."

She started to get up. "Since I can't entice you into coming back to bed, would you like me to fix breakfast?"

"No, thanks," Mike replied. "You just stay there. I'll just grab some coffee and a piece of toast on the way out."

Downstairs in the kitchen, while waiting for the coffee to finish perking, he poured a glass of juice from the refrigerator and dropped a slice of bread in the toaster. Eating hurriedly, he returned upstairs to say goodbye to Jen. He knelt down beside the bed to give her a kiss. "Don't forget we have a date for tonight."

"How could I?" she replied coyly.

Stepping outside, Mike noticed that the sky had begun to brighten to the east. The sun was still well below the horizon, however. "Going to be another hot one," he said to himself as he turned the key in the ignition of his aging Fiat Spyder. After complaining for a few seconds the engine sputtered to life and soon was purring smoothly.

"I wonder how much longer this pile of junk is going to last?" he muttered under his breath as he shifted into reverse. As sports cars go, it wasn't much, but he still hated to part with it.

Before backing out of the driveway he reached up, unlatched the convertible top, and eased it back into its compartment behind what passed for a rear seat. Driving through the Maryland suburb, the cool morning air felt good on his face. Most of the houses were still dark, their occupants still fast asleep. Turning onto Indian Head Highway, he headed north toward the Beltway. He was well ahead of the early-morning rush hour, and traffic was still relatively light. Although he liked to complain, in reality he didn't mind the early-morning drive to the Pentagon. It gave him time to think and plan his day. This morning, however, his thoughts were on his marriage and Navy career.

Except for three tours of shore duty, including one year at Monterey, California, attending General Line School, he had spent his entire career aboard destroyers, culminating in his being given command of the destroyer USS *William R. Rush (DD-714)*. Last year, while on the *Rush*, he had been singled out as one of the Navy's rising young stars and deep-selected for captain. Shortly thereafter, he had received orders to his current job as Director of Foreign Ship Training in OPNAV [Naval Operations]. Reflecting back, he realized that without Jen's help and support none of it would have been possible.

They had met while he was on summer leave between his junior and senior years at the Naval Academy. When he returned to Annapolis, they began to correspond with each other. It wasn't long before he knew she was the person he wanted to marry. He was also smart enough to realize that a woman like Jen came along but once in a lifetime.

When she visited Annapolis during spring break, he took her out one evening, to have dinner at the Harbor House. During dessert he proposed to her, and she accepted. Upon graduation they were married, and they spent their honeymoon driving across the country on the way to his first duty station. During their first year of their marriage his ship operated in and out of San Diego, affording them an opportunity to be together and become familiar with each other's needs and wants.

In June 1950 the Korean War broke out, and in July the destroyer division to which Mike was assigned was ordered to the Western Pacific [WESTPAC]. Saying goodbye to Jen at the pier was one of the hardest things he had ever had to do. His four years at the Naval Academy had done little to prepare him for this aspect of Navy life. Somehow they had gotten through it, as well as with the many separations that followed. As the years progressed, Jen steadily became more independent and self-reliant, and in many ways she handled the long separations better than he.

By now, Mike had arrived at the South Parking Lot of the Pentagon. Stopping at the guard house, he reached into his pocket for his ID card and showed it to the civilian guard on duty, a retired Navy chief boatswain's mate. Glancing at it perfunctorily, he said, "Good morning, Captain. You're in early as usual."

"I know," Mike replied. "The only good thing is that I miss the rush-hour traffic." While putting away his ID card, he asked, "How are things going with the protesters, Chief?" He was referring to the group of young people who gathered outside the building daily, demonstrating, demanding an end to the war.

"For chrissakes, Captain, it seems like more of them are showing up every day," the guard replied. "The only good thing is that they don't arrive until afternoon, timing it to make sure they get a big play on the evening news."

"That figures," Mike said, shaking his head. He remembered from an earlier conversation that the guard had a son serving in Vietnam. "By the way, Chief, when's that youngster of yours up for rotation?"

"He's already back. Arrived at Travis last week," the chief replied. "Would you believe, before they would allow him off the base he had to change out of his uniform into civilian clothes so he wouldn't be harassed by a bunch of those goddamn hippies camped outside the gate?" He paused for a moment. "What the hell kinda country have we become, Captain, when you don't dare wear your uniform in public?"

"I wish I had an answer, Chief," Mike replied, easing the car into gear. "All we can hope for is that it's over with soon, but I'm glad he's home safe."

"Thanks, Captain. So am I," the guard replied.

As he drove through the parking lot, Mike thought over his conversation with the security guard. Having gone through two tours in Southeast Asia, he was keenly aware of the mess in which we had become involved, and wanted it to end as much as anyone else.

The thing that was most troubling to him was the hostility the general public directed at those in uniform. Up until the present, the military had always enjoyed a special relationship with the American people. Now, after witnessing the brutal scenes from the war played out on the evening news, they had become increasingly frustrated. Needing someone to blame, they found the military the most convenient target on which to vent their rage. What they failed to take into account was that they, the military, were the real victims of the war. *They* were the ones who were coming home in the body bags.

He hoped that the politicians had learned their lesson about the limitations of military force, particularly when the objectives were ill-defined and our national interests were not at stake. He also knew it would be a long uphill struggle to rebuild morale once this was all over.

By now he had arrived at his assigned parking space, a cherished perk reserved only for officers in the grade of 06 and above. Parking the car, he raised the rag top and refastened the latch.

It was now 0620. Entering through the south entrance, he climbed the stairs to the third floor. At this time of the morning the passageways were nearly deserted. Proceeding a short distance around the B ring, he took an inter-connecting passage to the C ring, where his office was located. Distinguishing it from the myriad other doorways was a sign on the bulkhead, reading "Captain Michael Canfield USN, Division of Foreign Ship Training." Unlocking the door, he stepped inside and turned on the light. His office consisted of a three-room suite, a reception area and two cubicles. One was his office and the other was that of his assistant, Commander Jack (Buzz) Laroque.

Only slightly larger than his stateroom on the *Rush,* the offices were filled with the same style of Spartan gray steel furniture he had on board ship. Obviously, the Navy did not want its officers becoming too comfortable with being ashore.

In deference to his rank, however, his office was equipped with an oversized wooden desk and a large leather swivel chair. A gray fake-leather sofa, end stand, and coffee table completed the standard furnishings, to which Mike had added some pictures and a few personal items.

Hanging up his coat, he settled in the chair behind his desk, and soon became lost in the various directives and requests filling his action basket.

At 0745 the quiet was broken by voices in the outside passageway. Shortly the door opened, and Buzz entered. Knocking on the open door to Mike's office, he peered in. His eyes were bloodshot. "Morning, Boss. Mind if I come in? I sure could use a cup of coffee!" Before Mike had a chance to reply, Buzz was stretched out on the sofa, looking like he was about to get sick.

"For God's sake, Buzz! What the hell happened?" Mike asked. "You look like hell."

"It's the perils of being a bachelor in Washington," Laroque replied, his eyes shut.

Tall and slender, Buzz had a boyishly handsome face, the kind most women found irresistible. An A6 pilot, he had just returned from a tour of duty on a carrier stationed off Vietnam. While there, on a mission over the north, his plane had taken a hit from a surface-to-air missile, but luckily neither he nor his bombardier were seriously injured. Limping back to the coast, they ditched offshore, where they were rescued a short time later by a helicopter from a destroyer on station nearby.

A few moments later, the door opened again. It was Peggy Holle, their joint secretary and receptionist. From Lincoln, Nebraska, with strawberry blonde hair and freckles, she had the fresh, scrubbed look one associated with a young woman from the Midwest. She had come to Washington two years earlier, recruited directly out of high school by the General Services Administration to fill the insatiable appetite of the Washington bureaucracy for secretaries and clerks.

"Good morning, Captain. Good morning, Commander," she said, cheerfully. Seeing Buzz lying down on the couch, she added, "Good gosh, Commander! What happened to you? You look absolutely awful."

"Commander Laroque is trying to make up for all the time he was at sea, Peggy," Mike interjected. "Right now I think he could use a cup of coffee."

"I'd say so," she said disapprovingly, turning to leave. A few moments later she returned with two cups of coffee in hand. By now, Buzz was halfway sitting up.

"You still dating that E-5 yeoman up at BUPERS?" he asked, looking up at Peggy.

"Yes, I am," she replied, "but it's nothing serious. Besides, he's about due for rotation."

"If you decide to look around, I'd be glad to make myself available," Laroque said, partly in jest.

Not appreciating his last remarks, she set his cup down roughly on the coffee table, spilling some of the contents in the saucer. Spinning on her heels, she turned to leave. Pausing at the door, she looked back over her shoulder. "Commander Laroque, you should be ashamed of yourself." She then added, "During orientation they warned us about dating aviators and—especially older men."

"That really hurts," Laroque replied, feigning a pained expression on his face. He was now sitting upright.

"Okay, Buzz. Now that you have been cut down to size, could you get me an update on the status of the ships in training?" Mike asked. "I have a staff meeting with the admiral at 0900."

"Right away, boss," Laroque replied, slowly dragging himself up off the sofa.

In the beginning, Mike had had a difficult time getting used to Buzz's aviator persona. For the most part, he chose to dismiss it as part of the psyche of all aviators, and as time went on they had come to develop a fairly close working relationship.

With the Navy bringing a whole new generation of ships on line, a surplus of ships was left over dating from World War II. In an effort to retrieve some of the costs, the General Services Administration [GSA] had decided to offer them up for sale to allied governments, rather than sell them for scrap or place them into the mothball fleet.

Before turning the ships over to the foreign governments, they were placed in the shipyard and put into peak operating condition. Additionally, the Navy assumed responsibility for training the foreign crews. This is where Mike came in. It was his job to shepherd the ships and crews through the turnover process.

Along with strengthening the navies of our allies, it afforded the United States with the opportunity to evaluate the foreign officers assigned to the ships, with the realization that many of them could become future leaders, either military or political, in their respective countries. At the completion of the turnover all personnel involved in the process were extensively debriefed, and the information obtained forwarded to the various intelligence agencies to be filed away for future reference.

Usually things went along without a hitch, but at times the harsh disciplinary methods common to foreign navies was a problem with which Mike had to deal. Although he tried to refrain from becoming involved in the internal affairs of the ships in training, he occasionally found it necessary to counsel the offending skippers when such behavior tended to get out of hand. Even though they appeared out-wardly sympathetic to his views, Mike was enough of a realist to know that the changes in the behavior of the offending skippers was probably only temporary. As soon as they left the States they would undoubtedly revert to their old ways.

Nothing of importance came up during the staff meeting with the admiral. When he returned to his office at about 1000, Peggy handed him his phone messages, calling his attention to one in particular.

"Captain Cayhill called about 15 minutes ago," she said. "He wants you to call him back right away. He said it was extremely urgent."

Mike recognized Captain Cayhill to be the chief of staff to Admiral Larkin, Commander Naval Base, Norfolk, Virginia. Asking Peggy to return the call, he went into his office.

A few moments later Peggy buzzed him on the intercom.

"Captain Cayhill's on the line," she said.

Mike picked up the phone. "Captain Cayhill, this is Mike Canfield returning your call."

Dispensing with any pleasantries, Cayhill got right to the point. "Captain Canfield!" he began. "I'm calling about that Turkish destroyer of yours tied up at the Dessub [destroyer/submarine] piers." From the way he said it, Mike had a feeling that this was not going to be pleasant.

"Yes sir. What about her?" he asked.

"Early this morning I had a phone call from the port director. While he was making his rounds of the piers, he noticed something strange going on aboard the *Selrik*. The crew was building a large wooden scaffolding on the fantail. He thought it looked suspiciously like a gallows.

"After he hung up, I informed the admiral what the port direc-tor had said. He directed me to get hold of the *Selrik's* skipper and have him report to his office immediately. With that, I phoned Commander

9

Kudasis and told him that Admiral Larkin wanted to see him straight away.

"A little while later, this little shithead showed up in my office and I escorted him on in to see the admiral. After exchanging a few niceties, the admiral asked him about the construction project on board his ship."

Cayhill paused briefly to catch his breath. "Kudasis then went on to tell the admiral he was building a gallows, and that he intended to hang one of his crew members tomorrow morning, after quarters. He even had the balls to invite the admiral to come down and witness the hanging! The admiral let him know in no uncertain terms that there wasn't going to be any hanging while the *Selrik* was tied up alongside his pier. At that, this little piss-ant had the gall to remind the admiral that his ship was Turkish real estate, that he, the admiral, had no juris-diction, and further, he would do as he damn well pleased on board his ship. With that, the admiral went totally ballistic and ran him out of his office, using a few choice parting words I won't bother to reiterate here."

By now, Cayhill had worked up a full head of steam. "Captain," he continued, "You had better get hold of this goddamn idiot and read him his rights! Holy shit! Could you imagine what would happen if the press got hold of this?" Contemplating the thought, his voice trailed off. Mike took advantage of the lull in the conversation to try and calm the situation.

"Look, Captain. Give me a chance to see what I can do. I'll be back in touch."

"Okay, but don't be too long about it. Admiral Larkin is really pissed." With that, Cayhill hung up the phone.

"Peggy," Mike called out. "Get Commander Kudasis on the phone."

Waiting for the call to go through, Mike recalled an incident that had occurred during a port visit to Izmir, Turkey. On the day of their arrival, two men had been hanged in the town square, and as was the custom, the bodies were allowed to hang from the gallows until sunset, whne they were cut down.

Shaking his head, he tried to put the grisly scene out of his mind. He thought back to the one and only time that he had met Kudasis. It was when he and Jen had attended the commissioning ceremony of the *Selrik* at the Philadelphia Navy Yard. He remembered how, on the drive back to Washington, Jen had mentioned her feelings of dislike for the skipper. What made the incident stick in his mind was that it was so unlike her to express such feelings.

Reports of the shipriders assigned to the *Selrik* didn't mention anything out of the ordinary other than that the skipper was something of a sundowner. In itself this was not unusual, as many foreign skippers tended to be severe disciplinarians.

The sound of the buzzer on his intercom interrupted his train of thought. It was Peggy saying that she had Commander Kudasis on the phone.

Mike picked up the receiver. Kudasis' voice came on the line. Speaking in a thick Middle Eastern accent, he said, "Ah, good morning, Captain Canfield, I have been expecting your call. I presume Captain Cayhill has told you of my conversation with your Admiral Larkin."

Mike got right to the point. "Yes, I have spoken with Captain Cayhill. He informed me of your plans to hang a member of your crew in the morning."

"This is true, Captain," Kudasis replied. "You see, this man has been convicted of a serious crime and has been sentenced by a court-martial to be executed by hanging. Unlike in your country, we in Turkey believe that punishment should be swift, and in public, in order to serve as a deterrent to others."

"It is not my position to comment on your country's laws," Mike replied calmly. "However, I want to make it perfectly clear to you that there will be no one hanged while you are in a United States port. I needn't remind you that you are a guest of the United States government."

"You do not understand, Captain Canfield," Kudasis replied. "My ship is sovereign territory, and therefore subject only to the laws of my country."

"That may be so in international waters, but right now you are in a United States port," Mike reiterated firmly.

"I am sorry, Captain, but I do not take orders from you or from your Admiral Larkin," Kudasis angrily retorted.

Mike came to the conclusion that it was now time to play a little hardball. He remembered an old Navy saying. "If you grab them by the balls, their hearts and minds will follow." He decided to go for the balls. "If this is your position, Captain, then I must warn you that as soon as I get off the phone I intend to call your ambassador here in Washington and advise him of your plans and also of the possible political consequences of your proposed action. In the unlikely event that your ambassador is unwilling to listen to reason and order a stop to this execution, then I intend to recommend to the Chief of Naval Operations that your ship be declared persona non grata and that it be ordered out of port." Mike knew he was getting way out on a limb, but he hoped his bluff would work.

"Before you reply, I would strongly suggest that you carefully think it over. Are you sure your government will back you up, or will it, as I think most likely, sacrifice you to overriding political considerations?"

There was a moment of silence on the other end of the phone while Kudasis considered his options. Concluding that his government would not likely back him up, his voice took on a more conciliatory tone.

"Captain Canfield, I do not wish to destroy our otherwise good relations, nor do I wish to be viewed as being inhospitable, so I will honor your request. I will agree to postpone the execution until we are out to sea."

Mike breathed a sigh of relief. He realized that a postponement of the hanging was probably the most he could hope for under the circumstances.

"I also think it would be wise for you to write a letter of apology to Admiral Larkin before he decides to make an issue of this incident. I would not want to see you get into any trouble," Mike added, sarcastically. Thoroughly subdued by now, Kudasis readily agreed.

Pressing on, Mike said, "I can expect to see the scaffolding coming down this afternoon, then?"

"You have my word," Kudasis replied.

After he hung up the phone with Kudasis, Mike put in a call to Captain Cayhill.

"Mike Canfield here."

"How did you make out with that shithead?" Cayhill asked.

"He has agreed to postpone the execution until they are out to sea," Mike quietly replied. "The scaffolding will be dismantled this afternoon, and Admiral Larkin should be receiving a letter of apology from Commander Kudasis shortly."

Cayhill was taken aback. He had not expected the Turkish skipper to be so easily dissuaded.

"Mind if I ask how you went about convincing him?" he asked.

"I just reminded him of the possible consequences of his action," Mike replied, deciding not to go into any of the details of his conversation with the Turkish skipper. "I'll give you a call later on this afternoon to make sure he keeps his word, although I don't anticipate any problem."

"We'll keep our eye on him. Don't worry," Cayhill replied. "By the way, Mike, good work," he added.

From inside his office, Buzz overheard part of the phone conversations going back and forth. He was curious as to what was happening. Waiting for a couple of minutes to make sure Mike was off the phone, he knocked on his door.

"Ready for some lunch, Captain?" he asked.

13

"Sounds good, Buzz," Mike replied, getting up out of his chair.

Over lunch in the cafeteria, Mike filled Buzz in on the morning's events. After he had finished, Buzz asked, "Do you really think you could have gotten him thrown out of port?"

"I guess we'll never know the answer to that, but taking risks is what we get paid for, isn't it?" Mike replied.

Later, back in his office, Mike went through the incoming mail. One large brown envelope, from the Bureau of Naval Personnel, marked "Personal," piqued his attention. Opening it, he found a set of orders inside that read:

> *From: Chief of Naval Personnel*
> *To: Captain Michael R. Canfield 249 20 8924/1100*
> *Subject: Temporary Additional Duty*
> *You will report at 0900 on 10 September 1968 to the president of line commander selection board to convene at the Navy Department, Arlington Annex for temporary additional duty as a member of the board.*
>
> > *Robert M. Donnelly*
> > *Vice Admiral, USN*
> > *Chief of Naval Personnel*

Mike took a few moments to sit back and reflect on his upcoming assignment. Like most officers in the Navy, he had always wanted to be on a promotion board, but he knew that the selection process was quite rigorous. The Navy Department carefully reviewed the records of each potential member in order to ensure that the membership of the board reflected the same characteristics it desired in its future officers. By doing so, it hoped that the board members would, in turn, seek out these same characteristics in the officers up for consideration.

At 1600 Mike phoned Captain Cayhill. "Captain, this is Mike Canfield. Just called to find out what's happening down there."

14

His voice sounding relieved, Cayhill replied, "Mike, I don't know what you told him, but whatever the hell it was, it sure as shit worked. The gallows are down, and Kudasis had a formal letter of apology hand-delivered to the admiral. By the way before I forget, Admiral Larkin wanted me to pass along an 'attaboy' to you for a job well done."

"Tell the admiral thanks. I am glad it worked out," Mike replied.

Changing the subject, Cayhill asked, "What do you think the odds are that he'll hang the poor bastard after they get under way?"

"I'm guessing that he'll probably go through with it."

"Yeah, that's my feeling too," Cayhill replied.

Later that afternoon Mike and Buzz were going over the schedules for the other ships in the pipeline when Peggy poked her head in the door to say goodnight.

A short time later Mike looked down at his watch. "Sorry, Buzz, I've gotta run. Promised Jen I'd be home early tonight."

"Sounds like a heavy date to me."

"I'm just an old married man, remember."

"Sure, boss. I hear ya."

CHAPTER 2

Jen Canfield arrived home from work at about 4:20 p.m. Her day had been filled with staff and faculty meetings, in preparation for the beginning of classes next week. Beginning a new job at the college this year did not make life any easier, but she was looking forward to the upcoming year and to the challenge her new position promised.

While beginning preparations for dinner, she reminisced on the time she first met Mike. She had gone to a dance with a girlfriend when, early in the evening, she noticed a good-looking young man casting admiring glances in her direction. Thinking back on it, she had to admit that she was attracted to him as well. A short time later, he had sauntered over and asked her for a dance.

While in his arms, something stirred inside her she had never felt before. He must have felt the same way, since he asked to drive her home. Pressing his body against hers while he kissed her goodnight, he asked if he could see her again the next day. Trying not to appear too enthusiastic, she agreed. During the next week they spent nearly every waking minute together, and by its end she suspected she was falling in love. Unfortunately, she was returning to college at Ohio Wesleyan, and he was heading back to the Naval Academy to begin his senior year.

Mike invited her to join him in Annapolis for Thanksgiving. They were together again at Christmas. At Easter, Mike proposed, and in June they were married in the Navy Chapel at the Academy. Loading up their few belongings in Mike's beat-up 1946 Chevy, they set out for California.

Upon their arrival in San Diego, they found a three-room furnished apartment in Mission Bay, moved in, and commenced their married life together. In March, she found out she was pregnant. The Korean War broke out in June, and Mike's ship received orders for Westpac [Western Pacific]. She was not prepared for the overwhelming feeling of sadness she felt as she watched the ship back away from the pier, nor for the terrible loneliness she felt upon returning to their now-silent apartment, but at least she had a part of Mike with her, growing inside her.

To help relieve the loneliness, the captain's wife, Bea Jameson, who had lived through many separations during World War II, organized weekly coffees and luncheons for the wardroom wives to get together. Not only did this get Jen out of the apartment, but it also gave her something to look forward to each week.

Candi was born in the Balboa Naval Hospital a short time before Mike's return in December. During the next few years the baby kept Jen busy and her life was full, balancing the duties of being a wife and mother, as well as surrogate father, when Mike was away. Although the long separations were particularly difficult to deal with, she took comfort in knowing that Mike was doing what he loved to do.

With time on her hands after Candi started school, she started thinking about returning to college. Not getting a degree had always been a source of disappointment to her. She talked it over with Mike, who encouraged her to go back to school, realizing that her life at home was probably very boring while he was away at sea.

That fall she enrolled in a community college, taking a few classes. Transferring from school to school each time Mike received orders to a new duty station, she persevered, and finally received her B.S. degree, and later her master's in zoology from Pembroke while they were stationed in Newport, Rhode Island, where Mike was serving as the exec of a destroyer.

Shortly afterward, she began teaching, and came to realize that she related well with young people. She loved teaching, and was secure in the knowledge that she was very good at it.

Completing the preliminary preparations for dinner, Jen went upstairs to the bedroom to shower and dress before Mike arrived home.

"I hope he's is not late tonight," she mused to herself as she took off her clothes.

Standing under the shower, the hot stream of water bouncing off her back and shoulders, she could feel the tensions of the day slowly erode away.

Turning off the water, she toweled off and returned to the bedroom to dress. Stopping in front of the full-length mirror, she paused to examine her body. "I could stand to lose a few pounds," she said to herself, "But then I guess I still don't look too bad for a thirty-eight-year-old woman," she concluded.

From the beginning of their marriage, she and Mike had shared an ardent relationship.

In front of the closet, she debated what to wear. Musing to herself, she said, "I think I'll wear the white sun dress. It will probably be the last time I'll be able to wear it this year." In addition to revealing the curves of her body and emphasizing her tan, it was also one of Mike's favorites. At the last minute, she decided to omit putting on a bra and panties. She liked to surprise Mike, and she knew this would turn him on as soon as he discovered she wasn't wearing anything under her dress.

As she was putting the finishing touches on her makeup, she heard the distinctive sound of the Fiat pulling into the driveway. A short time later, the back door opened and she heard Mike call out for her.

"I'm up in the bedroom, getting dressed," she answered.

Mike ran up the stairs to the bedroom. At the sight of her in the white dress, he temporarily forgot what he was about to say. "Wow, you look great!" he exclaimed. Putting his arms around her, he kissed her hard on the lips. Mumbling in her ear, he asked, "How was your day?"

"Exhausting," she replied.

"I hope not too exhausting," Mike responded.

Jen ignored his last remark. Feeling him grow hard against her, she pulled away. "You're just going to have to wait until after dinner," she said. It was time to change the subject.

"How did your day go?" she asked.

"Not bad," he replied. "Among other things, I saved a sailor from being hanged tomorrow."

"You're not serious?"

"Yeah, it's true," Mike said, going on to recount what had transpired earlier in the day between him and the skipper of the *Selrik.*

"What do you think will happen after they get under way?" she asked.

"Most likely they will go through with it," Mike replied. "Unfortunately, there's not much we can do."

Changing the subject, he continued, "On a more pleasant note, I do have some good news. I received a set of orders to serve on the commander selection board convening next month."

"That's great, Mike," Jen replied. "You've always said you wanted to be on a board."

"I admit I'm looking forward to it, but I'm afraid you won't be seeing much of me for the next few weeks, as I have a feeling that I'm going to be putting in some pretty long hours."

While he stripped off his clothes, Jen lay across the bed watching him.

"Stop staring at me like that. You're making me nervous," he said.

"I was just inspecting the merchandise, that's all," she teased.

19

"You keep this up and we won't get dinner," Mike replied, pulling up his trousers.

Sitting down to dinner, with candlelight and wine, Mike could feel the pressures of the day slowly fade away into the background. After they had finished with their coffee, he turned down the lights in the living room and put a record on the turntable. While slowly dancing to the mellow saxophone strains of John Coltrane in the background, he unzipped the back of her dress and slipped the straps down over her shoulders, allowing it to fall slowly to the floor. It was then he noticed she wasn't wearing anything under her dress. In the soft light his eyes wandered over her body.

"God, you're beautiful!" he exclaimed.

"I thought you might enjoy something different," Jen said, laughing at his totally predictable reaction. Upstairs in the bedroom, she lay down on the bed while he hastily undressed. Soon they became lost in the intensity of the moment. After it was over, Mike rolled over on his back.

Jen nestled up against his shoulder. "You're quite a lover, you know."

"You're not so bad yourself," Mike replied.

With their bodies pressed tightly against each other, they fell sound asleep. Jen awakened after midnight. Going downstairs, she gathered up her clothes, strewn around the living-room floor, and turned off the lights before returning to bed.

Mike was still fast asleep.

CHAPTER 3

September 10, 1968, Arlington, Va.

Dressed in his service dress blue uniform, Mike continued up Columbia Pike instead of turning into the Pentagon. Arriving at the Arlington Annex, he turned into the parking lot.

A gigantic four-story building, the Annex, as it was commonly called, rivaled the Pentagon in size. With eight perpendicular wings, it was built during World War II to house the Bureau of Naval Personnel [Bupers]. It stood on a hill overlooking the Pentagon. The front of the building faced Arlington National Cemetery across the street to the north. With the Vietnam War at its peak, the sound of the rifle volleys echoing from across the road was an all-too-familiar sound to those who worked there.

Pulling up to the guard house, Mike brought his car to a stop, reached for his orders, and showed them to the civilian guard on duty. Checking his name off a list, the guard gave him a parking permit and directed him to a section reserved for selection board members, just to the east of the gate. Parking his car, Mike walked across the lot to the ground floor of the seventh wing, where the selection board area was located. In the Selection Board Services Office, he presented his orders to the secretary. Taking them from him, she escorted him across the passage to the room assigned to the Commander Board and introduced him to Commander Ed Anderson, the recorder for the board.

As Mike approached, Anderson held out his hand. "Good morning, Captain," he said. "Welcome aboard. We'll be getting started as soon as the admiral arrives. In the meantime, please help yourself to a cup of coffee."

Taking a paper cup, Mike filled it with coffee from the large urn sitting on a table by the door. Adding a teaspoon of creamer, he stirred it into the coffee while he looked around the room. Lined up around its outside perimeter were a series of gray metal desks. Alongside each desk was a gray wooden cart with two V-shaped troughs, one above the other.

Several other captains were already present in the room, none of whom Mike recognized. From the insignias pinned over their breast pockets, he could tell that all three branches of the unrestricted line— surface, aviation, and submarines— were represented. With coffee cup in hand, he walked over, introduced himself, and joined in the conversation.

At 0750 Vice Admiral Wilkerson arrived. With a neatly trimmed red beard, craggy eyebrows, and piercing gray eyes, he cut an imposing figure. Over his left breast pocket was a set of gold dolphins. Over the right one he wore a single light blue ribbon with five white stars.

There was something about his carriage and demeanor that gave one the impression that he was more used to giving rather than taking orders.

Well known throughout the Navy for his exploits during World War II, "Rusty" Wilkerson was renowned for daringly piloting a submarine into Tokyo Bay, sinking a Japanese cruiser tied up alongside a pier in Yokosuka. For this action he had been awarded the Congressional Medal of Honor.

Pausing briefly at the door to speak to Anderson, the admiral made his way around the room, greeting each member of the board in turn. When his turn came, Mike introduced himself.

"So you're Captain Canfield," Wilkerson said. "I've heard a good deal about you recently."

Mike was taken by surprise. "I hope it wasn't all bad."

"On the contrary," the admiral replied. "I had lunch with Admiral Larkin the other day, and he told me about the situation on board the *Selrik*. He was very impressed with the way you handled the incident."

"It took only a little friendly persuasion," Mike replied.

Wilkerson cracked a slight smile before moving on.

At 0830 the board members made their way to an auditorium where they were to receive some preliminary briefings before commencing their work.

Once they were gathered, Rear Admiral Hollings, the vice chief of naval personnel, greeted them. In his remarks he sought to impress upon them the importance of the task which they had been called upon to perform: sitting in judgment on one's fellow officers; deciding who should and who should not be promoted. Concluding his remarks, he said, "You are indeed fortunate to have Admiral Wilkerson as your senior member. I would strongly urge you to seek his advice as you go about your work."

Captain Grisham from Pers B-12 was the next speaker. He sought to provide them with an insight into what went into putting together a promotion board. From early on Congress had taken a special interest in the promotion of officers in the military. Encoding their wishes into law, the legislators set forth not only how often promotion boards were to be convened, but also who could serve on them. The law further stipulated that the members of a promotion board must be senior in grade to those under consideration, and further prohibited anyone from serving on two consecutive boards considering officers of the same rank.

To this the Navy had added some of its own requirements, the most important one being to require that any member assigned to a promotion board must be a "due course" officer, never having been passed over for promotion to any grade.

Finishing his presentation, Commander Smith from the planning section, Pers A, went on to brief the board on how the number of officers to be selected was arrived at.

The primary thing the Navy Department wanted to do was make sure that each officer "enjoyed" equal opportunities for promotion. In order to accomplish this, it would first be necessary to determine the number of projected vacancies for the upcoming year. Once this had been done, the number of officers to be considered by the board was adjusted so that each officer coming before the board for the first time would have the same chance of being promoted as those in previous years. These officers would then make up the "new field." The board, in addition, would consider those officers who had been previously considered or passed over by previous boards.

Following the morning's briefings, Mike joined several of the board members in the Bupers cafeteria for lunch. Going through the line, they sat together at a table in the section of the dining area reserved for captains and above. Over lunch, their conversation revolved mainly around the upcoming board.

During a lull in the conversation, Jim Lansky, one of the surface warfare officers, asked Chuck Diesel, "I see you're a submariner, Chuck. I was wondering if you'd ever worked for Admiral Wilkerson?"

"One time," Chuck replied. "When I had command of a boat in Pearl, the admiral was COMSUBPAC."

"I've heard tell he's quite a bear to work for," Don Brown, one of the aviators, interjected.

"Well, he's not one to mince any words, particularly if you screw up, but I found him to be fair enough if you did your job," Chuck replied. "You've got to admire him, though, for taking his boat into Tokyo Bay. Getting through the net undetected was one thing, but getting out after the Japs knew he was there—that must have been hairy. Instead of hightailing it for the entrance after he let loose his torpedoes, he headed up the bay, where he lay on the bottom in shallow water, while the Jap destroyers concentrated their attention on the harbor entrance. Once they had given up, thinking he had escaped, he tailed a merchant ship coming out of Yokohama through the anti-submarine net, hiding in its wake."

"I guess he proved the old adage. In combat, always do the unexpected," Mike said.

"I think we're all in for an interesting couple of weeks," Lansky commented as they got up to leave.

After lunch the board gathered in the tank, a windowless projection room with the walls and ceiling painted entirely in black. Up front were four large projection screens. Facing the screens were three tiers of leather reclining chairs, similar to those found in the "ready room" on an aircraft carrier.

Joe Grieves from selection board services was the briefing officer. "You had better get used to this room, as you're going to be spending a lot of time in here during the next couple of weeks," he warned. Pausing, he continued, "I would like to call your attention to several features on each of your chairs. You will notice that each of you has a flashlight pointer, a small lighted writing table, and an electronic voting module. It's the voting module I want to talk about.

"This is the device which looks like a little black box. On it you will find five buttons marked A, B, C, D, and E. It's with this module that you'll be casting your vote on the records projected on the screen.

"Since the law requires that to be selected for promotion an officer must receive a simple majority of 'yes' votes, you are probably wondering why the five choices. Why not a simple 'yes' or 'no'? As you get into your deliberations, you'll find that most of the officers voted on will receive a majority of 'yes' votes. After all, most of them will be qualified for promotion. However, your job is not merely to select those who are qualified, but those who are 'best fitted.' within the numbers allowed." He paused for a moment.

"This requires a more definitive means of making a decision other than a simple 'yes' or 'no'. This is the reason we have five choices. The A, B, C, and D buttons all register affirmative votes, while allowing you to weight your vote depending on your confidence in the individual being able to perform the duties of the next higher grade. For example, an A vote represents a 100 percent confidence in the individual, a B vote 75 percent, C vote 50 percent, D vote 25 percent and the E button is zero percent confidence, a 'no' vote.

"Once all members have voted, the results are tabulated electronically, and the number of 'yes' and 'no' votes, along with the average confidence level, are automatically projected on the electronic scoreboard above the center screen. As you get into your deliberations, you will find yourselves voting several times on some individuals before arriving at a final decision."

Once he had finished, the members returned to the board room, where they were sworn in by the recorder.

Now with the board officially convened, the first order of business was to come up with a set of ground rules for going about their work, to ensure that each officer got a full, impartial hearing in front of the board.

After much discussion, the board finally decided to review the records of the new field first, followed by the old field. They also decided to have each record reviewed by two members before it was projected for voting. In the event the two members could not agree on a grade, the record would be sent to a third member for arbitration.

While they were in the tank, the recorders had filled the carts by each desk. Picking up the first record, Mike opened it. It was separated into two parts. One was the fitness report file, containing detailed evaluations of the officer's performance from the time he was commissioned, while the other included the individual's biography, photograph, and other information relevant to his career.

With the record were summary sheets, portraying the information contained in the individual fitness reports. These would be used by the board members as worksheets to be projected in the tank. After the board was over, these sheets would be destroyed by burning.

Soon Mike was absorbed in his work. He lost track of time. Glancing up around 1830, he noticed that the room was almost empty. Most of the others had already left for the day. Finishing up with the record he was working on, he placed it in the bottom of the cart and went home.

CHAPTER 4

Traffic on the Beltway was heavy, and Mike did not arrive home until after 7:30 p.m. When he arrived, Jen was in the study. Hearing his car pull into the driveway, she got up and greeted him at the door. Giving her a kiss, he went upstairs to the bedroom to change out of his uniform.

Later, as they were having dinner, he asked, "How are things going at work?"

"Really well," she replied. "I'm especially pleased with the help I've received from the staff. The head of my department is a retired brigadier general. He would like to meet you, and he's invited us to have dinner with him and his wife whenever it's convenient."

"I'm afraid it's going to have to wait until I finish up with this board."

"I'm sure he'll understand," Jen answered. Changing the subject, she asked, "And what about your day?"

"I spent most of the day listening to briefings," Mike replied. "After tonight, better not wait dinner. I'll just grab something to eat when I get home."

The next morning, as he was getting dressed, Mike's thoughts were preoccupied with the board. While tying his tie, Jen opened her eyes. Sleepily, she said, "What time is it?"

"It's five o'clock," Mike replied. "Go back to sleep."

Jen closed her eyes. Mike came over and kissed her lightly on the lips. "I'm leaving now," he said quietly. "Please don't wait dinner."

When he arrived in the board room, several other members were already there. Pouring a cup of coffee, he carried it over to his desk and soon was lost in his work. By now he had begun to establish a routine.

The first thing he did when starting a new record was to look at the photograph of the individual. Having a face to relate to served to remind him that he was dealing with a real person, whose future at this moment was in his hands.

He then read through the officer's biography before going to the fitness report folder, which would be the main factor in determining whether the individual would be selected for promotion.

Annually, all commanding officers were required to submit an evaluation report on each officer under their command. In this report the individual was graded on his leadership and professional ability. He was also compared numerically with the other officers in the command of the same rank. There was also a place for the commanding officer to give his personal impressions of the individual's overall capabilities.

At 0700 Admiral Wilkerson arrived in the board room. Stopping briefly to speak to the recorder, he sat down at his desk. Before beginning his work, he announced that the first session in the tank would be at 0900.

Around 0850, the members of the board, coffee cups in hand, began straggling down the passageway to the tank. Once everyone was present, the lights were turned down and the first group of summary sheets were flashed up on the screen. The admiral was the briefer for the first record.

"I've asked the recorder to project this record first. I thought it would be helpful, if I kicked things off," he said.

Using his flashlight pointer, he went of to dissect the first individual's career from beginning to end, noting trends, weaknesses, and strong points. It was a masterly job, making the others feel a bit uncomfortable knowing they had to follow this act.

Clearly a "head and shoulders" type, the individual received nine 'yes' votes, with an 87 percent overall level of confidence.

The board spent the next hour and a half looking at and voting on records. It was sometimes difficult not to identify with the person, and perhaps overstate the true performance. One of the briefers was soon to learn the dangers of doing so when he went on to exaggerate about the job the individual had done.

Growing irritated, the admiral began to tap his fingers on his writing table. Finally, unable to control himself any longer, he broke in.

"Dammit, Captain," he said. "Let's cut the crap. It's pretty obvious this officer doesn't hack it. Stop wasting our time."

Turning around in his chair, he directed his next remarks to the entire board. "Before we go any further, let's get something straight. As a briefer, your job is not to sell anything. Just tell it like it is, and let us make up our own minds. If we all do this, it will make our jobs that much easier. As far as this particular record goes, I think we have all heard enough. Let's vote." The electronic board lit up, while an uncomfortable silence enveloped the room.

The days that followed were one continuous blur of reviewing records and voting in the tank. Mike soon came to find out that deciding who should and who should not be promoted was not as simple as he had at first thought. Many factors had to be considered. How did one weigh performance relative to the difficulty of the assignment, or account for different grading standards by the various reporting seniors? These matters, as well as many others, needed to be thoughtfully evaluated before deciding on a grade.

In many cases the officer's performance was such that his promotion was virtually assured. These were the easy ones, and the board spent very little time with these "water walkers" or "shoo-ins," as they were referred to. On others, the board members would agonize for hours before casting their votes.

In the beginning, the members were hesitant in expressing their views, but after a few tank sessions they gained confidence and began to openly voice their opinions. In some cases the discussions became quite heated.

Slowly, however, their views began to converge, as they developed a collective sense of the qualities they were looking for in a selectee. Coming from a warrior class, they homed in on reports covering wartime and combat situations, giving a great deal of weight to what the commanding officers had to say in these instances.

Trends in performance were closely scrutinized as well. It was obviously better to receive lower marks at the beginning of an assignment and improve, rather than the reverse. How the individual was compared with his peers, and the commanding officer's written comments, were also carefully noted. When it came time to vote, each individual member had to take all these factors into account and decide, by himself, in the darkened room what level of confidence he placed in this officer's ability to perform the duties of the next higher rank.

No matter how hard they worked, there seemed to be an unending supply of records to review. At long last, on Tuesday morning of the second week, the recorder announced they had finished up with the new field. Although each record had been screened and voted on, no one had yet been selected to be promoted.

At this point in the proceedings Admiral Wilkerson scheduled a tank session to review the voting and make some interim decisions on whom they would select. 'A great deal of discussion ensued, with the board members reluctant to commit many numbers until they had a chance to look at the old field and to take another look at the group scoring in the lower middle. Eventually they decided to tentatively select those individuals who scored higher than 75, leaving twenty-three numbers.

31

Before they began with the "old field," the admiral cautioned the board to keep in mind that the individuals they were now going to look at had all been passed over by a previous board. To select an officer from this group would in effect be second-guessing that decision. He also warned against placing too much stock in fitness reports written after an officer had been passed over, as many commanding officers tended to inflate the performance of these officers in an effort to get them promoted. With these cautionary thoughts in mind, the board began its review of the old field.

In most cases it was readily apparent why the individual had been passed over. One record, however, stood out from the others. The officer's name was Jake Edward Barnes.

As Mike leafed through the folder, he was surprised by the fact that Lieutenant Commander Barnes, as an ensign, had been awarded a Bronze Star during the Korean War.

His interest piqued, he delved into the record further. He noted that Barnes had been an NROTC graduate from Rice Institute. Receiving his commission, he had been assigned to an APD stationed off the east coast of Korea. A little further on in the record, Mike came across the action report accompanying the citation for the Bronze Star.

According to the report, South Korean Intelligence had located a mine-storage depot in a cave dug into a hillside just outside a small fishing village located about 100 miles north of the 38th parallel, in the vicinity of Sonjin. The area was thought to be lightly defended by a home guard.

A high priority was assigned to taking out the depot, since a number of ships had recently been sunk by floating mines. Unfortunately, the terrain ruled out the possibility of an air strike. Weighing his options, Commander Task Force 95 decided to go with a night raid, utilizing a company of Marines.

The operation order called for the Marines to be put ashore after midnight on a secluded stretch of beach about a mile from the village. Leaving a platoon behind to guard the beachhead, the remainder of the group was to proceed inland over a low ridge to the target area. Once the target had been destroyed, the raiding party was to make its way back to the landing zone for pickup before dawn.

Ensign Barnes was the boat group commander in charge of the landing and recovery. As they made their way to the beach, a gibbous moon provided just enough illumination to effect a landing through the surf, but not enough to silhouette the boats against the horizon.

The landing went off without a hitch. With the defensive perimeter set up, the remainder of the raiding party silently proceeded inland toward their objective. Waiting for them to return, Barnes ordered his boats to retract from the beach and "lie to" outside the surf line.

As they approached the depot, the raiding party was suddenly ambushed by three companies of North Korean regulars. All hell broke loose. Badly outnumbered and outgunned, the Marines fell back toward the beach, the company commander urgently requesting covering fire and immediate extraction.

Receiving the message, Barnes ordered his boats back onto the beach. Dropping their bow ramps, they anxiously stood by, awaiting the retreating Marines. A destroyer nearby was dispatched to the scene to provide fire support, but did not arrive in time to be of any assistance.

From his boat, Barnes could hear the sound of gunfire growing near. It was apparent an intense fire fight was under way, and the situation was rapidly deteriorating. A short time later, the first Marines appeared out of the darkness and headed for the waiting boats. Loading the other boats first, he ordered them to retract and standby outside the surf line, ready to provide fire support. Once they had safely retracted, he ordered the remaining Marines to collapse the perimeter toward the beach, where he was standing by to recover them. With the North Koreans in hot pursuit, the last group of Marines ran toward his boat, scrambling on board, dragging several of their wounded with them.

Under a hail of bullets, Barnes backed his boat out through the surf to safety.

In the award citation, accompanying the report, Barnes was cited for coolness under fire, exhibiting superior leadership ability, and risking possible capture in order to rescue the last remnants of the raiding party.

Turning to the fitness report record, Mike noted that Barnes, with one exception, was always rated number one among his peers and was consistently graded outstanding in all categories. Comments from his commanding officers were generally glowing, describing him as levelheaded, unruffled, a born leader, cool in stressful situations, exhibiting an ability to quickly grasp the situation, a stellar performer, etc.

The exception was one fitness report covering a seven-month period in 1961. That report, in contrast, described him as a hothead, easily rattled, and further charged him with disobeying a direct order. This was puzzling. Mike muttered to himself. "What the hell happened that would have caused him to screw up so badly? Maybe I'm missing something here?"

He decided to ask for another opinion. Getting up from his desk, he walked the record over to Jim Lansky.

"Jim, would you mind taking a look at this record, and let me know what you think?" he asked.

A short time later, Lansky came over, record in hand. Giving it back, he said, "Something's wrong here. Hell, except for that one report, this guy would have been a shoo-in. Also, in case you didn't notice, this report was signed by a damn civilian, and you know how much stock we have placed in those. I gave him a B. It would have been an A-plus except for that one report. There's no way this guy should've been passed over."

"I agree," Mike replied. "That's why I asked for your opinion. I sure as hell would be interested in finding out what went on in last year's board."

34

After Jim left, Mike set Barnes' record on the corner of his desk. He thought about talking it over with the admiral, but decided to wait, to let it settle for a while. Taking a coffee break before the afternoon tank session, he walked over to Selection Board Services and asked Joe Grieves if he could see the list of members on last year's board.

"No problem, Captain," Grieves replied. "It's a matter of public record."

Getting up from behind his desk, he walked over to a nearby filing cabinet, pulled out the precept, the document convening last year's board, and handed it over to Mike.

Reading through the list of members, Mike recognized only one name, Captain Harry Gibson. Known throughout the destroyer force as "Hoot," he had been the operations officer on CRUDESLANT's [cruiser, destroyer force, Atlantic fleet] staff when Mike was skipper of the *Rush*. They had met on a couple of occasions when Mike had attended commanding-officer conferences in Norfolk.

Mike remembered him as a hulking, bombastic individual who perpetually chewed on an unlit cigar. He was regarded as a no-nonsense straight shooter who pulled no punches, regardless of the consequences. Mike had a gut feeling that he would have been a staunch supporter of Jake Barnes.

Handing the precept back to Joe, he placed a call to his office. Peggy answered in a cheerful tone of voice. "Foreign Ship Training, may I help you?"

"Peggy, this is Captain Canfield."

"Captain, how are you? We sure do miss you around here. When will you be coming back."

"Sometime next week," Mike replied. "But, right now, I would like you to look up a home phone number for me. Name is Captain Harry Gibson. I think he may be stationed in Norfolk. When you find it, leave a message for me here at Selection Board Services."

35

Upon his return from the afternoon tank session, there was a phone message on his desk from Peggy with Captain Gibson's number on it.

CHAPTER 5

September 1968, At Sea Off the Virginia Capes

The LSD *Plymouth Rock* was steaming along at 12 knots, in company with the LPH *Valley Forge*, LSTs *Wood County* and *Grant County*, and a second LSD, the *Ft. Snelling*, as part of Task Group 28.2. Two days earlier, the task group had embarked a battalion of Marines at Morehead City, North Carolina, to participate in PHIBEX 8-4, an amphibious training exercise scheduled to take place at Camp Pendleton, the Virginia National Guard Training Area on the coast about ten miles south of Virginia Beach. The task group was steaming in a modified box formation, with the helicopter carrier *Valley Forge* in the center.

In the early predawn hours, everything on board the *Plymouth Rock* was quiet. Other than those on watch, the crew was still asleep. Entering the door of the empty chart house, Lieutenant Commander Jake Barnes walked over and poured a cup of coffee from a pot setting on a warmer on the starboard bulkhead. From its murky appearance, he suspected it had been left over from the mid watch. Although he preferred his coffee black, if it was particularly bad he would add a spoonful of sugar. This was one of those times.

Picking up the message board hanging alongside the chart table, he began to read through it while he took a sip of his coffee. "I should stop drinking this crap," he grumbled. "Anything that tastes this bad can't be good for your gut."

Finishing with the messages, he refilled his mug and made his way through the darkened pilot house and out onto the port wing of the bridge.

Resting his arms on the high gunwale, he gazed out over the sea. Away from the lights on shore, the sky was filled with stars. Low in the eastern sky the winter ellipse, with Orion's belt near its center, could now be seen. As the days moved closer to winter, it would begin to rise earlier and earlier until it would be visible throughout the night.

The warmth from the coffee mug, cupped in his hands, felt good in the chill of the early morning air. He never seemed to tire of looking out over the sea. It was one of the few remaining places on Earth where man's impact was still not apparent, even though he knew that before long even the sea would be littered with the trappings of civilization. "If only I had lived in the days of the old square-riggers." he thought. "Life was so much simpler then."

Jake looked forward to this time, being alone in the dark. It gave him a chance to mentally prepare himself for the upcoming day, but mostly it afforded him the opportunity to savor the experience of being at sea. Having been passed over for promotion, he knew these times were numbered.

As he stood alone in the darkness, he thought back over his career. Other than a tour of shore duty, he had been with the amphibs ever since his commissioning. He had been part of the many changes that had occurred in amphibious warfare since World War II.

The voice of the boatswain's mate of the watch jarred him back to the present. "Captain's on the bridge," he called out.

Dressed in his pajamas and bathrobe, Captain George Allman stepped into the pilot house to speak to the OOD [officer of the deck] before making his way out onto the open bridge.

Seeing Jake standing there, he said, "Morning, XO. You're up early." By force of habit, he went over to the pelorus and checked the ship's course on the gyro repeater.

"I need time to get started in the morning," Jake replied.

Turning away from the pelorus, the captain asked, "What do the 'weather guessers' have to say about conditions in the landing area?"

"Skies clear with the wind out of the southeast at about 15 knots," Jake replied. "There's also a message on the board from the Seal team. They did a beach recon at 0200. Their report indicated a three-foot surf, with a five-second interval and one knot of long shore current."

"What did they have to say about the beach gradient?"

"About 10 percent, which should minimize the risk of the boats broaching."

"What about sandbars?"

"One located approximately 15 yards offshore, but it's deep enough, so it shouldn't present a problem," Jake replied.

Standing alongside each other, staring out into the darkness, they fell silent. Allman was the first to speak. "What time's reveille?"

"0430, with early chow for the boat crews and Marines at 0445. I recommend setting the sea detail at 0510," Jake replied. "I have also told Damage Control Central to ballast down to the well deck by the time we reach anchorage."

"Hold off loading the Marines as long as we can," Allman said. "They're going to have a long enough day as it is."

"Aye, aye, sir. I figure on loading them at 0530."

The captain turned to leave. "Looks like you have things well in hand. I think I'll get some breakfast before it hits the fan."

After the skipper had left, Jake resumed his position at the gunwale. Soon his mind went back to his previous thoughts.

With the helicopter a whole new dimension had been added to amphibious warfare. It was called vertical envelopment. To test and develop this new concept, the Navy had converted one of its older aircraft carriers, the *Valley Forge*, to a helicopter carrier, followed a short time later by the first LPH, a ship designed from the keel up to carry helicopters and troops.

For the first time in history there was now a dependable, effective way of introducing troops deep behind the beach. Until now, the only way of doing this had been to the use paratroops, whose overall effectiveness was spotty at best. Now, however, there was a way to introduce troops behind enemy lines with precision, ready to fight as soon as they hit the ground. The battlefield had now become much more difficult to defend. The enemy commander would be forced to look to his rear as well.

Besides the helicopter, newer, heavier tanks and vehicles were also coming on line, requiring larger, newly designed ships and landing craft to accommodate them. Of these, the LSD, Landing Ship Dock, was fast replacing the older APAs and AKAs as the primary amphibious assault ship. Introduced late in World War II, the LSD was designed to carry landing craft in a large well inside the ship instead of on deck. This not only permitted the carrying of larger landing craft, but also allowed pre-loading them, thereby reducing the time in the landing area.

In order to load the boats in the well, large ballast tanks were filled with sea water, causing the ship to sink down in the water. Once the well was flooded, a large gate in the stern was lowered, allowing the landing craft to be driven into the well under their own power. Once secured in place, the stern gate was raised and the ballast tanks pumped out, leaving the boats stored high and dry until arrival in the landing area. Expanding on this earlier design, the Navy had brought on line a newer, larger class of LSD, with a helicopter deck installed over the well. The *Plymouth Rock* was one of these.

The sound of the boatswain's mate of the watch piping reveille interrupted Jake's train of thought. Picking up his coffee mug, he returned to the chart house, where the quartermaster of the watch was busy breaking out the charts for the landing area. Even though he knew the area by heart, having participated in numerous landings here, Jake took a few moments to look them over before going below.

Stopping by his stateroom to freshen up and shave, he made his way to the wardroom. A number of the ship's officers and Marines were already present. As president of the mess, he took his place at the head of the first table. He was in the process of removing his napkin from its silver ring when Abalos, the first class steward, appeared at his side carrying a fresh pot of coffee.

"Good morning, Commander," Abalos said cheerfully. It was customary for the exec to be called commander irrespective of his rank.

"What can I get you for breakfast?" he asked.

Jake ordered a couple of eggs over easy with baked beans.

While he sipped his coffee, Mark Germo, the Marine company commander, entered, dressed in battle fatigues.

"Mind if I join you, Commander?" he asked, approaching the chair to Jake's left.

"Not at all," Jake replied. "Please sit down." Waiting for the Marine to give his breakfast order, he continued, "I hope you've enjoyed your brief stay on the *Rock*, Captain."

"It couldn't have been better, Commander. The troopers and I sure do appreciate your hospitality."

"We're always glad to hear that," Jake replied.

Before they could continue, Abalos came with Jake's breakfast. The conversation was put on hold while Jake concentrated on eating. Finishing, he folded his napkin and placed it back in its holder.

"You'll have to excuse me, Captain, I have to get back up to the bridge."

"What's the weather look like?"

"Pretty good," Jake replied, standing up to leave. "It shouldn't present any problem."

As he stepped out onto the open bridge, the first hint of daylight was visible in the eastern sky. Soon the skipper appeared and took over the conn to guide the ship into position.

41

Moments later the quiet of the morning was broken as the first wave of CH-46 assault helicopters, laden with troops, rose from the flight deck of the *Valley Forge*. Once airborne, they formed up in a line abreast, and dropped down until they were skimming the tops of the waves. With their rotors thumping as they bit into the cool morning air, they turned and headed for the still dark shoreline off to the west.

The *Plymouth Rock* was now riding low in the water, with her 390-foot well deck awash. Her stern gate was cracked open. The eight LCM-8 assault boats, stored in the well, each carrying one M-60 tank, were loaded and ready. Hearing the anchor chain rattling on the fo'c'sle as the anchor was let go, Jake issued orders to flood the well and lower the stern gate. Once the valves to the gravity tanks, underneath the well deck, were opened, the well quickly filled with sea water. It wasn't long until the "Mike 8s" were floating. The wave action accentuated inside the confined space caused them to bounce around and bang against each other. It was imperative to launch the 62-ton boats as quickly as possible, to prevent damage to the boats or risk injuries to personnel.

"Request permission to launch the boats, Captain," Jake called out from his station on the after wing of the bridge.

"Permission granted."

"Aye, aye, sir. Bosun pass the word, Away all boats."

As soon as they heard the word "away," the coxswains of the two Mike 8s, nearest the stern, shifted into reverse and rammed their throttles to full. The remaining six boats followed suit in tandem, and soon all boats were free and clear. Reaching the relative calm outside the well, the boat crews and embarked Marines breathed a collective sigh of relief.

Once clear, the Mike 8s formed two circles, one off each quarter, and stood by to await orders from the boat group commander on when it was time to head for the line of departure [LOD]. From there they would make their final dash to the beach.

It was now light enough to make out the other ships anchored nearby. Through his binoculars, Jake looked over at the *Ft. Snelling*, anchored off the port beam. Her stern gate was down, and she was in the process of launching her load of 20 LVT-5s.

The Landing Track Vehicles, or LVTs, as they were commonly known, had largely replaced the open boats from World War II. True amphibians, they were capable of operating on land as well as in the water. Most were outfitted to carry a complement of 25 Marines, although some of them were configured to carry a single 105mm howitzer cannon instead. Completely enclosed, they were capable of speeds up to eight knots in the water. Once ashore, they were able to move swiftly inland on caterpillar tracks at 40 miles an hour.

Once they were launched, the LVTs formed up into waves of five each. Barely visible above the waves, they began to make their way toward the LOD, 1,000 yards offshore. The shoreline in the distance was now visible as the sky continued to brighten to the east.

Joining Jake on the wing of the bridge, Captain Allman said, "Well, Jake, so far, so good."

"Let's hope this wind doesn't pick up after sunrise," Jake replied. "The Mike 8s will be all right. They're pretty seaworthy, but the LVTs are another matter. They don't have a helluva lot of freeboard. If anything should go wrong, they would sink like a rock."

"I don't know whether I'd prefer riding the LVTs or the helicopters," the skipper replied. "I guess you could say, for a Marine, getting to your place of work could be the most dangerous part of the job."

While Jake and the captain were talking, the boat group commander led the first wave of LVTs toward the LOD. On arrival, he took up station, and took control of the arriving waves of boats, dispatching them toward the beach at five-minute intervals.

By now, the helicopters had dropped off their first load of Marines and were on their way back to the *Valley Forge*. Landing on the flight deck, they quickly reloaded, and soon were on their way back to the landing zones This would continue until all the troops and equipment were ashore.

Jake climbed up into the swivel chair on the port side of the pilot house and listened to the progress of the landing over the PRI and SECTAC radio speakers piped into the pilot house. The first wave of the Mike 8s had now landed, unloaded their tanks, and safely retracted from the beach. They were now on the way to the *Ft. Snelling* to pick up the beachmaster unit.

Once ashore, they would take over control of the landing, supervising the unloading of the boats and movement of materiel inland.

At H+60 minutes, the beachmaster declared the beachhead secure. It was now time for the LSTs, *Grant County* and *Wood County*, to begin their approach to launch the pontoon causeways carried alongside. Once in place, the LSTs married up and began to unload the vast quantity of support cargo, trucks, and other heavy equipment. All the while, the helicopters and boats continued their round trips back and forth, ferrying materiel and supplies from the ships offshore.

By 1100, the landing phase of the operation was complete. All equipment and troops were now ashore. The task group commander dissolved the task group and detached all ships to proceed independently back to port, once they had recovered their boats and helicopters.

While waiting for the Mike 8s to return from the beach, Captain Allman came up to Jake on the wing of the bridge.

"How about having lunch with me in my cabin before we get under way?" he asked.

"It would be my pleasure," Jake replied. "What time?"

"Make it 1200," Allman said, turning around to leave.

Below in his stateroom, while he changed out of his working uniform into a fresh set of khakis, Jake thought about his time on the *Plymouth Rock* and his relationship with the skipper. For the most part it had been a good one, with the captain granting him a great deal of freedom in running the ship.

Although the billet of executive officer on this class ship called for a full commander, Jake's detailer believing him to be a shoo-in for promotion, had issued his orders prior to the promotion boards reporting out. Unfortunately, when the list was published his name was not on it. Considering what had happened back in '61, it did not come as a surprise, although he allowed himself to hope that it was part of the past. Having been "passed over," Jake knew that one word from the "old man" would get him replaced, but the captain had made a special point of requesting the Bureau to keep him on in his present assignment.

At 1200 sharp Jake knocked on the door of the captain's in-port cabin. Allman called out from the bedroom, "Come on in, Jake. Make yourself comfortable. I'll be out in a couple of minutes."

Jake sat down on the sofa and picked up a copy of the *Naval Institute Proceedings*. He had just begun to leaf through it when Licksi, the captain's steward appeared with a glass of iced tea in hand.

"Good afternoon, Commander," he said, setting the glass down on the coffee table in front of Jake.

"Good afternoon," Jake replied. "What's this I hear about you getting orders to the White House mess?"

"Yes sir, Commander, it is true."

"If you don't mind my asking, how did you go about arranging that?" Jake asked.

"My brother, he already stationed there, and he recommend me," Licksi replied in pidgin English.

"Well, when you get there, give my regards to the President," Jake replied.

Licksi didn't quite know what to make of Jake's last remark. Deciding not to say anything, he hastily beat a retreat back to the galley.

The captain's quarters on the *Plymouth Rock* were spacious. The combination sitting and dining area was nicely appointed with sofa, end tables, occasional chairs, and a dining table that could seat up to eight when fully extended.

Today the table was set for two, with white china rimmed in gold and emblazoned with the ship's commissioning pennant. A white napkin folded like a fan sat in the middle of each plate.

Captain Allman appeared from the bedroom wearing freshly starched khakis.

"I hope you like salads, Jake."

"Sure thing, but then anything would sound good about now," Jake replied.

"Well, let's get with it, then," Allman said, motioning toward a chair at the table opposite from his. "It's been a long time since breakfast."

During lunch, the captain kept the conversation focused on routine ship's business. Jake was beginning to wonder why the skipper had invited him to lunch.

When they had finished eating, Licksi cleared the table and filled their coffee cups before returning to the galley. Measuring out a teaspoon of cream, Allman slowly stirred it into his coffee.

After he had finished, he looked over at Jake, his voice taking on a more serious edge. "A couple of days ago I saw in the *Navy Times* that the commander board is in session."

"I know," Jake replied. "However, I don't think there's much chance of my being picked up, having been passed over last year."

"I want you to know that I sent in a special fitness report, highly recommending your promotion."

"Thanks, Captain, I really appreciate it, but I know the odds are stacked against me," Jake replied. "No doubt this will be my last tour of sea duty. After I leave the *Rock*, I'll probably be sent to some backwater foreign shore duty assignment to finish out my twenty."

Allman did not comment on Jake's last remark, saying instead, "For the life of me, Jake, I can't understand why you weren't picked up the first time. You're without a doubt one of the finest officers I have ever worked with." Pausing, he shook his head in disbelief.

"I don't mean to pry into your personal affairs, Jake, but is there something in your past I don't know about?"

"Yes sir, there is, but I can't talk about it. It's still classified. The most I can say is, I got in way over my head, and screwed it up."

"I've a hard time believing that you screwed up, Jake," Allman replied. "If there's anything I can do, please let me know. All of us here on the *Rock* are pulling for you." His voice trailing off, he added, "Some things just don't make any sense."

"Thanks, Captain. Your confidence in me means a lot," Jake replied, sincerely touched by the skipper's concern for him.

Leaving the captain's cabin, Jake went below to his stateroom to catch up on some paperwork before it was time to set the sea detail. No matter how hard he tried, he had a difficult time concentrating on his work. His mind kept wandering as he thought of the past and worried about his future.

It was during his sophomore year at Rice that he had met Emily. Although he had dated other girls during high school, she was the first girl he had ever felt serious about. From the beginning they had planned on getting married as soon as he graduated.

Upon his commissioning in June, he received orders to a small amphibious transport [APD] out of San Diego. They were married at her home in Little Rock the following week, and two weeks later he reported to his ship. A few days after their arrival in San Diego, the Korean War broke out, and his ship was soon en-route to Westpac. Em had a difficult time adjusting to being alone. During the time he was away, she became almost a recluse, rarely leaving their apartment.

Jake returned home to a person totally different from the one he had left. Their marriage slowly began to disintegrate. Even though she didn't say it, he could sense she blamed him for abandoning her. Things improved somewhat during the time he was at home, but his second deployment had proven too much for her.

He remembered the day, while on station in the Yellow Sea, when he received a letter from her. Inside was a single page on which she had written that she was leaving him and was returning to Little Rock to stay with her family while she tried to pull her life back together. He had never felt so alone in all his life. Even though the news was not unexpected, seeing it in writing gave it a certain finality.

They saw each other one more time after he returned from Korea, when he took leave and visited her in Little Rock. During the visit, little was accomplished toward saving their marriage. She had firmly made up her mind to leave him. She didn't want anything more to do with the Navy. A week after he returned to San Diego, she filed for divorce. It had now been fourteen years since he had last heard from her.

Then there was that incident back in 1961 that had crippled his career. Now he was faced with just marking time until he completed his twenty years.

What then? Until now, the Navy had been his whole life. He had given it his best. In return it had destroyed not only his marriage, but his career as well.

CHAPTER 6

Tuesday, September 17, 1968, Washington

Mike Canfield pulled into the driveway just as the sun sank below the horizon. Opening the door to the house, he called out Jen's name. When she didn't answer, he guessed she must be upstairs.

Jen had just finished showering and was standing naked in front of the mirror, brushing her short blonde hair. Entering the bedroom, Mike brushed her lips with a light kiss. In an absent sort of way, he said, "I see you have dinner started."

Jen sensed something must be troubling him. Normally, finding her naked would have elicited a response from him, and, more than likely, they would have ended up on the bed, making love.

Later on during dinner, Mike was unusually quiet. He poked at his food, even though she had prepared one of his favorite dishes.

While serving coffee, she asked, "Is there something wrong, Mike? I've noticed you've been awfully quiet this evening."

"Something happened today that has been bothering me," he said. "Today, in the board room, I reviewed a record of an officer who had been passed over by last year's board. Since then I haven't been able to get it out of my mind. I have a gut feeling something's wrong." He paused to shake his head. "Hell, Jen, this guy has a better record than most of the officers we have selected. It just doesn't add up."

From past experience, Jen knew that Mike needed time to sort it out in his mind. She allowed him to go on without interrupting.

"If his record were average I could understand, but except for one brief period, he virtually walked on water. For the life of me, I can't understand how the last board could have overlooked him."

Jen did not comment, and Mike lapsed back into silence.

Finishing his coffee, he excused himself. "I think I'll go into the study and give Buzz a call," he said. "I need to touch base with him and check on the status of things back in the office."

The study was his and Jen's private sanctuary, a place where they could escape when they needed some time to themselves. Jen had furnished it with soft brown leather furniture, and a large mahogany desk she had bought for him at an antique auction, as an anniversary present. One wall was lined with bookcases, while the other three were covered with family pictures, framed certificates, and plaques from his various duty stations. On the oak floor was a red and black Oriental rug.

Sitting down at the desk, Mike dialed Buzz Laroque's home phone number. On the second ring, Laroque picked up the phone. Recognizing Mike's voice, he said, "Hi, boss, when are you coming back to work?"

"Probably by the middle of next week."

"I can't wait," Laroque replied. This 'black shoe' Navy stuff is way out of my league. You've got to remember that I'm used to dealing with things that have wings. Up until I arrived here, I thought boats were only used to haul airplanes around."

"Welcome to the real Navy, Buzz, and by the way, they are ships, not boats. Boats are things that are carried on board ships, just like airplanes are."

Laroque ignored Mike's last remark. "By the way, before I forget," he continued. "Your old buddy from the *Selrik*, Commander Kudasis, called today and asked me to pass on a message to you. He said he was getting under way tomorrow, and would be heading back to

Turkey, after making a brief stop outside the 12-mile limit to take care of some unfinished business. He said you would know what he meant."

Mike had figured all along that Kudasis would go through with the hanging, but he was a little surprised that he would have made a point to let him know.

"I think he's actually looking forward to hanging that poor bastard. Isn't there something we can do?"

"I wish to hell we could, Buzz, but unfortunately, once he's outside our territorial waters he is free to do pretty much as he pleases. All we can do is make note of it in our briefing report. Other than that cheerful bit of information, what else is new?"

"Not much, except the destroyer we are transferring to the Dutch has been delayed in the yard for another week to fix some electronic problems."

"Okay, keep me informed. It sounds like you have things well in hand." Seeking to put an end to the conversation, he continued, "Look, Buzz, you'll have to excuse me now."

"Okay, skipper. Look forward to having you back. I can't wait to get the skinny on what it takes to get promoted."

After talking with Buzz, Mike returned to thinking about Jake Barnes. He fingered the message in his pocket with Hoot Gibson's phone number on it, debating about whether he should call him or not. He worried about how he might react. Certainly it might be considered inappropriate to talk with someone from the previous board. Still, he felt compelled to find out as much about Jake Barnes as possible. He rationalized that he hoped someone would do the same for him, given similar circumstances.

Slowly, he dialed the number Peggy had given him earlier. A gruff voice on the other end of the line answered, "Captain Gibson here."

"Captain Gibson, this is Mike Canfield. I don't know whether you remember me."

"Sure I do. You were skipper of the *Rush* when I was at CRUDESLANT. Congratulations on your promotion."

"Thanks, Captain," Mike replied.

"Call me Hoot," Gibson shouted into the phone. "Now, what can I do for you?" Mike moved the receiver away from his ear.

"I'll get right to the point. I am on the line commander board now in session. I know that you had served on the same board last year."

"Yes, I did. So----?" Gibson questioned.

Mike was beginning to think his calling Gibson had been a bad idea, but it was too late now. Tentatively, he plunged ahead. "Today in the board room I reviewed a record of an officer who had been passed over by your board. I was wondering if you might remember him."

Before he could continue, Gibson interrupted. "Before you go any further, Mike, you damn well know that the proceedings of a selection board are secret. You are way out of line talking to me about it."

"Yes sir," Mike replied, sheepishly. He sought to end the conversation as gracefully as he could. "You're right. I am sorry to have bothered you at home."

"Don't worry about it. I may have come on a little strong. Off the record, what's this guy's name?"

"Jake Barnes," Mike replied.

There was a long silence on the other end of the line. For a while Mike thought that Gibson had hung up.

"I had a suspicion it might be about him. He really got a royal screwing."

"But how?" Mike asked.

"My better judgment tells me I should end this conversation, but I'm still pissed over what happened. From now, on everything I am about to tell you is off the record—understood?"

"You have my word," Mike replied.

"You asked if I remembered Barnes? The truth of the matter is, his case caused quite a conflict in our board." He paused for a few seconds before continuing, "The fact is, Mike, our board did select him."

"What?" Mike exclaimed, surprised by what he had just been told.

"You heard it right, Mike. Barnes was selected for promotion."

Mike was now thoroughly confused. "But why then wasn't he promoted?"

"Because his record had been flagged. That's why," Gibson replied.

"Flagged?" Mike asked.

"Your first board, right?"

"Yes sir, it is."

"As you will soon find out, whenever the board finishes up its work, the names of the selectees will be turned over to the performance people for them to take a look at it before it's sent over to the Secretary of the Navy's office. Sometimes they have information on the officer that's not in the official record. If they think the board needs to know, then they'll brief the board on the circumstances, giving them an opportunity to reconsider their decision. Mostly the type of information is personal, like the guy's wife's an alcoholic, or maybe he's a womanizer. Stuff like that.

"In the case of Barnes, though, it was something else. When this captain from Pers F came down to brief the board, all he'd say was that Barnes' record had been flagged. As you can imagine, we weren't exactly too happy with this half-assed explanation. This guy Barnes, as you already know, was strictly a heads-and-shoulders type. We wanted some straight answers, but all this puke would say is that the matter was classified, and that if we selected him his name would be stricken from the list. The board about had a fit. Everyone was pissed. We weren't too happy with being told what to do. The president of the board even went up to see the Chief of Naval Personnel, but all he could get out of him was that the order to flag Barnes originated at a higher level.

"We debated for the better part of a morning about whether we should just go ahead and select him anyway, but finally decided that if his name was going to be taken off the list, we might as well not waste the number. Instead, we selected someone else in his place. I'm still not sure we did the right thing. Well, Mike, now you have it. That's about all I know, but whatever it was this guy Barnes did, he sure as hell got himself cross-wise to the current and made some high-ranking enemies."

Mike was silent while he tried to digest what he had just heard.

"Mike, if you are thinking about pursuing this matter, better be careful. Someone pretty far up the line has gone to a great deal of trouble to keep whatever happened under wraps, and they aren't going to take kindly to anyone caught nosing around."

"Thanks for the advice, Hoot. I've got to let it sink in a little before deciding what to do."

Mike slowly put the phone back into its cradle. He settled back in his chair, running his hands through his hair, thinking about what Gibson had just told him. He hadn't been wrong after all about Barnes, but he still didn't have any answers as to what had happened back in 1961. And then there was all this stuff about his record being flagged. What the hell was that all about?

While Mike was busy on the phone, Jen had changed into her nightgown. Opening the door to the study, she said, "I thought I heard you hang up the phone. Is everything okay?"

"To tell you the truth, I don't know," Mike replied. "I found out that I had been right about Jake Barnes, and I also found out why he was not promoted. I also learned there is still a lot I don't know."

"What are you going to do now?" Jen asked.

"I don't know yet," Mike replied.

Looking up at her, he said, "Gosh, you are beautiful."

CHAPTER 7

Wednesday morning

Driving into the Annex the next morning, Mike mulled over in his mind what he should do about Jake Barnes. Should he just forget what he had been told by Hoot Gibson last evening, or should he pursue the matter further?

Parking the Fiat, he walked across the parking lot to the selection board area. On the way to his desk he stopped briefly to say hello to a couple of board members already in the room.

Jake Barnes' record was still sitting on the corner of the desk where he had left it the previous evening. He briefly considered taking it up with the admiral when he arrived, but once again decided against it for the present. Besides, what could he say? He had given Hoot Gibson his word.

Opening up Barnes' record, he went through it once again, thinking perhaps there was something he had missed that would give him a clue as to what had gone wrong back in 1961.

The only thing in the record covering this period of time was the one fitness report written by a Mr. Ray Belcher, head of Field Office 12, located in the Pentagon. Not only was the report classified, but so were the duties to which Barnes had been assigned. That he had been involved in some sort of secret operation was readily apparent.

It's got to be the CIA, Mike thought, but what had been going on back in 1961 that Barnes could have been involved in? Thinking back, he tried to remember—Central America, Africa, the Middle East, or Southeast Asia. It could have been any one of these, but, why someone like Jake Barnes? If he were a Special Forces type, or perhaps an aviator, it would have made more sense. He had known several ex-aviators who had been recruited in the recent past by the CIA to fly supply missions into the Congo, but in their cases they had been civilians. What skills did Barnes have that the CIA needed?

Looking back through the summary sheets, it suddenly dawned on him. "Hell, it's obvious!" he muttered to himself. Barnes had spent nearly his whole career with the amphibs. He was an expert in amphibious warfare. Mike thought back. He then remembered how in 1960 Fidel Castro had been making up to the Russians, and President Eisenhower had asked for, and had been given, secret permission by Congress to mount a military operation to oust him from power, using a group of Cuban expatriates. That had to be it. They needed Barnes to train the Cubans in amphibious warfare.

This part of the puzzle was solved, but it still didn't explain away the bad fitness report. Everyone knew the landing at the Bay of Pigs had been a fiasco, but most of the blame was political, not military. What had happened to cause Barnes to fall on his sword?

"Where do I go from here?" Mike asked himself. "I still don't know a helluva lot about Barnes' involvement, or what was behind him getting such a bad write-up."

Mike's immediate problem, however, was what he should do with Barnes' record. He still didn't have anything of substance to go on, except a suspicion that he was involved in the Bay of Pigs debacle. Mike decided to set the problem aside for a while and move on to the other records stacked in the cart beside his desk.

Returning from the morning tank session, he approached Jim Lansky and invited him to lunch. "Why don't we go over to the Arva restaurant? I'm getting a little tired of this cafeteria food," Mike suggested, wanting to talk with him alone.

"Okay with me," Lansky replied.

The Arva Motel, across the street from the west entrance to Arlington Cemetery, was a favorite lunch spot for military personnel stationed at both the Annex and Ft. Myer. When they arrived there were already a number of Army personnel in the dining room.

While waiting for their food to arrive, Lansky looked over at Mike. "Okay, Mike, you didn't ask me out to lunch because of my looks. Somehow, I suspect it has something to do with this guy Barnes."

"You're right, Jim, it does," Mike replied. "I've been stewing over this since yesterday, and somehow I think there's a lot more to this story than we know." He then went on to relate his theory about the Bay of Pigs.

"Come to think of it, I think you have something there," Lansky replied. "But it still doesn't explain the bad fitness report."

"I know," Mike said. "I'm beginning to suspect that maybe I've become too close to the situation. This is one of the reasons I wanted to talk with you. I would like your thoughts about where I should go from here."

"As I see it, you don't have much choice, Mike. Let the record go through and see what happens," Lansky replied.

"I sure as hell would hate to see this guy get passed over again."

"Look, Mike, I know it's difficult not to sympathize with Barnes, but be careful. Remember what happened that first day in the tank. You also have to realize that there's going to be a helluva lot of resistance from the board, and especially from the admiral, in picking up a 'passed over' officer. You can count on me to back you up, but you've got to let the record speak for itself."

Returning to his desk after lunch, Mike jotted down on a note pad what little information there was on the questionable fitness report.

He then placed the file in the bottom of the cart along with the other completed records.

Jake Barnes' record did not come up in the afternoon tank session. On the way back to the board room, Mike stopped by Selection Board Services and called his office. He wanted to see what he could find about the civilian who had written up the report on Barnes. Peggy answered the phone.

"Peggy, this is Captain Canfield. Is Commander Laroque around?"

"He's in his office. Just a moment, Captain, I'll get him," she replied.

A few seconds later, Laroque picked up the phone. "Hi, skipper, what's up?"

"Buzz, I need you to look someone up for me. He's a civilian, by the name of Ray Belcher. Back in 1961 he was assigned to the Pentagon, to a Field Office number 12. I have a feeling he may be CIA. How about digging around and see what you come up with? Give me a call at home tonight, and let me know what you find out."

"I'll get right on it," Laroque replied.

Mike was glad Buzz hadn't asked any questions.

The Beltway was choked with traffic, and it was after 7 when Mike arrived home. As he and Jen were finishing dinner, the phone rang. Jen answered. After a short conversation, she put her hand over the mouthpiece. "It's Buzz," she said.

"I'll take it in the study," Mike replied, getting up from the table.

Sitting down at his desk, he picked up the phone. "Hi, Buzz. How did you make out?"

"You were right about Belcher being a CIA type. In fact, he is now head of the Directorate for Operations over at Langley."

The Bay of Pigs certainly didn't hurt *his* career, Mike thought to himself. Over the phone, he said, "Anything else?"

"Yes sir. I tracked him down here in the Pentagon. He worked here for an eight-month period back in 1960 and '61. From what I've been able to find out, the operation was strictly hush-hush.

"I suspect it had to do with the Bay of Pigs," Mike replied. "What I'd like for you to do now is nose around and see if you can get the names of any of the other people who were assigned to that office."

"Right, boss. I'll get on it first thing tomorrow morning. Anything else?"

"Not for now, Buzz. Just let me know what you come up with."

Hanging up the phone, Mike reclined back in his chair, thinking over what Buzz had uncovered. He mused to himself, I guess we now know who was responsible for flagging Barnes, but what was it that Belcher had against him?

CHAPTER 8

Thursday Morning

Jake Barnes' record was the third one to come up in the morning tank session. Before beginning his briefing, Mike reminded himself. Remember Jim's advice. Play it cool. Be objective. Let the record speak for itself.

Starting at the beginning of Jake's career, he first recounted the action that had earned Jake the Bronze Star. From there he went on to review the rest of his record, noting performance scores and comparison results, trying to be as objective as possible. Pretty soon a pointer appeared on the screen, focusing on the Belcher report.

"What happened here, Mike?" Don Brown questioned.

"I was about to get to that," Mike replied. "As you can see, Lieutenant Commander Barnes' record is one of consistently high performance, except for this one period back in 1960-61. Unfortunately, this report contains little to account for the low marks. Since it is so out of keeping with the rest of his record, I have asked the recorder to project it on the screen so you all can have a look at it."

Giving the board a couple of minutes to read the report, he went on, "As you can see, there isn't much to go on, as most of it is classified, including Barnes' duties."

"What do we know about this guy Belcher, other than that he's a civilian?" one of the other members asked.

"I thought someone might ask about that, so I checked into it," Mike replied. "What I found out is that Mr. Belcher is currently head of the Directorate of Operations over at Langley. It would be my guess he was also CIA-connected at the time this report was written."

"Sounds to me like Barnes might have been involved in some sort of secret operation," Don Brown speculated. "Do you have any idea of what it might have been, Mike?"

"It's difficult to say, Don, but given his background in amphibs and the time frame of the report, my guess is it was the Bay of Pigs," Mike replied.

"That might explain why the report is classified, but it still doesn't account for the low marks or comments, 'Hot headed,' 'easily rattled,' 'disobeying a direct order.' These are pretty damning accusations," Ron Allen interjected

"But if it were true, in particular the disobeying an order, why wasn't he given a court-martial?" Brown countered.

"I wish I had some answers," Mike said. "The perplexing thing to me is that this report is so out of character compared with all the others."

Jim Lansky, who had sat silent until now, broke in. "As you can see, I was the second reviewer for Barnes' record," he began. "The thing that I can't understand is why he wasn't selected by the last board." Pausing for a moment, he continued, "Do we throw out an offi-cer with an outstanding record of performance because of one report covering a measly six-month period? And written by a CIA type to boot!" Jim was fully aware he was playing on the distrust with which most military officers viewed their CIA contemporaries.

Admiral Wilkerson was growing impatient. "Gentlemen, let's not forget, Barnes has already been passed over by a previous board. Obviously, they must have felt the information in this one report was reason enough to deny him promotion. We also need to consider that this report was written not by just any civilian, but someone who is now the head of a directorate at Langley. I recommend we vote. We have wasted enough time already."

The electronic score board lit up as the members cast their vote. The recorder read off the results: "8 yes, 1 no, with a 73 percent confidence level."

On the way back to the board room after the tank session, Jim Lansky came up alongside Mike.

"Good job, Mike," he said quietly, slapping him lightly on the back.

"Thanks, Jim," Mike replied.

"I wonder who it was who put in the no vote," Jim wondered out loud. "If I had to guess, I would bet on the admiral."

"Or maybe Ron Allen," Mike suggested.

"That's also possible," Jim replied. "But, in either case, I think he might have scored high enough to end up being selected. If it weren't for that one no vote, he would've been a shoo-in."

Getting him selected might be the easy part, but getting him promoted, well, that might be another story, Mike thought to himself.

To Jim he replied, "I guess we'll just have to wait and see. By the way, thanks for the support."

When he returned from lunch, Mike had a message on his desk that Commander Laroque had called. Walking across the passageway to the phone booth, he put in a call to his office.

Buzz picked up the phone on the first ring.

"Buzz, this is Captain Canfield."

"I thought it might be you, skipper. I just wanted to let you know what I've come up with. This guy Belcher did in fact head up the field office here in the Pentagon. There also was a Navy type by the name of Barnes assigned to the office, along with a Marine gunnery sergeant by the name of McCormick."

"Good work, Buzz. That didn't take long."

"You don't know how many little old gray-haired secretaries I had to charm," Laroque replied. "I hope this earns me some Brownie points on my next fitness report."

"It most certainly will," Mike replied. "How about something like, Commander Laroque has a way with older women?"

"Gee, thanks."

"Seriously though, Buzz, I do appreciate your help. Now, can you get me a phone number on McCormick."

"Peggy already has," Laroque replied. "He is stationed at Quantico. Here are his home and office phone numbers." He paused while Mike wrote them down. "I also found out that this guy Barnes is stationed on the *Plymouth Rock,* currently at sea."

"That's okay, I won't be needing to talk with him anyway," Mike replied. "If you come up with any more names, give me a call."

"Sure thing. I'll keep working on it."

That evening after dinner, Mike went into the study and dialed Sergeant McCormick's home phone. A woman's voice answered.

"Good evening. My name is Captain Canfield. Could I speak with Sergeant McCormick, if he's available?"

"Just a moment. I'll get him," she replied. Mike could hear her voice in the background calling out for her husband.

"There's a Captain Canfield on the phone. He wants to talk with you."

There was a short pause, after which a man's voice came on the line. He was breathing hard.

"Yes sir, Captain. You'll have to excuse me, I was downstairs in the rec room. What is it I can I do for you?"

"Sergeant, I'm serving on a Navy promotion board in Washington and I've been working on the record of an officer named Lieutenant Commander Barnes. I understand you served with him back in 1961. Is that so?"

The line fell silent. Finally, McCormick spoke. There was a worried sound to his voice. Tentatively, he said. "Yes sir. I knew him."

"I wonder if you could tell me anything you might know about him, and about what went on during this period of time?"

"Look, Captain, the operation we were involved in is still classified," McCormick replied. "I'm sorry, but really, I can't talk about it."

"Sergeant, I am not asking for any details or for you to reveal anything classified. I just would like for you to give me your impression of what kind of an officer Lieutenant Commander Barnes was?"

"Honest, Captain, I just can't say any more. I don't want to get into any trouble. I've a wife and three kids to think about. I just want to get my twenty in. Maybe you should talk to Jose' Ramirez."

"Where can I get hold of him?" Mike asked.

"I'm not sure. It's been a long time. Last I heard he was a lawyer in the Miami area."

"Thanks a lot, Sergeant. You've been a big help, and as far as I'm concerned, this conversation never took place," Mike said, trying to reassure him.

"Thanks, Captain, I really appreciate that. I'm sorry I couldn't be of more help."

Hanging up the phone with McCormick, Mike dialed Buzz's home phone.

"I'm sorry to bother you at home, but I need another favor from you."

"Ask away," Laroque replied.

"I need you to look up someone else for me. His name is Jose' Ramirez. I believe he's a lawyer in the Miami area. That's about all I know."

"I'll get on it first thing tomorrow," Laroque replied. "By the way, Captain, I hope someday you will fill me in on what the hell is going on. I didn't realize that selection-board duty involved all this cloak-and-dagger stuff."

"Neither did I, Buzz. Neither did I."

CHAPTER 9

Friday, September 20, 1968 Washington, D.C.

Upon his return from the morning tank session, Mike found a phone message on his desk from Buzz asking him to return his call. Walking across the passageway to the phone booth, he dialed his office number.

When the phone rang, Buzz answered. Recognizing Mike's voice, he said. "I think I located your man Ramirez. There's only one attorney with that name listed in the Miami directory. If you've got a pencil, I have his office phone number right here."

Mike reached into his coat pocket looking for something on which to write. Finding the memo containing the telephone message, he said, "Okay, Buzz, let me have it."

"The number is 486-3973."

After he finished writing down the number, Mike said, "Thanks again, Buzz. Remind me to buy you lunch after this is all over."

Hanging up the phone, Mike returned to the board room and continued reviewing records. Just before noon Jim Lansky stopped by, and asked if he were ready to go to lunch.

"You go on ahead, Jim. I've a phone call I need to make first. I'll catch up with you in the cafeteria as soon as I finish."

After Lansky had gone, Mike walked across the passage and placed a long-distance call to the number in Miami. A young woman with a soft Spanish accent answered the phone.

"Good morning. Ramirez and Associates, attorneys at law. How may I help you?"

"Hello, my name is Mike Canfield. I would like to speak with Mr. Jose' Ramirez, please."

"Just a moment," she replied. "I'll see if he is in." A moment later, a man's voice came on the line.

"This is Jose' Ramirez. What can I do for you, Mr. Canfield?"

"Mr. Ramirez, I am a Navy captain currently serving on a selection board in Washington. One of the officers being considered by our board is a Lieutenant Commander Jake Barnes. If I am speaking to the right person, I have reason to believe you might know him."

He was met with silence on the other end of the line.

"Why is it whenever I mention Jake Barnes' name, everyone goes silent on me?" he thought to himself.

When, Ramirez finally answered, his voice took on a guarded tone. "Yes, Captain, I know Jake Barnes, but I haven't seen or heard from him in a number of years."

"I wonder if you would be willing to talk with me about what occurred back in 1960-61," Mike said.

"Captain, how do I know you are who you say you are, and why should I talk to you about Jake Barnes?"

"I can understand your concerns, Mr. Ramirez. In your position, I'm sure I would feel the same way," Mike replied. "I can only assure you my interest in this matter is strictly limited to determining Barnes' fitness for promotion."

Before answering, Ramirez took a few seconds to think over what Mike had said. "All right, Captain Canfield, I will agree to talk with you, but only in person, and only after you have provided me with some proof of your identity."

"Fair enough," Mike agreed. "Since the board is about to complete its work, time is rather critical, however. Could we possibly meet this weekend at a place of your choosing?"

"I could meet you tomorrow here in Miami. Perhaps we could have lunch together. "

"That's agreeable with me," Mike said. "However, I'll need to make some travel arrangements first. Can I confirm the appointment with your secretary later on this afternoon?"

"Certainly, Captain. I look forward to meeting you. When you call, my secretary will provide you the address and directions to the restaurant."

Hanging up the phone, Ramirez leaned back in his chair. The events of the past came rushing back. Perhaps it was time that it all came out in the open. Something in his gut told him he could trust the man he had just talked with on the phone. Even though it happened a long time ago, the nightmares of being in prison in Cuba still caused him to wake up at night in a cold sweat. Yes, it was time to let the truth be known.

Hanging up the phone with Ramirez, Mike again dialed his office.

"Peggy? Has Commander Laroque gone to lunch yet? I need to talk with him. It's somewhat urgent."

"He just walked out the door," Peggy replied. "Hold on a minute. I'll see if I can catch him."

A few seconds later Buzz picked up the phone. "What's up, Captain?" he asked.

"Buzz, I need to meet with someone in Miami tomorrow. What's the possibility of your checking out a plane over at Andrews for the weekend?"

"Now you're talking, boss. Let me see what I can do. I'll call you back in a little while, okay?"

"I need to know by 1600, as I have to confirm an appointment by then."

"I'd better get off the phone, then," Laroque replied.

Hanging up the phone, Mike walked over to the sixth wing, where he joined Jim for lunch.

Apologizing, Mike said, "Sorry, Jim, something urgent came up."

"No problem, Mike, but why is it that I have a feeling it has something to do with Jake Barnes?"

"You're right, it does. There's still a lot we don't know about what happened back in '61. I'd feel a lot more comfortable if I knew. Maybe he did screw up, like Belcher said in his report."

"But you still can't refute his record, Mike. For chrissakes, the guy walked on water up until then, and also since. It just doesn't figure."

"That's what I keep telling myself, but there still has to be some truth in what Belcher wrote."

"Don't let it get to you, Mike," Jim counseled. "All we can do is act on the information that we're provided."

Shortly before they were due to go into the tank for the afternoon session, the secretary from Selection Board Services delivered a message to Mike that Commander Laroque had called.

Crossing the passageway, Mike put in a quick call to his office. Buzz answered the phone.

"I've got good news," he said. "I've arranged to check out a T33 for the weekend. We can leave any time after 0800. Now, how's that for service?"

"Where and when can I meet you?"

"How about we meet at the Navy Terminal over at Andrews at 0730?"

"Okay, Buzz. 0730 it is."

At dinner that evening, Mike informed Jen of his plans for the weekend. A disappointed look came over her face.

"This is not what shore duty is supposed to be all about," she complained. "Besides, Candi is coming home for the weekend, and she's bringing her roommate along for us to meet."

"I'm really sorry," Mike replied. "Can't you tell Candi we'll drive over to Fredericksburg next weekend and take them both out to dinner?"

Sensing his feeling of guilt, she hastened to add, "It's okay, Mike. I'll explain to Candi. She'll understand. Goodness knows she's used to your being called away on a moment's notice. I know you're all wrapped up in this Barnes thing, but I'll have to admit I'll be glad when this selection board is over."

That was about as close as Jen ever got to being critical of the Navy.

"It's only for a few more days. After that things should return to normal, and I promise, I'll make it up to you," he said.

"I'm going to miss you. What time do you expect to get back?"

"By Sunday afternoon at the latest," Mike replied. Getting up, he went over to her and put his arms around her.

"Thanks again for being so understanding," he said.

CHAPTER 10

October 1960, Little Creek, Virginia

Jake walked into his office at the Amphibious Operational Training Unit [AOTU]. His khaki uniform was wrinkled and sweat-stained. He had just returned from the beach, where he had spent the afternoon evaluating boat crews doing practice landings. Taking off his hat, the one with the gold officer's crest and chin strap that had long since turned green from salt spray, he tossed it onto a coat rack in a corner of the room. Before sitting down at his desk to write up the exercise reports, he went to the head to wash up. By the time he had finished with the reports, it was after 1700. Everyone in the building, except for the duty section, had already left for the day.

On the way to his room at the BOQ [bachelor officers quarters] he thought about Em, and how he had naively thought they would be together for the rest of their lives. Now all he had to look forward to was another night sitting alone in his room, eating dinner in front of the TV. He decided to stop by the club and have a beer.

By the time he arrived, the after-work crowd had already thinned out. Only a few diehards remained sitting at the bar. From their speech, it was evident they had had a few too many to drink. Not wishing to become involved with a couple of drunks, he took a seat at a table off in a corner of the room.

Seeing him enter, Cindy, the cocktail waitress, came over and set a basket of chips on the table in front of him. "What can I get you, Jake?" she asked.

"Make it the usual, a Miller's draft," he replied, scooping up a handful of chips.

A few minutes later she returned with his beer. Setting the mug down in front of him, she stayed on to talk.

As she stood next to him, Jake became conscious of the nearness of her body, detecting a faint hint of the perfume that she was wearing. Moving slightly, her leg accidentally brushed against his bare arm. The sensation startled him, causing him to become even more aware of the closeness of her body.

Jeez, it's been a long time, he thought. After his divorce from Em he had buried himself in his work, feeling no desire to be with another woman. As Cindy continued talking, his mind wandered, filling with the memories of his life with Em, back to the time when they were in college. Deep down inside he still harbored a hope that she would come back one day.

In the background he could hear Cindy's voice. "Jake, I've been watching you come in here, sitting at a table off all by yourself. You sure look like you could use someone to talk to. Why don't you and I go out after I get off work at 7 o'clock and get something to eat ?"

She stood waiting for his reply while he thought it over.

"What the hell, why not?" he said to himself. Anything beats sitting in front of the TV all evening.

Looking up at her, he said, "I think I would enjoy that. If you like seafood, I hear there's a crab house at the foot of the Lynnhaven Bridge that is supposed to be pretty good."

"That sounds good to me," she replied. "I haven't had seafood in a long time."

Polishing off the rest of his draft, he pushed his chair back from the table and stood up to go.

"Okay then, I'll pick you up out front at seven. That'll give me a chance to change out of this sweaty uniform."

Getting into his car, Jake drove across the base to the BOQ. In his room, he stripped off his uniform, stepped into the shower, and turned on the water. For the first time in ages, he felt somehow alive again. He was beginning to look forward to the evening, to having a woman to talk with for a change.

A slim, petite, brunette, Cindy had been attracted to Jake since he began coming into the club, making a special point to wait on him. In spite of her subtle flirtations, Jake had not paid a great deal of attention to her. Even though it had been almost seven years, he still hadn't gotten over the breakup of his marriage.

Turning off the water, he toweled off in the shower before returning to the bedroom to dress, putting on a fresh pair of chino trousers, a black polo shirt and loafers. After he finished dressing, he drove back to the club. Cindy was standing out in front when he arrived. She had changed out of her waitress uniform into a sleeveless white blouse and dark blue skirt. She looked stunning. Jake wondered why he hadn't noticed her before. As he drove up, she ran over to the car, opened the door to the passenger's side, and slid into the seat alongside him.

"Hi, Jake," she said, a little breathless. "Gee, I'm hungry."

When they arrived at the restaurant, the hostess told them it would be half and hour before there would be a table available.

"Why don't we wait in the bar?" Jake said.

When the waitress arrived, he ordered a draft beer for himself and a whiskey sour for Cindy.

Waiting for the drinks to arrive, Jake looked across the table at her. "You know I don't even know your last name."

"It's Kramer," Cindy replied, holding out her hand.

"Mine's Barnes," Jake replied, taking her hand.

"I already know that," Cindy replied. "I've seen it on the name tag on your uniform."

"And what is there to know about Cindy Kramer?" Jake asked.

"There's really not much to tell," she replied. "My dad was a Navy chief. I grew up right here in Norfolk. After I graduated from high school I got married to a sailor, became pregnant, and now have a seven-year-old son, Jimmy. Jim, my husband, couldn't take being married, having a family and all. We are now separated, waiting for the divorce to become final." Her voice took on a harder edge. "He's now back on sea duty, which suits me just fine. I'm fortunate my mother lives nearby, so she's able to watch Jimmy while I'm at work. I don't know what I would do without her." Before she could continue, the hostess came over to advise them that their table was ready.

Seated at a table for two by a window, they could watch the boats making their way in and out of the inlet. Taking a look at the wine list, Jake ordered a bottle of a dry white wine from California.

Returning a short time later with the wine and a bucket of ice, the waitress poured a small amount into Jake's glass. He nodded his head in approval. She filled each of their glasses and placed the bottle in the chiller before leaving. Holding up his glass, Jake said, "Well, here's to you, Cindy Kramer. I am glad you suggested going out to dinner."

"I hoped you wouldn't think I was being too forward," she replied. "You just looked like you needed a friend." She couldn't tell him that she'd been hoping he would ask her out ever since she had started working at the club.

While they were eating, Cindy asked, "Now that I have told you the Cindy Kramer story, how about telling me the Jake Barnes story?"

"Fair enough," Jake replied. He then told her about his marriage to Em and how they had divorced because she couldn't handle being alone while he was away at sea.

After he had finished, Cindy said, "How ironic—your wife couldn't handle the separations, and my husband couldn't stand being at home."

"This conversation is getting pretty morose," Jake replied. "Why don't we talk about something more pleasant?"

"You're right," Cindy said. "Why don't we forget about the past for tonight?"

For the remainder of dinner they each talked about their hopes and plans for the future. She became enthused as she told him about taking some courses at Old Dominion University, so that she could get a better job. He talked about his life in the amphibs, and how he hoped some day to command his own ship.

Time passed quickly. For the first time in a long while, Jake was truly enjoying himself. He hated to see the evening come to an end. Lingering over coffee, they both became quiet. Cindy reached across the table, putting her hand on his.

"I've really had a good time, Jake," she said.

"So have I, Cindy Kramer," he replied.

While Jake was paying the check, Cindy excused herself to go to the ladies' room. Before leaving, she stopped in front of the mirror to freshen her makeup and reapply her lipstick. Conscious of the wet feeling between her legs, she said to herself, "God, I haven't felt like this in ages."

Even though they were both in a quiet mood on the drive back to Little Creek, Jake was keenly aware of her presence on the seat next to him. Arriving back at the club, he pulled into the parking space alongside her car. She slid over next to him, reached up, and kissed him. As his lips met hers, he felt a passion he had not felt in a long time. Holding her close, he kissed her long and hard.

"You are an exciting woman, Cindy Kramer," Jake said, kissing her again. Cindy turned in the seat to press her body against his. He began to fumble with the buttons on her blouse. Pushing his hand aside, she proceeded to deftly undo them. With her blouse open to the waist, Jake reached inside her bra and cupped his hand over her breast. It was larger than he had expected.

"God, it's been a long time since I held a woman like this," he said. Lying back on the seat, she started to pull him down on top of her.

Jake protested, "No, not here. I have a better idea," he said, reaching for a beach blanket in the back seat.

Getting out of the car, Cindy giggled, "Where are you taking me, Jake?"

"You'll see," he said, leading her across the parking lot toward the golf course. Hand in hand, they climbed the small hill behind the trees toward the eighteenth green, where he laid the blanket down on the close-cropped grass.

Lying down beside her on the blanket, he began to slowly run his hands over her body. Reaching up under her skirt, he tugged at her panties. She lifted up slightly, allowing them to slide down over her hips. Raising up, Jake knelt between her legs and undid his trousers while she hiked up her skirt until it was bunched around her waist. In the soft moonlight, Jake's eyes wandered over her body.

Watching him drop his trousers, she said, "You don't have to worry, Jake, I already have a diaphragm in. I put it in when I went to the ladies' room back at the restaurant."

As he bent down to kiss her, she said, "Hurry, Jake." Reaching down, she guided him toward her. He entered her with one long, slow thrust. Her body tensed while he began to slowly move inside her. Clasping her arms around his back, she kissed him hungrily on the neck. With each stroke her body eagerly rose to meet his.

As he began to move more rapidly, she dug her fingers into his back and began making sounds in his ear. Realizing she was about to climax, he thrust into her one last time, his body shaking from the spasms.

They remained in the same position, both too exhausted to move. After a while he reluctantly got up and pulled up his trousers while she stepped into her panties, adjusted her skirt, and re-buttoned her blouse. As they made their way back to the parking lot, she clung close to him. Both were silent. Stopping alongside her car, he held her close, not wanting to let her go.

"Much as I hate to, I have to go now, Jake," she said, pulling herself away. "My mother is baby-sitting. She's going to wonder what happened to me."

Before releasing her from his grasp, he whispered in her ear. "Thanks, Cindy Kramer. You've made me feel like a man again."

Getting into her car she turned on the ignition and rolled down the window. Blowing him a kiss, she said, "You're an exciting man, Jake Barnes. Maybe next time you'll be the one to ask me out."

Before he had a chance to reply, she put the car in reverse and backed out of the parking space.

Jake watched her drive off into the night. Then he got into his car and slowly drove back to the BOQ. Along the way, he thought to himself. "It's time you put your life back together, Jake Barnes. Em is not coming back, not now, not sometime, not ever."

CHAPTER 11

The next day

At quarters the following morning, the exec [executive officer] informed Jake that Captain Ervin would like to see him after they were dismissed. Making his way to the captain's office, he knocked on the door.

"You wanted to see me, sir?" he asked.

"Good morning, Jake." Captain Ervin replied, motioning toward a chair. "Come on in and sit down. How about a cup of coffee?"

"Yes, thanks," Jake replied.

Ervin pressed the buzzer on his desk. In a moment, his steward appeared in the doorway.

"Liutenant Barnes and I would like some coffee," he said.

A short time later the steward reappeared with a tray containing a silver coffee service, which he set down on the coffee table.

"I imagine you're probably wondering what this is all about," Ervin said, as he poured each of them a cup of coffee.

"I'll admit I'm curious."

"I had a call late yesterday afternoon from the assignment desk up in Bupers. They wouldn't tell me a great deal, but I gather they are in the process of putting together some sort of an operation requiring the services of an officer who is an expert in amphibious operations.

They wanted me to recommend someone to fill the billet, and you were the first one who came to mind."

He paused, giving Jake a few moments to think it over.

"Well, Jake, what do you think?" he asked. "Would you be interested?"

"Right off hand, I can't say," Jake replied. "It sounds interesting. Do you know anything more about what the job would entail?"

"Not much, other than that it's a secret operation, and participation is strictly voluntary. I would guess it could be dangerous as well. If you're interested, they want to interview you for the job. It might be an opportunity to further your career, although I would hate to lose you for six months."

"How long before they need an answer?" Jake asked.

"By the end of working hours today," Ervin replied. "Why don't you think it over? I'm sorry I don't have any more information."

Setting his coffee cup down, Jake got up to leave. "I'll get back with you this afternoon, and let you know what I decide."

During the course of the day he weighed the decision in his mind. He enjoyed his job here at AOTU, and now there was Cindy. His mind went back to last night. She made him feel like living for the first time in years. He wanted to be with her again. On the other hand, it would only be for six months.

By mid-afternoon he had made up his mind to at least go for an interview. He informed Captain Ervin of his decision.

Around 1600, the buzzer on his desk rang. It was the skipper. He asked that he drop by his office. Jake made his way down the passage to the captain's office.

"You wanted to see me, Captain?" he asked.

"You'd better get your bags packed, Jake. They want you in the Pentagon tomorrow morning for an interview. The personnel office is cutting a set of orders for you to fly up commercial, and by the way, they want you to report in civilian clothes."

Jake had a feeling that his life was about to take a new turn. He only wished he knew more about what he was getting into.

On the way back to the BOQ, he thought about stopping by the club to see if Cindy was working again tonight, but decided against it. He would wait until he returned from Washington.

Early the next morning he drove his car to Norfolk International Airport, where he caught the morning flight to Washington. Arriving at National Airport, he hailed a cab to take him to the Pentagon.

The office where he was to report was on the second floor of the D ring. Arriving outside the door, he noticed that except for a room number it was unmarked. Opening it, he stepped inside.

A pretty young secretary looked up from her desk and smiled at him. "You must be Lieutenant Barnes," she said.

"I have an appointment with Mr. Belcher," Jake replied.

"Just one moment," she said, getting up from her desk. Opening the door to an inner office, she went inside and closed the door behind her. Jake could hear her speaking with someone, but could not make out what was being said.

A few seconds later she came back out and resumed her seat behind the desk. "Mr. Belcher will see you in a few moments, Mr. Barnes. In the meantime, please make yourself comfortable."

While she resumed her typing, Jake took a seat in a chair against the wall. Picking up a magazine from the table in front of him, he began to leaf through it.

About five minutes later the door to the inner office opened, and an athletic-looking man about his own age, with closely cropped blond hair, came out. Striding across the room, he extended his hand.

"Lieutenant Barnes, thanks for coming by. My name is Ray Belcher."

Everything about him, from his self-confident manner to his expensively tailored clothes, exuded Ivy League. Having been born into an affluent family in Connecticut, he had spent his high school years at Staunton Military Academy in Virginia, and his summers playing tennis at an exclusive country club in Connecticut, where his parents held a membership. Like his father, he had graduated from Harvard with a degree in international relations. He had planned to enter the Foreign Service upon graduation, but when CIA recruiters visited the campus during his senior year, he had decided to accept a position with the agency.

After undergoing training at Camp Perry outside Williamsburg, Virginia, he was assigned to covert operations. One of his early assignments was to Honduras, where he had been involved in funneling aid to the rebels in Guatemala.

"Why don't you come on in so we can get to know each other?" Belcher said, motioning toward his office.

Inside, there was another person seated on the couch.

"Lieutenant Barnes, this is Dick Harris from over at State."

In contrast to Belcher, Harris was a slightly built, scholarly type with prematurely gray hair. Shaking hands, Jake took a seat on the sofa.

"I know you've had an early morning," Belcher said. "How about something to drink?"

"Coffee would be fine," Jake replied.

Belcher pushed a button on his desk, and soon his secretary appeared with a tray containing three cups of coffee, along with cream and sugar.

"Jake, you are probably wondering why all this hush-hush business. You don't mind if I call you Jake, do you?" Belcher asked. "We try to be on a first-name basis around here."

"Not at all," Jake replied.

"Before we get started, I want to emphasize that what I'm about to discuss with you is top secret and is not to go beyond this room."

"Yes sir, I understand," Jake replied.

"I am sure you're aware of what's going on in Cuba," Belcher said.

"Just what I've read in the papers," Jake replied.

"Well, to fill you in, our intelligence sources have recently learned that Mr. Castro has struck a deal with the Soviets to obtain military hardware, along with Russian advisors to provide training in its use. In exchange, Castro has given the Russians permission to build bases in Cuba. Not only is this is a clear-cut violation of the Monroe Doctrine, but to allow the Russians to gain a foothold there would represent a serious threat to our national security as well. Could you imagine nuclear missiles positioned just ninety miles off our coast? Hell, they could hold our whole country hostage!" He paused in order to emphasize the gravity of the situation.

"Congress is so concerned with what's going on down there that they recently passed a secret resolution authorizing the president to mount a covert operation to get rid of Castro, using a group of Cuban expatriates. The CIA has been assigned the task of implementing this resolution, and I have been selected to head up the operational part of the task force.

"The president wants to be rid of Castro as soon as possible, and at the latest before he leaves office in January. To put it simply, Jake, our job will be to organize a Cuban brigade, train them, and put them ashore in Cuba."

Jake now realized why they wanted someone who was an expert in amphibious warfare.

Looking him in the eye, Belcher asked, "Well, Jake, what do you think? Would you be interested in joining our group?"

Jake's mind was spinning. From what he had read in the newspapers, he realized that Castro was a closet communist who had gained power the previous year by pretending he was going to free the Cuban people from the tyranny of the Batista regime. The only thing was, as it is with most zealots, that once he seized power he quickly established another repressive, doctrinaire regime worse than the one it had replaced. As soon as the Cuban people found out what Castro was all about, there was a mass exodus to the United States, coming mostly from the educated and professional classes. Setting up residence mainly in South Florida, they had become a very vocal and militant group advocating the overthrow of Castro by whatever means necessary.

Looking up, he realized that Belcher and Harris were waiting for his reply. Still, he had some unanswered questions

"What would my role be in this venture?" he asked.

"You would be primarily responsible for the amphibious part of the operation, as well as a full partner in the planning and execution of the entire mission," Belcher replied. "I guess I don't need to tell you this is going to require a lot of work, not only in planning, but also in training the Cuban Brigade. We plan to put the Cubans ashore at night, somewhere in the vicinity of Havana."

A night landing—that's risky, Jake thought. Normally, night landings were used only for small operations conducted by highly trained specialized forces, such as the Navy Seals.

Expressing his doubts, he said, "I don't see how we can take a bunch of civilians and turn them into an effective amphibious landing force in four months, let alone conduct a night landing."

"Look, Jake, all we have to do is get them safely ashore. Once they have landed, according to our intelligence, the Cuban people will join in and rise up in revolt against the government. It should be a piece of cake."

Jake was wary of people who tended to oversimplify complex situations. His Navy training had taught him to prepare for the worst and then hope for the best.

"What kind of resources will we have to conduct this operation?" he asked.

"We are in the process of contracting for five civilian freighters from a Mr. Garcia, a ship owner in Central America. In addition to the freighters, we have two converted LCIs in our inventory."

"How about landing craft?"

"The Navy has been tasked to provide whatever we might need," Belcher replied.

"What about air and naval support?"

"The Navy has already committed one carrier and six destroyers, and the Air Force will provide reconnaissance and fighter cover from Homestead."

Harris, who had sat quietly listening in, interrupted, "Jake, you need to understand that this is to be primarily a Cuban operation. We are only responsible for providing logistics, training, and transportation to enable the Cubans to accomplish their mission."

"How do you plan to keep an operation of this size and scope secret?" Jake asked.

Belcher was becoming impatient. Before Harris could answer, he said, "Jake, let me worry about leaks." Pressing him for an answer, he asked, "Well, what do you think?"

Jake thought it over for a moment. "I guess you can count me in, as long as I get a free hand in running the amphibious part of the show," he replied.

"That's great, Jake," Belcher said enthusiastically. "It's good to have you on board. Officially, you will be attached to the Naval Support Group at Andrews, where your records will be kept. However, you will be working out of our field office in Miami. First thing in the morning, I'll have a set of message orders on the wire, ordering you to report as previously directed. Pack whatever gear you think you might need, but leave your uniforms at home. There's already a staff of officers and enlisted personnel on site in Miami, as well as a representative from the Cuban Brigade. Once you arrive, I want you to take charge. I'll put out the word from here."

Jake suddenly realized things had progressed much farther than he had thought.

Bringing the meeting to an end, Belcher stood up behind his desk. "Dick and I will be shuttling back and forth between here and Miami. We'll keep you posted on our schedule."

Jake stood up to leave. "Before I go, I need to know where to report."

"Right," Belcher said. "Talk to Sally on the way out. She'll give you the address in Miami."

As he was leaving, Jake stopped by the secretary's desk and picked up the phone numbers and address. Taking a cab back to National, he caught a flight back to Norfolk.

The plane was not crowded. He had a row of seats to himself. Sitting next to the window, he gazed absently at the river-inundated landscape of Virginia drifting by below. He understood the need to keep the Russians out of Cuba. What made him uneasy, however, was Belcher's confidence that this was going to be a cakewalk. Jake harked back to an earlier time in Korea when a small, relatively straightforward operation had gone wrong. From that, he had learned, in amphibious warfare nothing can be taken for granted.

It was late by the time he arrived in his room at the BOQ. Taking a quick shower, he went straight to bed.

After quarters the next morning, he stopped by Captain Ervin's office. "Got a minute, Captain?" he asked as he knocked on the door.

"Sure thing, Jake. I was just about to give you a call. Come on in." He waited while Jake sat down. "I take it you haven't seen the message board."

"Not yet," Jake replied, thinking he was talking about his orders.

"The lieutenant commander list came out yesterday," Ervin said. Jake knew the board was in session, but with everything else going on during the past couple of days it had slipped his mind.

Before he had a chance to reply, Captain Ervin reached across the desk and extended his hand. "Congratulations are in order, Lieutenant Commander Selectee Barnes."

"Thank you," Jake said, obviously elated.

"I can't think of anyone who is more deserving," Ervin added.

He paused for a moment to give Jake a chance to savor the news before continuing. "By the way, how'd things go up in Washington yesterday?"

"I decided to accept the assignment," Jake replied. "They want me to report tomorrow. I wish I could give you more details, but the operation is top secret. I was told I would be receiving a set of message orders sometime this morning."

"That's awfully short notice."

"If things go according to schedule I should be back by March or April at the latest," Jake said.

Leaving the captain's office, Jake had little time to think about his upcoming promotion. His orders were on the message board by mid-morning, and he spent the remainder of the day getting his affairs in order.

Around 1700 he returned to the BOQ and began to pack. Finishing up around a quarter to seven, he got into his car and drove to the "O" Club. He looked forward to sharing the news of his promotion with Cindy.

Seeing him enter, she came over to greet him. She was upset that he hadn't called her. "I missed you the past couple of evenings. How come you didn't at least call?"

"I had to go to Washington yesterday, and didn't get back until late last night," Jake replied. "How about having dinner with me tonight?"

"I don't know whether I should," she replied.

"Come on. Let me make it up to you," Jake said. "Besides, I have some news I want to share with you."

"Oh, all right, but first let me call home and tell my mother I'll be late." Waiting for her to return, Jake sat at the bar and ordered a draft. When Cindy returned, she had changed into a short-sleeved light blue dress. Clinging tightly against her body, it accentuated her beautiful figure.

Walking over to where he was sitting, she said, "Okay, I'm ready."

Jake stood up. "You look beautiful," he said, approvingly.

On the way out to the parking lot he asked, "You feel like Italian? There is a little place I sometimes go to out on Pleasure House Road."

"I love Italian food," she replied. Arriving at the car, Jake held open the door for her. She waited while he went around to the driver's side before asking, "Now, what's the news you wanted to tell me?"

"I'll tell you during dinner," Jake replied. "Right now I just want to tell you how great you look, and what a good time I had the other evening. Since then I haven't been able to get you out of my mind."

Cindy slid over next to him and kissed him on the cheek. "I had a good time too, Jake," she said. "But when you didn't come to the club the last couple of evenings, I wondered what had happened. I was afraid I would never see you again."

"I'm sorry. I should have called," he said, feeling guilty.

As they entered the restaurant, the owner came over to greet them. Shaking Jake's hand, he asked, "Jake, where've you been? I haven't seen you in a while."

"I've been pretty busy lately," Jake replied.

"Well, whatever the reason, it's good to see you again, and also to see that you have brought someone along for a change. Such a nice-looking young lady, too," he said, looking at Cindy approvingly. "Follow me, I have a special table just for you."

When the waitress arrived, Jake ordered a bottle of chianti. Returning a short time later with the wine, she filled each of their glasses and set the bottle on the table. After she had gone, Jake looked into Cindy's eyes and raised his glass. "Here's to a wonderful and beautiful woman," he said.

"Why, thank you, Jake," Cindy replied. "Now what's the news you wanted to tell me. I am dying to find out."

"I'll have you know, Cindy Kramer, you are having dinner with newly selected Lieutenant Commander Jake Barnes."

Cindy reached over to squeeze his hand. "Oh, Jake, I'm so happy for you. When will it become official?'

"It'll still probably be another month or two before my number comes up," he replied.

Before they could continue, the waitress came up to take their order. Jake held back telling her the other news, that he would be gone for six months. He decided to save it for later.

After dinner, as they were holding hands across the table, he thought about the past week. All of a sudden his life had turned around. He was having dinner with a beautiful woman. He had been selected for promotion, and he was starting a new job. At the thought of the latter, his face clouded over. He hated leaving Cindy so soon after they had found each other.

Seeing his frown, Cindy said, "What's wrong, Jake? You look like something's troubling you."

"I guess I might as well tell you the other piece of news," he said, looking down at the table. He didn't want to see her reaction to what he had to say. "I'm going to be out of town on TAD [temporary additional duty] for about six months," he said.

Cindy's heart sank. Under her breath she said, bitterly, "The damn Navy. All it's ever done is mess up my life. I should've known better than to date another sailor."

Seeing her reaction, he tried to console her. "It'll only be for six months. After that I'll be coming back to AOTU. In the meantime I'll call and write. I promise."

They left the restaurant in a funk. Cindy was silent during the drive back to Little Creek. Jake had a feeling she was about to cry.

Arriving back at the base, he asked, "Would you like to come up to my room for a while?"

"Okay," she said weakly. On the way up the stairs, she clung desperately to his arm.

Inside his room, she fell into his arms, sobbing. "You don't know how much I'm going to miss you, Jake. I'm so afraid you'll forget about me."

He held her close, kissing away the tears. "I could never forget you, Cindy Kramer. I only wish we had met a long time ago." Undoing the back of her dress, he said, "I want you so badly. Let's just think about tonight."

They went on to undress each other, between kisses. Cindy was now naked except for high heels. Jake stepped back. "Let me look at you. I want to remember you like this while I am away."

His eyes ran over her, trying to etch every detail of her body into his memory. Unable to control himself any longer, he carried her to the bed. Lying there, with the dim light coming in the window silhouetting her body, he kissed her passionately, murmuring, "You don't know how much I'm going to miss you, Cindy Kramer."

"I'm going miss you too, Jake, but right now let's celebrate your promotion," she replied, pulling him over on top of her.

The next few moments were lost in a blur of passion. They couldn't seem to get enough of each other. It was over too soon. Rolling over on his back, she snuggled next to him, her head on his shoulder. Quietly she began to sob. Holding her tight, he stared at the ceiling and contemplated their future.

He tried to soothe away her fears. "Don't worry, I'll be back in no time at all." They held each other this way for a long time, neither wanting to see the evening come to an end. Finally, around 3 o'clock, Cindy pulled away. "Jake, I have to go now. I want to be home before Jimmy gets up for school."

After they had dressed, Jake drove her back to the club parking lot. Standing alongside her car, they held each other for a long time before she broke away.

"You take care, Jake. I'm going to miss you," she said, trying to hold back the tears.

"Goodbye, Cindy, I'll call when I can," Jake said, as he watched her drive off. She didn't look back. He knew she was crying.

As he got back into his car, Jake realized that the Navy could be a very jealous mistress.

CHAPTER 12

Saturday, September 21, 1968, Andrews Air Force Base

Mike Canfield awoke at 0530 and slowly dragged himself out of bed. The twelve and fourteen-hour days were beginning to take their toll. As he turned on the water in the shower he thought to himself, "I need to slow down and take some time off when this is all over. It isn't fair to Jen, for her to be left alone so much of the time."

Old habits die hard. After years of taking Navy showers, turning off the water while soaping down, Mike was always sensitive to wasting water. This morning, however, he deliberately let the water run, luxuriating in the feel of it running over his body. Finally, unable to handle the guilt any longer, he turned off the faucet. Drying off, he wrapped a towel around his waist and stepped out of the shower stall. Turning on the water in the sink, he let it run hot. As he was shaving he scrutinized his face in the mirror. Now that he had turned 40, it had lost its boyish appearance and had begun to take on a more mature look. There were some streaks of gray along his temples, and a few lines had begun to appear under his eyes, the result of spending too many hours on the bridges of ships, squinting in the bright sunlight.

"Jeez, I'm getting old," he said to himself. Turning away, he returned to the bedroom, where he glanced over at Jen. She was still asleep. As he was getting dressed, she slowly opened her eyes.

"Good morning," he said. "I tried not to awaken you."

"That's okay," she replied, stretching. "I wanted to get up and have breakfast with you anyway." Yawning, she added, "After that, I intend to go back to bed and sleep in 'till noon."

"That not fair," Mike replied. "Nevertheless, I would enjoy your company."

While Mike packed his overnight bag, Jen put on her robe and went downstairs to the kitchen, where she turned on the coffee maker and set the table for breakfast. As usual, they ate in silence. Finishing breakfast, Mike returned upstairs to pick up his suitcase.

Before going out of the door, he gave Jen a kiss and held her close for a moment.

"Thanks for being so understanding. I should be back by tomorrow afternoon. I'll give you a call before we take off from Homestead."

Being the weekend, Indian Head Highway was nearly deserted. At the Beltway, Mike turned east, toward Andrews Air Force Base. Passing through the main gate, he continued on to the Navy side of the field, where he parked his car in the lot across from the terminal building.

Buzz was already suited up. Seeing Mike enter the building, he walked over and saluted.

"Morning, Captain. Everything's all set to go as soon as we get you suited up. Our bird is already standing by on the flight line. I just finished checking the weather, and it looks like we're going to have a great day for flying."

"Are you sure you have a license to fly this thing, Buzz?" Mike asked in jest.

"Boss, I cut my teeth on this type of aircraft," he replied.

91

While Mike put on his flight suit, Buzz went over the flight plan with him. After he finished, they made their way toward the sleek blue jet parked outside on the flight line. As they approached, the crew chief, standing alongside the aircraft, snapped to attention. "Good morning, Captain...Commander, she's all checked out and ready to go."

Assisting Mike into the rear seat, he helped him fasten his harness, and went on to brief him on the cockpit controls, along with the procedure for operating the rocket ejection seat. Once he was satisfied that Mike was familiar with the emergency procedures, he stepped down and took up a position off the right wing, where he was visible to the cockpit. Giving the aircraft one final visual check, he gave Buzz the hand signal to power up.

With the help of the APU, the Pratt & Whitney jet engine came to life. Sputtering for a few seconds, it soon settled down to a dull roar. Once the wheel chocks were pulled clear, the crew chief gave Buzz a thumbs-up.

"We're ready to roll, boss," Buzz relayed over the radio. "Time to close the canopy." Releasing the brake, he eased out onto the taxiway, completing the pre-flight check as they made their way toward the end of the runway. Once he had received clearance for takeoff, he pointed the small jet down the runway and eased the throttle forward. Mike felt himself being forced back against the seat as the aircraft rapidly accelerated. Lifting off, he felt the wheels slam home. Buzz dropped the right wing and made a sharp turn to the south. After leveling off on course, he eased back on the stick. Mike felt the nose lift as they commenced a steep climb up through the scattered cumulus clouds toward their assigned cruising altitude. Looking out of the cockpit canopy, he noticed that they were coming up on Chesapeake Bay. The altimeter on the instrument panel read 30,000 feet, and the air speed indicator indicated 450 knots. Buzz eased back on the throttle and leveled off.

"Everything okay back there?" he asked over the radio.

"So far, so good," Mike replied, settling back to enjoy the flight. Soon they were "feet wet" over Cape Hatteras. It seemed like no time at all before the shoreline of Florida came into view off the starboard side of the aircraft. Shortly thereafter, Buzz eased forward on the stick to begin their descent into Homestead Air Force Base.

Receiving clearance to land, he set the small jet down on the long runway and taxied up to the flight line, where ground personnel were standing by to direct him. As he shut down the engine, a government sedan pulled up. An Air Force lieutenant colonel stepped out.

Approaching Mike, he saluted. "Welcome to Homestead Air Force Base, Captain Canfield. My name is Johnson. Colonel Marsh asked me to meet you and confirm that everything is okay. I have arranged accommodations for you and Commander Laroque at the VOQ [visiting officers quarters]."

"Thanks, Colonel, I appreciate your stopping by," Mike replied.

"Colonel Marsh also asked me to inform you that his car and driver are available should you require transportation."

"Please pass along my thanks to the colonel," Mike replied, "but I won't be needing it. I have already arranged for a rental car."

"Yes sir. Just let us know if there is anything you need, and enjoy your stay while you are here in the Miami area." With that, he got back into his sedan and drove off.

While Mike was talking, Buzz was busy making arrangements with the flight line crew to fuel and service the aircraft. At Base Operations he checked on the weather forecast and filed a flight plan for the following day. When he had finished, they picked up the rental car and drove to the VOQ. There they checked in with the airman at the front desk.

"You're welcome to come along with me, Buzz."

"I might as well. I don't have anything else to do. Besides, I am curious as to what the hell's going on."

"Okay then, give me a few minutes to freshen up. I'll meet you back here in the lobby."

Inside his room, Mike changed clothes, putting on a sport coat and tie. When he came down, Buzz was already waiting. Exiting the base, they turned north onto the Florida Turnpike toward Miami. On the drive into the city, Mike gave Buzz a quick rundown on the reason for the trip.

"I gather this also has something to do with your asking me to look up information on this guy by the name of Belcher," Laroque said. "But what does he have to do with Jake Barnes?"

"All I know is that Barnes worked for him, and I suspect it has something to do with the Bay of Pigs. I'm hoping the gentleman we are going to see, Mr. Ramirez, can shed some light on that."

Arriving in the city, they took the MacArthur Boulevard exit toward downtown. Buzz was busy reading the directions, trying to find the street where the restaurant was located.

"I think I've found it," he said. "Turn right at the next light, go five blocks and then turn left."

"That's it up ahead," Laroque said. "See the sign out front, El Cacique."

Parking the car at the curb, they got out and walked up the street to the restaurant. At the door, they were met by the maitre d', who greeted them in Spanish. "*Buenas tardes. Puedo servirle en algo, senores?*"

Mike replied in English, "We are here to meet with Mr. Ramirez."

Shifting to English, the young man replied, "You must be Captain Canfield. Mr. Ramirez just called. He asked me to inform you that he will be along in a few minutes. He suggested you have a drink while you are waiting."

Motioning for them to follow, the maitre d' escorted them to a table by a window. Sitting down, Mike took a look around. In the center of the room was a large, ornately decorated water fountain sur-rounded by tropical plants. Most of the tables were full.

After they were seated, the maitre d' handed each of them a menu and departed. Soon a young waitress appeared, carrying a tray with two tall glasses of white sangria.

As they were sipping their wine, Mike noticed a man enter the restaurant. He was alone. Dressed in an expensive-looking dark blue suit, he appeared to be in his mid-forties. He glanced around the room as if he were looking for someone. Mike guessed that this might be Mr. Ramirez.

The maitre d' walked up to greet him. After a short conversa-tion, he pointed in their direction.

As he approached, Mike and Buzz stood up.

"I assume you must be Mr. Ramirez," Mike said, extending his hand. "I am Mike Canfield and this is my assistant, Commander Jack Laroque."

Shaking hands with each of them in turn, he said. "*Buenos tardes,* Captain Canfield, Commander Laroque. It is my pleasure to meet you."

"Please sit down," he said, signaling for the waitress. She soon appeared with a another glass of sangria.

"Would either of you gentlemen care for another drink?" he asked. Both Mike and Buzz declined.

"If not, shall we order now? If you are undecided, I highly recommend the Cuban seafood salad. It is quite excellent here."

Mike and Laroque both decided to accept his recommendation.

Turning to the waitress Ramirez said, "In that case, we will have three seafood salads, and would you please bring us a bottle of my favorite white wine."

A short time later she returned with the bottle of wine, along with a basket of warm Cuban bread.

"Would you care to sample the wine, Captain?" Ramirez asked.

"It would be my pleasure."

Giving Mike a chance to taste it, he asked, "Well, what do you think, Captain?"

"It's very good," Mike replied. "You have excellent taste, Mr. Ramirez."

While they waited for their entrees to arrive, Ramirez looked over at Mike. "Captain Canfield, on the phone yesterday you said you were serving on a Navy promotion board."

"That's correct," Mike replied. Recalling how Ramirez had wanted to see some proof of his identify, he reached inside his coat pocket, removed a copy of his orders, and handed them across the table.

Taking them from him, Ramirez read through them carefully. Satisfying himself that they were legitimate, he handed them back.

"Now, what is it I can do for you, Captain?"

"As I indicated on the phone, Lieutenant Commander Barnes is one of the officers before our board as a candidate for promotion. In going over his record, I noticed that in 1961 he was assigned to an operation which I have reason to believe was run by the CIA. I also know you were a part of this operation."

Mike noticed Ramirez raise his eyebrows slightly. "I would be interested in finding out what you know about Barnes, as well as anything else you would care to tell me about what happened back then."

Ramirez sat silent for a few seconds before replying. "You have done your homework well, Captain Canfield. Yes, it is true. I know Jake Barnes. We were both part of Operation Cuba Libre, or Operation Pluto, as you Americans called it. We first met in Miami in late October 1960."

Before he could continue, the waitress arrived with their food. While they ate, the discussion of Jake Barnes was put on hold. The conversation shifted to the food, an excellent combination of green vegetables and fresh seafood, with a hint of calamari.

"This is excellent, Mr. Ramirez," Laroque said.

"I am glad you are enjoying it, Commander Laroque," he replied.

While they were having coffee, Mike steered the conversation back to Jake Barnes. "You were saying you and Lieutenant Commander Barnes worked together on Operation Cuba Libre?"

"Yes, in fact we worked quite closely together," Ramirez replied. Glancing out the window, a startled look came across his face. Quietly, he said, "I think I may have been followed here, Captain."

Mike started to turn around.

"Wait! Don't look now," Ramirez said. "There is a car parked across the street. Leaning against it are two men dressed in dark suits. They were not there when I arrived."

"Well, if they are staking out the place, they sure as hell aren't being very professional about it," Laroque interjected.

"No, that's not it. I think they wish to be recognized," Ramirez replied. "They are trying to convey a message to me."

The thought seemed to make him even more nervous. Pushing his chair back from the table, he stood up.

"I am sorry, gentlemen, but there is nothing more I can tell you. I must go now. Will you please cover for me for a few moments? Hopefully, once I am gone, our friends will depart."

"Is there something we can do, Mr. Ramirez?" Mike asked.

"No, I will be all right after you have gone," he replied.

"If you should change your mind, we'll be at the Visitor Officers Quarters at Homestead Air Force Base until tomorrow morning."

"Thank you, Captain Canfield, but I don't think I will," he replied. "I may have said too much already. I am sorry to have wasted your time." Leaving the table, he stopped to say something to the maitre d' before disappearing into the rear of the restaurant.

Mike and Buzz looked at each other, neither of them knowing what to make of this turn of events. Quickly downing his coffee, Mike motioned for the waitress and asked for the check.

"It has already been taken care of," she said.

As they left the restaurant, Mike saw the two men across the street get into their car and drive off.

On the drive back to Homestead, Laroque said, "I wonder what spooked Ramirez? He looked like he'd seen a ghost."

"I'll be damned if I know," Mike replied. "This is getting to be really strange. I can't figure out what the hell is going on, except that someone doesn't want Ramirez talking to me. But why?"

"If that was their intention, it sure as hell worked," Laroque replied. "Boss, if you want my opinion, I think, for a couple of Navy types, we're getting in way over our heads."

Mike wasn't listening. He was busy with other thoughts. Who were these two men? It has got to have something to do with Jake Barnes, or why else would they be here? Somehow, this guy Belcher must have found out we were coming down here, and he is trying to keep Ramirez from talking to me.

Recalling his conversation with the gunnery sergeant at Quantico, he asked himself, Why is it no one is willing to talk to me about Jake Barnes? And then there was the warning from Hoot Gibson.

Breaking the silence, Laroque asked, "What do we do now, boss?"

"There isn't much we can do, Buzz," Mike replied. "I don't think we are going to get anything out of Ramirez. Besides, the selection board is due to wrap up Tuesday, which doesn't give me much time."

Going back to what happened in the restaurant, Laroque said, "God, it's been a long time since I've seen someone so scared. Do you think those guys out in front of the restaurant might work for Castro?"

"No, I don't think so," Mike replied. "My guess would be they're CIA."

"But they're supposed to be on our team," Laroque replied. "Besides, how in hell would they have known we were coming down here?"

"They might have a tap on Ramirez' phone," Mike guessed.

"Either that or they found out I was nosing around asking questions back at the Pentagon."

"That's probably more likely," Mike said.

By now they had arrived back at Homestead. At the front desk, they picked up the keys to their room.

"What time do you want to meet for dinner?" Mike asked.

"How about we meet in the bar around 1700."

"Okay, Buzz, see you then."

In his room, Mike called home. "Jen, this is Mike. We've struck out down here. We'll be returning to Andrews in the morning. I should be home by early afternoon."

"I'm sorry it didn't work out, Mike, but I'll be glad to have you home," she replied, sympathetically.

After hanging up the phone, Mike laid across the bed. He tried to get some sleep, but his mind kept going back to what had occurred at El Cacique.

"Ramirez acted like he was truly frightened. I wonder what kind of hold Belcher has over him?" he said to himself. "Whatever it is that Ramirez knows, it's pretty apparent Belcher doesn't want me finding out. And without him talking, I've pretty much reached a dead end."

Around 1630, he got up, took a shower, dressed and walked across the street to the "O" Club. Buzz was already in the bar, seated at table by himself.

Seeing him enter, he stood up and motioned for Mike to come over.

For the next hour they went over what had happened back at El Cacique, speculating about who was involved and why. Giving up, they finally went in to dinner.

In the dining room, the hostess escorted them to a table. Before leaving, she gave a menu to each of them, informing them that in addition to the regular menu the club was featuring a Mongolian barbecue this evening. Since neither of them had eaten at one before, they decided to give it a try.

After the waitress left, Mike asked, "Would you like something to drink, Buzz?"

"No thanks, boss, I'm still getting over the wine from lunch. Besides, I have to fly tomorrow."

Getting up from the table, they made their selections from the wide variety of meats, exotic spices and vegetables arranged on the buffet table. At the end of the line, the contents of the plate were weighed to determine the cost, then sent off the kitchen to be stir-fried.

After dinner Buzz and Mike returned to the bar for a cup of coffee. Around 2000 Mike excused himself.

"I think I'll check it in for the night, Buzz. What do you say we meet for breakfast around 0700."

"0700 it is," Laroque replied. "Goodnight, skipper. I'm sorry things didn't work out."

"Thanks, sorry to have screwed up your weekend," Mike replied.

"Don't worry about that. I needed the flight time anyway."

When Mike arrived in his room, the message light was flashing on the phone. Dialing the front desk, he asked for his messages.

"Just a moment, Captain," the duty clerk replied, setting down the receiver. In the background, Mike could hear him rustling through some papers.

A few seconds later his voice came back on the line. "A Mr. Ramirez called earlier. He asked if you could meet him around 10:00 p.m." He then gave Mike the address of a supper club in Coconut Grove. "He also asked that you not call him back. He said, if you can't make it, he would understand."

Mike hung up the phone, puzzled by the message he had just received.

"I wonder what caused Ramirez to change his mind?" he asked himself.

Leaving the room, he hurried back across the street to the club. Buzz, was still there, engaged in aviator talk with a couple of Air Force officers.

Seeing Mike, he excused himself and walked over. From the look on Mike's face, he sensed something was wrong.

"What's up, boss?" he asked.

"You're not going to believe this, Buzz, but when I got to my room I had a message from Ramirez. He wants to meet me at 2200 in Coconut Grove."

"That doesn't give us much time," Laroque replied.

CHAPTER 13

Ramirez waited anxiously inside the men's room at El Cacique. When the maitre d' informed him that the men outside the restaurant had left, he phoned his office and asked his secretary to reschedule his afternoon appointments, telling her that he wasn't feeling well. He felt guilty about canceling the appointments, but today he would not have been able to give his clients the attention they deserved.

During the drive to his home in Coral Gables, he thought about the past. He had been born in Havana into an affluent family. His father was a prominent physician and his mother was a renowned Cuban painter whose paintings of natural landscapes were widely exhibited and acclaimed throughout Cuba.

From early childhood, he had attended the best private schools in Cuba. Later on, he attended college in the United States, obtaining a law degree from Georgetown University. Returning to Havana, he set up a law practice, and shortly thereafter he met Maria. They fell in love and were married a short time later in an elaborate ceremony attended by nearly all the prominent members of Havana society. Their first child, Anna, was born a year later. Eighteen months after Anna, Luis was born. These were years filled with pleasant memories. As his law practice flourished, his life was full with friends and family, and like most of his friends, he generally ignored the political events unfolding in the country.

Unknown to him at the time, at the other end of Cuba, in Oriente province, another person was growing up who was to have a profound influence on his life. He was Fidel Castro, born August 13, 1926, the illegitimate son of a well-to-do planter and a servant girl working in the Castro household. After the death of his wife, Fidel's father married his mother, Lina. Much like Ramirez, Fidel attended the best schools, including the prestigious Colegio Belen in Havana.

After graduating from high school, Castro entered the university, where he became involved with a number of radical organizations dedicated to the overthrow of dictatorships throughout Latin America.

Then in 1948 he married Mirtha Diaz Balart, the daughter of another prominent Cuban family. Continuing on at the university, he graduated in 1950. Becoming even more deeply involved in politics, he joined the Orthodoxo Party, and in 1952 he ran for the Cuban Congress, but was defeated. After that, he associated himself with groups dedicated more and more to violence. Increasingly disillusioned with his political views, his wife divorced him in 1955.

As a result of his revolutionary activities, Castro was deported from Cuba and moved to New York City. Following a short exile, he returned to Cuba, landing with a group of 80 rebels in Oriente province on the eastern side of the island. When President Fulgencio Batista found out about Castro's return, he ordered his arrest, along with that of his followers. In subsequent action, most of the rebels were killed, except for Castro and a few of his close associates, who managed to escape into the mountains. Once there, Castro set about recruiting another army and began to wage a guerrilla campaign against the government forces.

In the beginning, the upper classes paid little attention to Castro's activities, but as the movement gained momentum many of their members, including Jose' Ramirez and his friends, supported the revolution. They naively hoped that Castro's promised reform would get rid of the increasingly corrupt Batista regime and bring true democracy to their country.

Late in 1958, Batista's army rebelled against him, and in January 1959 he fled Cuba, seeking exile in Honduras. With Batista gone, Castro and his army, after a number of months of guerrilla warfare, triumphantly entered Havana and took over the reins of government. Once in power, he quickly moved to consolidate his hold over the country. Even though he had preached that Cuba would never again be ruled by a dictator, the true nature of his 26th of July Movement soon became apparent.

One of his first acts, after appointing himself premier, was to arrest anyone even suspected of disloyalty to his movement. To accommodate those not executed by firing squad, he embarked on an ambitious building program to dramatically increase the number of prisons. At the same time that he was purging the country of his perceived enemies, he began nationalizing and taking over private property, including that owned by foreign investors.

By this time, most of the Batista supporters had either been executed, were in prison, or had escaped the country. It wasn't long before the members of the Cuban professional and business classes came to realize that they had been betrayed, and they quietly began to make plans to move their families and money out of the country. Most of them came to the United States, where they set up residence in South Florida. Jose' Ramirez' family had been part of this exodus.

Once in Florida, the exiles formed a tightly knit community, dedicating themselves to the overthrow of the Castro regime. Joining in the movement, Ramirez assumed an active role in its leadership, resolving to return to Cuba one day and free his homeland.

"How naive I was," he thought to himself.

When he and the other leaders in the movement were approached in the summer of 1960 by the American CIA to help organize and lead a Cuban brigade to return to Cuba, he enthusiastically signed up. He envisioned himself riding into Havana at the head of a liberating army to the cheering throngs of his countrymen.

Instead, he ended up being captured, branded a traitor, and sentenced to twenty-five years in prison. Fortunately, he spent only a little over a year in prison before he was released.

When Castro sarcastically made a public statement that the prisoners were not worth five hundred tractors, the Cuban community in the States decided to take him at his word and organized a "Tractors for Freedom Committee."

Even though the tractors were never sent to Cuba, it spurred the Kennedy administration to press Castro for the release of the imprisoned members of the Cuban Brigade. Finally, after a year and a half of languishing in Cuban prisons, they were freed, and returned to the United States in exchange for $53,000,000 dollars in drugs and medicines. Most of the money was raised from private sources.

During the first month in prison, Ramirez had been subjected to nearly every indignity humanly possible. He was interrogated incessantly in an effort to make him confess to committing treason against the government of Cuba.

In the beginning his guards were content to beat and berate him. One day, however, he was confronted with a new group of interrogators from the newly formed Directorate of Scientific Application. Modeled after its Russian counterpart, its purpose was to elicit confessions from difficult cases and to indoctrinate them in communist philosophy, using so-called scientific techniques. In reality, it amounted to just a more sophisticated form of torture.

For a time, his tormentors forced him to listen to endless lectures on communist doctrine. Finally concluding he was not receptive, they fell back on more primitive methods.

One day, when he was brought into the interrogation room, he was ordered to remove all of his clothing. While he was sitting naked, they strapped him to a chair, and one of the guards dumped a bucket of cold water over his head. Another applied a cattle prod to his genitals. Each time he refused to cooperate, a jolt of electricity was sent coursing through his body, the cold water serving to intensify the effect of the current. After an hour of this treatment, he was reduced to blubbering, pleading and begging them to stop. He would do whatever they wanted.

Ordered to get dressed, he was taken to a radio station, where he read a prepared statement, confessing to being paid by the CIA to return to Cuba and pave the way for the return of Batista.

After his confession, his tormentors left him alone, giving up on trying to convert him to communism. However, he was to spend the remainder of his prison time locked in solitary confinement.

During Ramirez' imprisonment, Castro repeatedly refused to allow the International Red Cross or any other neutral organization access to the prisons. For good reason! The food was poor and the quarters squalid, with few if any sanitation facilities.

Ramirez' only link with the outside world was what he overheard from conversations between the guards. From them, he learned that Russian freighters loaded with military equipment were arriving daily in Havana, Santiago, and other Cuban ports.

After a while, he had begun to despair as to whether he would ever see his family again. This was harder for him to accept than the torture. At the time, he was unaware of the efforts of his friends and countrymen in the United States to secure his release.

Just before Christmas in 1962, he and 1,113 of his compatriots, including sixty who had been wounded, were released from jail and returned to the United States.

After his release from prison, Ramirez returned to Miami where he was reunited with his wife and children. Resuming his law practice, he vowed never again to trust anyone involved with any government.

Now they were after him again. Why couldn't they just leave him alone?

Pulling into his driveway, Jose' Ramirez got out of his car, walked briskly up to the house and unlocked the door.

"Maria?" he called out.

"I am out beside the pool," she replied.

Walking through the living room, tastefully decorated in pink and green pastels, he made his way to the screened-in pool area at the rear of the house. When he entered, Maria got up from the lounge chair, where she had been reading a book, to greet him. She was wearing a floral two-piece bikini bathing suit. Even after having had two children, her figure remained as trim and firm as it had been when they had met. Kissing her, he asked, "Is everything all right?"

"Yes, of course. Why?" she replied, noting the worried look on his face. "Is there some reason it shouldn't be?"

"Of course not," he said, giving her an extra squeeze. "Give me a minute to change into my bathing suit."

Turning to leave, he went into the bedroom, and changed out of his dress clothes, putting on swim trunks and a Cuban-style floral patterned shirt. Before returning to the pool, he stopped by the kitchen to mix up a pitcher of sangria. Placing the pitcher on a tray along with two tall glasses filled with ice, he rejoined Maria.

While pouring each of them a drink, he asked, "Where are the children?"

"Anna is next door and Luis is at soccer practice," Maria replied. "They should be home shortly."

Jose' sat down in a lounge chair, debating about whether he should tell Maria what had occurred during lunch. He decided not to worry her unnecessarily."

"How was your day?" she asked. "I thought you were going to work this afternoon."

"I was, but I decided to cancel my appointments. I wanted to be here at home with you."

Maria's wifely intuition sensed that all was not right. She hoped it had nothing to do with the past.

The afternoon passed quietly. She continued reading her book while he read the newspaper. The children returned home around 4, and joined them around the pool. While they exuberantly related their

107

day's activities to them, Jose' thought about how they were growing up so quickly. I must spend more time with them before they are all grown and move away, he thought.

Later, Maria fixed a light supper, which they ate together around the pool. After they finished eating, Jose' went into the family room to watch the evening news, while the children went across the street to visit with their friends.

Around 7 o'clock the doorbell rang.

"I'll get it," Jose' said, turning off the TV. Opening the door, he was startled to see two men leaning against the door frame—the same two he had seen earlier outside El Cacique.

"What do you want?" he asked brusquely.

The taller of the two, the one with black hair, replied, "Mr. Ramirez, we are with the government." Reaching into his inside pocket, he produced a badge, which he quickly flashed in front of Jose's face. "We've been asked to pass along a message to you."

"And what might that be?" Jose' inquired, even though he already suspected what they were about to say.

"We noted you had a meeting with a Captain Canfield today at El Cacique. I have been asked to remind you that there are some things in the past which would be best if they remained that way. Do you understand?"

"I understand. Now, if you will excuse me," he replied, shutting the door in their face.

"Who was that?" Maria asked from the bedroom.

"It was two of Belcher's men, warning me to keep my mouth shut," he replied, bitterly.

"Oh, no!" she exclaimed. "What's going on?" It was she who now had a worried look on her face.

"Yesterday I had a call from a Navy captain. He wanted to know what I knew about Jake Barnes."

"Why? I thought that was all behind us."

"I thought so too, but apparently he is now up for promotion. At lunch today I met with a Captain Canfield, who is on his promotion board. It was then that these men showed up."

"That explains why you came home early. You were worried about me," she said. Coming over to put her arms around him, she asked, "What are you going to do?"

"I don't know yet," he replied. "But it's time the truth came out. I am tired of being told what to do."

"But, Jose', they may harm you!"

"I don't think so. They are just bluffing, trying to frighten me to keep me from talking," he replied, angrily. He had made up his mind. "I am going to tell Captain Canfield what happened."

Removing his bathing suit, he changed into a casual shirt and slacks. When he had finished dressing he said, "I'm going out for a while, I'll call you and let you know where I will be, but be careful of what you say on the phone. They may be listening in." Seeing the frightened look come over her face, he added, "Don't worry, they will not harm me."

"Be careful," Maria called after him as he went out the door. "I couldn't bear to lose you again."

Backing out of the driveway, he drove around the neighborhood, frequently checking in the rear-view mirror to make sure he wasn't being followed. Once he was certain, he stopped at a pay phone in a service station and dialed the operator. When she answered, he asked for the number of the Visiting Officers Quarters at Homestead Air Force Base.

109

CHAPTER 14

October 1960, Little Creek, Virginia

Jake Barnes was sound asleep when the alarm went off at 0600. Reaching over to turn it off, he slowly climbed out of bed. In the bathroom, he turned on the water in the basin.

"God, that was a short night," he grumbled.

After he finished shaving, he put on a pair of khaki trousers and a sport shirt before going below to breakfast in the closed mess. The dining room was nearly full. Looking around the room, he found an empty seat at a table with some fellow officers he knew from over at UDT 22.

As he took a seat, one of them looked up. Noticing the civilian clothes, he asked, "Going on leave, Jake?"

"Nah. Just some TAD," Jake replied.

Hurrying through breakfast, he excused himself from the table and returned to his room, where he phoned for a base taxi. While packing, he had been careful to remove all military insignia from his clothing. As he picked up his bags, he thought about the dog tags hanging around his neck. He started to take them off, but hesitated. Thinking it over, he decided against it. He was still an American naval officer, and if anything happened to him he wanted to be treated as such.

Arriving at the airport forty-five minutes before his flight was due to depart, he proceeded to the ticket counter, where he checked in with the attendant.

Waiting for his flight to be called, he thought about the events of the last couple of days. He had to admit he was excited about being involved in a real operation for a change, but one thing that troubled him was Ray Belcher's attitude.

The two-hour flight to Miami International was pretty much uneventful, except for the young woman seated next to him who insisted on talking during the entire flight. At least it helped to keep his mind off Cindy.

Arriving in Miami, he picked up his bag and walked outside the terminal. There he hailed a taxi, giving the driver the address he had been given in Washington. A short time later the cab pulled up in front of an office building on Biscayne Boulevard.

Paying the fare, Jake picked up his luggage, walked into the empty lobby, and pushed the button to call the elevator. Getting off on the third floor, he made his way down the hallway, looking at the numbers on the doors. He noticed that were no names on them. They appeared to be unoccupied. This could explain why the agency had chosen this building for its Miami headquarters.

Suite 319 was at the very end of the hallway. Opening the door, he was surprised to find a pretty, young Hispanic woman seated behind a desk. She looked up at him. Before she had a chance to say anything, he introduced himself.

"Good morning, I'm Jake Barnes," he said, deliberately omitting his rank.

"Oh yes, Mr. Barnes," she said. My name is Eva. Mr. Belcher told me to expect you." Seeing his suitcase, she added, "I have made reservations for you at the same hotel where the rest of the staff is staying. If you'd like, I can have your bags sent over."

"Thanks," Jake replied.

"First let me show you to your office," she said, swiveling her chair around. Jake noticed her shapely legs as she uncrossed them while getting up from her chair. He briefly thought about Cindy.

She lingered in the doorway while he looked around. Jake surmised she had something she wanted to say to him. He looked at her quizzically.

"I suppose you are wondering about me, Mr. Barnes? What a Cuban girl is doing here, involved in a secret military operation such as this?"

"It crossed my mind," Jake said.

Speaking in a soft voice, she said, "During the great exodus, a couple of years ago, my father arranged for my mother and me to come here to Florida and stay with family friends, while he remained behind in Havana to take care of some business. I never saw my father again, Mr. Barnes.

"Shortly after we arrived in Miami, he was arrested, charged with being a traitor, and executed by that monster, Fidel Castro. I joined the counter-revolutionary movement, and when I heard about Operation Cuba Libre, I volunteered to do what I could and they sent me her."

"I'm sorry to hear about your father, Eva," Jake replied sympathetically. "I am sure he would be proud of what you are doing. Thanks for telling me."

She turned to leave. Jake followed her out of the room.

"I guess it's time I met the others," he said.

"They are in the conference room," Eva replied, motioning toward one of the other doors.

Inside the conference room a group of men in civilian clothes were seated around the table, talking. When he entered they stood up at attention.

He went around the table, introducing himself. Chief Engineman Lefty Gomez, his arms covered with a hodgepodge of tattoos, was the first person he came to.

Shaking hands, Jake said, "I hope you know your way around boat engines, Chief."

"Like yourself, Lieutenant, I'm an old gator sailor. Give me enough time and I can make anything run."

"How did you know I was with the amphibs?"

"You know how it is, Lieutenant," Gomez replied. Moving on, Jake shook his head. He was always amazed at how fast the word got around.

As he went around the table, Chief Bosun Joe Knisel, Chief Radioman Roy Custance, Gunnery Sergeant Mike McCormick, Chief Gunner's Mate Frenchie Lefebvre, and Lieutenant (junior grade) Jim McVie took turns introducing themselves.

The last person he came to was Jose' Ramirez.

"Lieutenant Barnes, my name is Major Ramirez. I represent the Cuban Brigade. Our commander, Colonel Juan Martinez, asked me to extend his apologies for not being able to be here."

Grasping his hand, Jake replied, "Glad to meet you, Major. I'm looking forward to working with you, and meeting the colonel."

"Colonel Martinez is in Washington attending a meeting of the Revolutionary Council. He should be returning to Miami shortly. You will have the opportunity to meet him then."

While he was talking with Ramirez, Bosun Knisel came over with a cup of coffee. Handing it to Jake, he asked, "Cream or sugar?"

"Neither, I drink it black," Jake replied.

Tall, with a square jaw and Slavic features that broadly hinted at his Eastern European origins, Knisel had more experience in amphibious warfare than anyone else in the room. His Navy career went back to World War II. As an assault-boat coxswain on a transport, he had participated in the battles for both Leyte Gulf and Iwo Jima. After the war, he was assigned to UDT 21, the Underwater Demolition Team

113

in Coronado. There he was charged with training boat crews. Although his hair had now begun to turn gray and his waist had thickened a little, he still conveyed the impression that he was not someone to mess around with.

Taking the cup from him, Jake said, "Thanks, Bosun. I'm glad to have you on board. I'm going to be leaning on you for help."

"You can count on me, Lieutenant," Knisel replied. Jake got the impression that he truly meant what he said.

Looking up at the clock on the wall, Jake noticed it was now 1215. He called for everyone's attention.

"Listen up. Why don't we break for lunch, but let's be back by 1330. I have a lot of catching up to do."

"There's a small place around the corner where we've been having lunch, Lieutenant," Knisel said. "You're welcome to join us, if you like."

"Thanks, Bosun," Jake replied.

Inside the cafe, the group sat at a large table in the center of the room. Chief Gomez was seated across from Jake. As they were eating, Jake noticed the chief was eating with his right hand.

"I thought you told me your name was Lefty?"

"Yes sir, it is," Gomez replied.

Jake gave him a puzzled look.

Gomez realized an explanation was in order. "That's a long story, Lieutenant. My old man was a big baseball fan, and about the time I was born, Lefty Gomez pitched for the Yankees. With our name being Gomez, the old man got carried away and decided to name me Lefty, after this guy. When I turned out to be right-handed, he about had a fit. Worse yet, I never took much interest in playing baseball. I was more interested in messing around car engines. The old man never quite got over it. He was real glad when I decided to join the Navy."

Listening in, the others would never let him forget it.

"Well, Chief, I for one am glad that you were more interested in fixing engines," Jake said.

114

After lunch, the group gathered back in the conference room. Jake took a seat at the end of the table, laying a yellow notepad and pen on the table in front of him.

He waited while they settled down before bringing the meeting to order.

"Before we get started, I would like to say a few words. I know all of you volunteered for this operation, and I don't need to tell you we have our work cut out for us. I need and expect your complete cooperation. I'm also looking forward to working with you and getting to know each of you better."

Pausing for a moment he continued, "Now that I have had my say, let's get down to business. How about we begin with each of you filling me in on your particular area of responsibility. Chief Gomez, how about going first."

"This morning I just received word that the Navy was transferring some landing craft, three LCUs and four VPs, to us," Gomez reported. "They are in the salvage yard in Bayonne, New Jersey."

"What kind of shape are they're in?" Jake asked.

"I don't know."

"Being in the salvage yard, I would hate to guess," Jake replied. "First thing tomorrow, I want you to catch a flight up to Bayonne. We need to get a reading on their status and what it takes to make them operational. Without boats, no one is going anywhere."

Moving on, he looked over at Knisel. "Bosun, how about the ships?"

"So far, all I have been able to find out is there are to be five merchant ships and two LCIs allocated to the operation," he replied.

"If that's it, how in hell are we going to transport the LCUs?" Jake asked. "For God's sake, everyone knows you can't hoist an LCU on board ship."

"That's a good point, Lieutenant, and as of now I don't have the answer," Knisel replied.

"This is something we need to get resolved pronto," Jake said. "Remind me to take it up with Mr. Belcher. In the meantime, I want you to get on board the ships as soon as possible to see what needs to be done."

Jake looked around the room for Chief Custance. "Chief, whenever Bosun Knisel visits the ships, I want you to go along and check out their radio gear."

Jake continued around the table. "Mr. McVie, where do we stand on logistics?"

"We have pretty well been given a blank check to procure anything we need, Lieutenant," he replied. "Right now I'm working on getting the training base set up in the Everglades. As soon as I finish with that, I'll be making up a load list for the actual operation."

"Good. Keep me informed," Jake said. Moving on to Gunnery Sergeant McCormick, he asked, "Gunny, when will we be able to commence training?"

"Next week," he replied. "The site allocated for training is an abandoned Navy auxiliary field in the Everglades, about fifty miles west of here. I toured the site the day before yesterday with Mr. McVie. It's in pretty rough shape, but a Reserve Seabee battalion is out there working on getting the utilities restored and the runway back in operation. They should be finished up with their work in a few days. After that, it all depends on how soon we can get the tents and mess kitchens delivered."

"Good! Let me know if there are any hang ups," Jake replied. Moving on to Jose', he asked, "Major Ramirez, can you give me a rundown on the status of your people?"

"As of now we have recruited over 1,000 men," Ramirez replied. "By the end of next week we expect to have 1,500 enrolled."

"Have any of them had any military training?" Jake asked.

"Not much in the way of any formal training, although some of them have participated in commando raids on the north coast of my country for the past year."

"I don't need to tell you of the need for secrecy," Jake cautioned. "If Castro gets wind of what we're planning, it will make things that much more difficult."

"There is no need to worry, Lieutenant," Ramirez replied. "All of our people hate Castro. They will not say anything to jeopardize the operation."

Bringing the meeting to an end, Jake went into his office. There he sat down at his desk and went over his notes. If they were to put a landing force together from scratch and have it ready in a little over three months, there was little time to be wasted.

"My God, what have I gotten myself involved in?" he thought to himself. Seven or eight landing craft from the scrap yard, five merchant freighters with God only knows who for crews, a couple of LCIs left over from World War II, and a group of Cubans with little or no military experience. The operation could turn into a friggin' Chinese fire drill.

He tried to put the thought out of his mind. The rest of the afternoon passed quickly, and around 1700 the members of the staff began to straggle into his office, requesting permission to depart for the day. Wrapping it up at about 1800 Jake put his notes away in the safe and locked up the office.

Taking the elevator to the ground floor, he walked to the hotel. It felt good being outside after being holed up inside an office all day. The weather had begun to cool off slightly. Arriving at the hotel, he checked in at the front desk, picked up his key, and went to his room. He stretched out across the bed for a few minutes. For the first time since early this morning, he thought about Cindy.

CHAPTER 15

The phone rang at 0600. It was the desk clerk with his wake-up call. Still half asleep, Jake put the phone back into its cradle, pulled himself out of bed, and made his way to the bathroom. Returning to the bedroom, he put on a fresh pair of khaki trousers and a sport shirt. It felt strange wearing civilian clothes. After he finished dressing, he took the elevator down to the lobby and made his way to the dining room. Bosun Knisel was already there, sitting at a table by the window.

Seeing Jake, he stood up and motioned toward him. "Care to join me, Lieutenant?" he asked.

"Thanks," Jake replied, pulling out a chair across the table from him. Shortly, the waitress appeared with a coffee pot in hand.

"Care for some coffee?" she asked in a cheerful voice.

"Sure thing," Jake replied, turning the cup right side up in the saucer.

Filling his cup, she stood by, waiting to take his order. After she left, Knisel said, "Mind if I ask you a personal question, Lieutenant?"

"Not at all," Jake replied.

"What the hell do you make of this rinkydink operation?" he asked.

"I'm not sure," Jake replied. "I'm a little uneasy about trying to mount an amphibious assault using a bunch of surplus boats left over from World War II, let alone using merchant ships leased from some backwater Latin American ship owner."

Knisel nodded his head in agreement. "I feel the same way. Why in hell couldn't they just to turn it over to us professionals instead of involving these CIA pukes? Then there's the Cubans, like Ramirez. He's a nice enough guy, but for chrissake, he's a lawyer. He doesn't know doodley squat about being a soldier."

"I'm sure that by the end of next week he'll have a pretty fair idea of what's involved after the gunny and his troopers get hold of him," Jake replied.

"You're not whistling Dixie about that."

The waitress arrived with Jake's breakfast. He concentrated on eating, while Knisel sat idly by, drinking his coffee. Finally, draining his cup, he pushed his chair back from the table. "Excuse me, Lieutenant. Guess I'd better get to work and see what I can find out about those merchies."

Still frowning, he picked up his check, and left a dollar bill on the table for the waitress. Turning to leave, he said, "See you back at the office, Lieutenant."

After he left, Jake thought about their conversation. "At least I hope we'll be able to use our own boat crews," he said to himself.

After breakfast, he walked to the office, taking the stairs to the third floor in order to get a little exercise. Slightly out of breath, he opened the door. Eva looked up from her typing.

"Good morning, Mr. Barnes," she said. "Mr. Belcher just called. He's at the airport, and expects to be here within the hour. He would like for you to set up a staff meeting for 9 o'clock. Afterward, he said he wants to inspect the training base in the Everglades."

"I wasn't expecting him until Monday," Jake replied. "Would you make sure the staff gets the word to meet in the conference room at 0900?"

119

At 0830 Ray Belcher arrived in the headquarters. With him were Dick Harris and a middle-aged Hispanic man.

"How about coming into my office for a moment," Ray said, shaking hands. "I want you to meet Colonel Martinez."

Following the group into Belcher's office, he closed the door behind him. Jake took a seat on the sofa next to Dick Harris.

"I presume you have met the rest of the staff, and they have briefed you on what's going on?" Belcher said.

"Yes sir, I got a rundown yesterday afternoon," Jake replied.

"Do you think we can be ready to go by the first week in January?"

"It's going to be pretty tight," Jake replied.

"When will we be able to set up shop in the Everglades?"

"Hopefully by the middle of next week. It depends on when the tents and mess kitchens arrive."

Breaking in, Colonel Martinez said, "It is important for us to get our people into camp as soon as possible. The longer we delay, the greater the chance that Castro will find out about our plans."

"I agree, Colonel," Belcher replied. "Jake, is there any way we can move the date up to the first of the week?"

"We'll have to ask McVie," Jake said.

At 0900 Jake accompanied the trio into the conference room, where Belcher took a seat at the head of the table flanked on either side by Colonel Martinez and Dick Harris. Jake sat down at the other end of the table.

Kicking off the meeting, Belcher said, "Good morning, gentlemen. Since I'm here in the area, I thought I would bring you up to date on where things now stand up in Washington. Both President Eisenhower and Mr. Cardona, the chairman of the counter-revolutionary coalition, have given the go-ahead to proceed with Operation Cuba Libre. They're both anxious to get things under way. We need to get on with training as soon as possible. Jake has informed me we are waiting on tents and mess kitchens. Mr. McVie, can you tell us when we expect them to arrive?"

"I have been promised they will be on site by Friday," McVie replied. "We should be all set up and ready to receive personnel first thing Monday morning."

"Good, let's keep on top of it." Shifting his attention to McCormick, Belcher asked, "Sergeant, are your people all set to go?"

"Yes sir. We're ready as soon as we get the word."

"Okay. Let's plan to move the training staff in over the weekend."

Concluding the meeting, he pushed his chair back and stood up. "I guess that about does it for now."

Jake followed him out of the room. "Before you leave, Ray, I need to talk to you."

"Okay. Come into to my office, but you'll have to make it quick. We don't have a lot of time to spare."

"I'll try to make it brief," Jake replied. "First, I would like to know when and where we can get a look at the freighters. We need to find out what kind of shape they're in. The other thing I would like to know is how we plan to get the LCUs to the landing area."

"As far as the freighters go, Jake, we are still in the process of negotiating with Garcia. I'll let you know as soon as the contract is signed. Concerning the LCUs, is there any reason we can't ferry them on board the ships?"

"No way," Jake replied. "The only way to transport a boat this big is in the well of an LSD."

"I guess that does present a problem," Belcher replied. "Let me talk with the Navy Department and see what they can come up with. Look Jake, I've gotta run."

"One last thing, Ray, before you go. What about boat crews?"

"We plan on recruiting them from within the Brigade," he replied. "Why, does that present a problem?"

"For chrissake, Ray!" Jake vehemently protested. "Do you know what's involved in training assault boat crews? It would make a helluva lot more sense to use American crews."

Dick Harris, who had been listening in, interrupted, saying emphatically. "Mr. Barnes, our orders are that no American forces are to set foot on Cuban soil until a provisional government has been set up ashore, and we receive a formal request from them for assistance."

"I don't mean to be difficult, Mr. Harris, but the boat crews will not be setting foot ashore," Jake rebutted.

Shaking his head for emphasis, Harris replied, "We can't risk it. Let's get it straight, once and for all, there will be no Americans in the boats."

"Okay then! We're going to need a training area where we can practice. We sure as hell can't conduct boat training in the Everglades," Jake replied. He was getting irritated.

Belcher interrupted them. "Gentlemen, gentlemen. Let's calm down. Look, Jake, give us some time. We'll get it worked out. As soon as I find out anything, I'll let you know." He turned to Harris. "Dick, could you give us a couple of moments alone."

After he left, Belcher leaned back in his chair. He began to twirl a ballpoint pen between his fingers. Adopting a patronizing tone, he said, "Jake, you worry too much. All we have to do is give these guys some basic training in how to use their weapons, and put them ashore. The Cuban people will take it from there."

Jake interrupted. "And if they don't, we are effectively sending 1,500 people to their death."

"Jake, I think you are over reacting a bit," Belcher calmly replied.

"Well, that may be, but a long time ago I was involved in an operation in Korea which was supposed to be routine, and we ended up losing damn near a whole company of Marines. We need to plan for the worst possible scenario."

"Your point is well taken, Jake," Belcher replied, trying to mollify him. "Believe me, there is absolutely no way we are going to let these guys die on the vine. The president has authorized the use of air cover and naval support. There will be a carrier and six destroyers standing by in case they're needed."

Jake was still upset. "It's too bad he didn't allocate a few amphibious ships as well, instead of relying on some beat-up old merchant ships."

Ray ignored his last comment. "Jake, look, you've just got to trust me on this. There are a lot of things going on behind the scenes you aren't aware of. The president is in this for the whole nine yards. He has extended the Monroe Doctrine to cover any nation around the world threatened by communism, promising them military assistance if necessary. If he would offer protection to other countries outside our hemisphere, he sure as hell isn't going to tolerate a communist government in our own back yard."

Jake was still not convinced.

Leaving the headquarters, Sergeant McCormick and Lt.(jg) McVie accompanied the group on their tour of the training site, while Jake remained behind at the office.

It was late when Jake returned to the hotel. He ate dinner alone before going up to his room. Exhausted, he went to bed early, but had a difficult time going to sleep. Tossing and turning, he thought about Cindy. "God, what have I gotten myself into?" he lamented. "My life was just beginning to get squared away again, and now this." He couldn't get rid of the uneasy feeling in his gut that something was very wrong.

CHAPTER 16

October 1960, The Everglades

Situated about fifty miles west of Miami, the training base contained few facilities except for a long-since-deserted landing strip and a few dilapidated buildings. Other than its proximity to Miami, the availability of a landing strip had been a primary consideration for choosing the site.

The first busloads of Cubans began to arrive early on Monday morning. From now until the operation was concluded they would have only limited contact with the outside world.

A group of men ranging in age from eighteen to over fifty, the members of the Brigade came from many walks of life and backgrounds. Some had fled Cuba for economic reasons, but most were political refugees. The one thing they all shared in common, however, was their determination to rid their country of Castro, many of them having had first-hand knowledge of his brutality.

As they stepped off the buses into a typical hot, humid South Florida morning, they were greeted by Sergeant McCormick and his group of drill instructors. Separated into companies, they got their first taste of what it was like to be a Marine recruit. The silence of the Everglades was soon broken by the voices of the drill instructors shouting out orders. The only difference between here and Parris Island, was that the dialogue was in Spanish instead of English.

As it is in all boot camps, the first order of business was processing. In order to fool Castro into thinking the force was larger than it actually was, the ID cards were numbered beginning with 2,500. Years later, each veteran of the operation would attach great significance to his number—the lower the number, the greater the respect to which he was entitled.

By the end of the week an additional 500 recruits had reported to camp, bringing the total to over 1,500. Training now began in earnest as Sergeant McCormick and his DIs took the first steps toward creating a fighting unit, instilling confidence in the men.

Comfortable with the knowledge that McCormick and his instructors had things well in hand, Jake returned to Miami on Tuesday, taking Knisel and Chief Radioman Custance with him. Chief Gomez was still in Bayonne.

Now that the Cubans were in camp, Jake focused his attention on the status of the boats and merchant ships. It was also time to take steps for planning the actual operation.

As soon as he arrived back in Miami he ordered three sets of hydrographic charts for the waters surrounding Cuba from the U. S. Navy Hydrographic Office in Washington, along with pilot charts, sailing directions, and tide and current tables. He also needed detailed topographical maps of the island. These he ordered from the Army Map service.

Chief Gomez arrived back in Miami on Thursday. Outside of Jake's office, he knocked on the door.

"It's me, Lefty, Lieutenant. Gotta minute?"

Jake looked up from his work. "Sure thing, Chief." Nodding his head toward a chair, he said, "Sit down. It's good to have you back." He waited for Gomez to sit down. "I have a feeling you don't have good news."

"You sure got that right," Gomez replied. "The boats are nothing but a pile of shit, if you'll pardon my French. The engines haven't been turned over in ten years, and the lowering gear for the bow ramps is all frozen up. To make it simple they need of a complete going-over from stem to stern."

"I was afraid of that," Jake replied. "Can you give me an estimate on how long it will take to put them back in shape?"

"It depends on how much help you can give me," Gomez replied.

"How many men do you need?"

"If you could get me ten first class enginemen and a few strikers, I think I could get them ready in about four weeks. We'll also need a crew of about five boatswain's mates for the hull work."

"Okay, Chief. Let me see what I can do," Jake replied. "In the meantime how about working up a list of the parts you're going to need."

Jake followed him out into the reception area.

"Eva, see if you can get Mr. Belcher on the secure line. I need to speak with him as soon as possible."

"Yes sir, Mr. Barnes," she said, stopping what she was doing.

Jake returned to his office to wait for the call to go through. A few moments later, Eva knocked on the door.

"Mr. Belcher's on the line."

He picked up the phone.

"Jake, good to hear from you. How are things going out in the Everglades?"

"Everything's pretty much on schedule," Jake replied. "McCormick and his troopers have things well in hand, but that's not the reason I called."

"What's up?"

"It's about the boats," Jake replied. "Chief Gomez just got back from Bayonne, and as expected, they're in pretty tough shape. We need to get some help from the Navy to make them operational."

"That shouldn't present a problem. I'll have someone from the Navy Department give you a call. Just let them know what you need."

Jake was surprised. He had expected Belcher to minimize the problem.

"By the way, is there any word yet on the ships?" Jake asked.

"I'm still working on it. We're still trying to tie up a contract. I should have some word by the middle of next week." Changing the subject, he asked, "By the way, have you given any thought toward selecting a landing site?"

"I've already started working on that," Jake replied. "The charts for the area are on order. They should be here by sometime next week."

"Good. Keep me up to date. There's a great deal of high-level interest in what's going on. Look, Jake, I've got a call on the other line. I'll talk with you later."

Jake spent the remainder of the afternoon working on his "must do" list, waiting on the call about the enginemen.

Shortly after 1600, Eva knocked on his door.

"Mr. Barnes, there's a chief from Norfolk, on the open line, who wishes to speak with you."

Jake picked up the phone on his desk.

"Lieutenant Barnes here."

"Lieutenant, this is Chief Riley from Epdolant [enlisted personnel distribution office, Atlantic fleet]. I understand you need some men for a special assignment. I have orders to give you anything you want."

"Great. For starters, I need ten first class enginemen and six strikers. I also need a first class boatswain's mate and four strikers. They are to report to Chief Gomez at the Bayonne Supply Center as soon as possible."

"Got it, Lieutenant. I'll get back with you in the morning."

"Thanks, Chief. I'll wait to hear from you," Jake replied, setting the phone back in its cradle.

He got up from his desk and went into the conference room. Chief Gomez was seated at the table, manuals and papers scattered all over. Pouring a cup of coffee from the warmer, Jake took a seat across the table and said, "I've got the men you wanted. We'll know by tomorrow when they are to report. As soon as we get the word, I want you to hightail it back up to Bayonne."

"I'm ready any time, skipper. This paperwork stuff is not my bag. I'm looking forward to doing something I'm good at." He hesitated for a moment, then added. "Don't you worry, sir, we'll have those babies purring like kittens in no time at all."

At 1000 the next morning, Chief Riley phoned to say that the men Jake had requested would arrive in Bayonne at 0800 Monday morning.

As Jake hung up the phone, he thought to himself, "Things are beginning to look up. Maybe Ray is right—I do worry too much."

CHAPTER 17

Miami, the following week

Belcher called on Wednesday to inform Jake that he would be in Miami the following morning along with Dick Harris and Miro Cardona, the chairman of the Cuban Revolutionary Council in New York. The purpose of their trip was to give Cardona an opportunity to meet with the members of the Cuban Brigade and to see at first hand how the training was progressing. After visiting the camp in the Everglades, they planned to stop by the Miami headquarters before their return to Washington.

After lunch on Thursday, Cardona, Belcher, and Dick Harris arrived at the Miami headquarters.

Miro Cardona was a scholarly-looking former law professor who had taught at the university in Havana. After the Castro coup he had settled in New York City, and was recently chosen to lead the Revolutionary Council.

Grasping Jake's hand, the chairman shook it vigorously. "Lieutenant Barnes, it is my sincere pleasure to meet you," he said. "The Cuban people and I will be eternally grateful to you and to the other members of your staff for your assistance in our great cause."

"Chairman Cardona, you can count on me, and the rest of the staff, to do everything we can to ensure the success of the operation," Jake replied.

In honor of the chairman's visit, Jake had arranged for refreshments and coffee to be served. After they were seated in Belcher's office, he signaled for Eva, who carried in the tray. After setting it down on the coffee table, she turned toward the chairman and curtseyed. He then realized who she was. Getting up from the sofa, he put his arms around her and kissed her lightly on both cheeks. Holding her hands in his, he said, "Eva, my dear, how you've grown. I barely recognized you," Continuing to hold her hands in his, he said, "I was so sorry to hear about your father. It was my good fortune to have been his friend back in Cuba. He was a good man and a true patriot."

"Thank you for your kind words, Mr. Cardona," she replied. "It is an honor to see you once again."

After Eva had gone, Jake went on to brief the group on the status of the operation. Once he had finished, Cardona excused himself to go into Jake's office to make some phone calls.

While waiting for him to return, Belcher said, "I have some good news for you, Jake. We have finally concluded the contract with Garcia for the use of the merchant support ships. He has been told to expect some of our people on board early next week to look things over."

"Where are they located?"

"They are anchored in Puerto Cabezas."

"What about the LCIs?" Jake asked.

"They're both in Pascagoula."

As he was talking, Belcher reached into his briefcase and got out a paper containing the phone number and address where Garcia could be reached. Handing it over to Jake, he said, "Just make sure you warn our people not to discuss the operation with anyone on board."

"Will do," Jake replied, folding up the paper and putting it in his pocket.

"One more thing, Jake. The State Department has been able to convince the president that the Cubans should be trained somewhere else other than in the United States. As a result, we've been directed to move the operation offshore as soon as practicable."

Jake expressed surprise at the change in plans. "How soon, and where to?" he asked.

"I'll let Dick fill you in," Belcher replied.

Dick Harris carefully removed his glasses and put them away in his jacket pocket before beginning.

"We are negotiating with the government of Guatemala to grant us a temporary lease for the use of one of their National Guard bases."

Interrupting, Jake asked, "When do you expect the negotiations will be completed?"

"We should know in the next few days. However, I don't anticipate any problems. They owe us a few favors," Harris replied.

"They sure do," Jake said under his breath, remembering the time in the 1950s when the Russians began to aggressively promote communism in Central and South America. Preoccupied with the spread of communism in Africa and Asia, the United States had been content with the status quo in Central America, choosing to ignore the growing unrest in the region.

When it became apparent that the Guzman government in Guatemala had been infiltrated by communists, the alarm bells in Washington went off. President Eisenhower issued an ultimatum stating that the United States would not tolerate a communist regime in the Western Hemisphere. Citing the Monroe Doctrine, he ordered a contingent of Marines to nearby Honduras, while at the same time tasking the CIA to provide covert assistance to the rebel forces of Carlos Castillo Armas. Ultimately, with CIA assistance, the Armas forces were successful in toppling the Guzman government. After assuming power, the Armas government quickly crushed the opposition and established a military dictatorship friendly to the United States.

His mind returning to the present, Jake asked, "How do we plan to move the Brigade down there?"

Harris looked over at Belcher.

"We plan on flying them in," Belcher said. "There's already an airstrip on the base. All we have to do is extend the runway to accommodate the C54s. I've already spoken with the Army, and they have agreed to do the work using an Engineering Battalion based in Panama. Once the work on the runway is completed, we plan to move the brigade down and load out all the equipment and materiel needed for the operation aboard the freighters. Once they are loaded, they will set sail for Guatemala to embark the Brigade. Until they then no one on board the ships will know where they are headed."

"Any word on training for the boat crews?" Jake asked.

"I've been in touch with the Navy Department. It looks like they're going to let us to use their facilities on Vieques Island off Puerto Rico," Belcher replied.

"We still have to get the LCUs to the landing area."

"Give me time, Jake. I'm still working on it. I'll let you know as soon as I find anything out." Growing impatient, he glanced down at his watch.

"Right now you'll have to excuse us. We need to get moving if we're to make our flight back to Washington."

As he was about to go out the door, he turned around. "One last thing, Jake. How are you coming along with selecting a landing site?"

"The charts haven't arrived yet. Give me a few more days," Jake replied.

"Okay. Let me know as soon as you come up with something."

After they had left, Jake asked Eva to get hold of Bosun Knisel, and have him come into his office.

Soon Knisel appeared in Jake's office, coffee mug in hand.

Taking a seat, he asked, "Any word on the merchies yet, Lieutenant?"

"That's the reason I wanted to see you," Jake replied. "I just got word that the contract's been approved. The freighters are at anchor in Puerto Cabezas."

"That's in Nicaragua, ain't it?"

"Right," Jake replied. "I want you to get down there and look them over. After you get there contact a Mr. Garcia." Reaching into his pocket, he handed over the address and phone number that Belcher had given him. "He has been told to expect you."

Knisel stood up to leave. "Before you go, Bosun, make sure you don't tell anyone on board what's going on," Jake cautioned. "Tell them they will be carrying military cargo. Nothing else. Once they get under way, we'll fill them in on the details."

"Okay, Lieutenant. I hope to hell they've built some hazardous-duty pay into their contract, as I've got a feeling they're gonna be earning it."

Jake ignored the last remark. "I want you to take Chief Custance along to look over their radio equipment."

"Yes sir. Will do. Any word yet on how we're going to transport the LCUs?"

"No, not yet," Jake replied.

"If that's it, I'll be on my way. Let's hope the ships are in better shape than Gomez' boats."

"You got that right. I feel like I've stepped back into the dark ages....LCVPs, LCIs," Jake muttered to himself.

The material from the Hydrographic Office arrived on Tuesday and the maps from the Army Map Service the following day. Jake decided to familiarize himself with the region before calling in Ramirez and McCormick. First he wanted to take a look at the pilot chart for January. This would give him an idea of what the weather and sea conditions would be for the month. The wind force and direction were of most interest, as these would determine the feasibility of when and where they could land. The pilot chart quickly confirmed what he already suspected—a beach assault anywhere on the north coast of the island would be next to impossible in January, as winds of 20 knots or greater out of the north were predicted during 80 percent of the month. If a landing were to take place in January it would have to be on the south side of the island.

A look at the hydrographic charts for the southern coast of Cuba ruled out the southwest coast. It was too shoal and inundated with numerous coral reefs and small cays. Any landing would have to be made farther to the east.

Before continuing, he decided to confer with Ramirez and McCormick. He put in a phone call to the training site, where he left word for them to meet with him at the Miami headquarters the following morning.

When they arrived the next morning, Jake was in the conference room, poring over the charts and maps.

Standing up to greet them, he said, "Thanks for coming by. We need to come up with some ideas for a landing site, and I wanted to get your input. I have already ruled out some areas." Before continuing, he placed the hydrographic chart and topographical map of the island side by side on the table, so they all could see.

"The weather in January makes a landing anywhere on the north coast too chancy, and the southwest coastline is too shoal. This leaves us little choice except to try to find a suitable site farther toward the east. But before we get down to business, I would like to find out about any special requirements you might have."

"As far as the landing force is concerned," McCormick said, "getting ashore undetected is the primary consideration. The longer before we are discovered, the better."

Jake interrupted him. "What you're suggesting, gunny, is a night landing. That sure as hell is risky, given the situation with which we're dealing."

"It's also risky getting caught on the beach in broad daylight," McCormick countered.

"You've got a point," Jake said. "We don't need to make a decision on that right now. I'm sorry I interrupted. Please go on."

"Something else we need to look for is whether the terrain is firm enough to support tanks and other heavy equipment. Otherwise we will have to lay down steel matting. That will take up a lot of time. Also, we will need access to paved roads if we hope to egress the area quickly."

"Anything else?"

"That's about it," McCormick replied.

"Okay, thanks, gunny. How about you, Jose'?"

"Before I begin, Jake, I don't know how much you know about our forces already in place on the island."

"Very little," Jake replied.

Using his pen, Jose' pointed to a location in Las Villas Province. "Our main force is located here in the Escambray Mountains. After the landing we need to link up with them as soon as possible." He then pointed to several other locations. "We also have forces here and here. Once they receive the signal that the landing is imminent, they will conduct diversionary attacks to keep Castro confused until we have had a chance to consolidate our forces."

"That narrows our choices down considerably," Jake said. "Let's take a look at the charts and see what we can come up with."

Over the next couple of hours they studied the charts and maps, exploring all possibilities. In the end, all agreed, the Playa del Giron, on the east side of the entrance to the Bahia de Cochinos, was the one location that most closely satisfied all their individual requirements.

There was plenty of deep water offshore, and the bay was protected on three sides. Although the Army maps indicated some swampy areas just behind the beach proper, there were two hard-surfaced roads leading out from the beach, one toward San Blas and the

135

Escambray Mountains off to the east, and the other to Jaguey Grande, in the direction of Havana. As a bonus, there was also a small airfield a few hundred yards from the landing site.

"Before we make a final decision, why don't we take a break?" Jake said. "That'll give each of us some time to mull it over."

After lunch the three of them gathered back in the conference room. Although McCormick expressed some concern about the swamps behind the beach proper, and Jake worried about the bottom conditions close in toward shore, they all still agreed that, everything considered, the Bahia de Cochinos site best met all their requirements.

Recalling how his instructor at Amphibious Warfare School had hammered it into their heads that there was no substitute for first-hand information, Jake worried out loud, "Before we go forward with this recommendation, I sure wish we could get a Seal team in there to take a look-see. There is no way of telling from the charts if there are any reefs or coral heads present. It would also be nice to verify the condition of the roads to see if they will support heavy equipment."

"Do you really think that 'Nervous Nellie' Harris, from the State Department, will go along with sending in a Seal team, Lieutenant?" McCormick snorted.

"If we don't, there sure as hell is no telling what we're going to run into, gunny," Jake replied. "These charts are over twenty years old." Even as he said it, Jake knew McCormick was probably right. There was little chance the State Department would go along with a live reconnoiter.

Still, there was one other alternative. Jake looked over at Ramirez. "Jose', do you think someone in the Brigade might be familiar with the area?"

"It's possible," he replied. "As soon as I get back, I will check into it."

"All right then, let's postpone a final decision until Jose' has had a chance to ask around," Jake said. "Meantime, I'm still going to broach the subject of a beach recon with Ray. In the meantime, how about briefing Colonel Martinez on what we've come up with, and see what he thinks?"

CHAPTER 18

Saturday, September 21, 1968, Miami

After leaving a message with the duty clerk at the VOQ in Homestead, Ramirez dialed his home number. On the first ring, Maria picked up the receiver.

"Maria, this is Jose'."

Before he had a chance to say anything, Maria interrupted him. "Jose', where are you? I have been worried."

"I am at a pay phone," he replied. "Before coming home, I think I will stop by to visit with Carlos." He knew that she would know what he was talking about, since Carlos Lopez, the owner of the La Paloma night club in Coconut Grove, was a close friend of theirs.

"Is everything okay with you ?" Jose' asked.

"Everything's fine," Maria replied. "The children are at home with me. We're in the family room watching TV. About what time can I expect you?"

"It may be late. I will call you before I leave."

"Please be careful," she pleaded, as he hung up the phone.

Getting back into his car, Ramirez drove around for awhile. It was still a couple of hours before his meeting with Captain Canfield. Besides, he wanted to think over what he was going to say. He remembered how, upon being released from prison, the members of the Brigade had been cautioned to refrain from talking about what had happened during the invasion.

It seemed like such a long time ago—first the dismal failure of the operation, then the time in prison, and finally his return to Florida in defeat. The first few years had been difficult, trying to readjust to normal life, and he knew it had been even more difficult for Maria. For her, it was first the agony of not knowing whether he was alive or dead, and then, once he had returned, dealing with his troubled nightmares. These had slowly begun to subside, and for the most part he now was able to sleep through the whole night.

As time went on, he became resigned to the fact that Castro was going to remain in power and that the United States government was not going to do anything about it. He remembered the frustration he felt upon his release from prison, when he learned that President Kennedy had struck a deal with the Russians, pledging not to invade Cuba if the Russians would agree to remove their nuclear missiles from the island, and about how Nikita Khrushchev had bragged that the Monroe Doctrine was not worth the paper it was written on.

Realizing that his country had been sacrificed to the self-interest of the United States, Ramirez drifted away from the revolutionary movement, concentrating his efforts instead on rebuilding his law practice and devoting time to his family.

A little after 9 o'clock, he arrived outside La Paloma. He parked the car in back of the club, where it would not be visible from the street. Seeing him enter, Carlos Lopez came over to greet him.

Putting his arm on his shoulder, he said, "Where is Maria?"

"She's at home," Jose' replied. "I'm here to meet someone. I have an appointment at ten o'clock." Seeing the look on his face, Carlos knew something was wrong. "Is there something you want to talk about?"

Jose' felt a need to talk with someone, and went on to tell Lopez about what had happened earlier in the day, about the call from Captain Canfield and the visit from Belcher's men.

139

Although they had not known each other at the time, Lopez, like Jose', had also been a participant in the ill-fated attempt to liberate Cuba back in 1961. Joining the revolutionary group as a pilot, he had flown one of the twelve B-26 twin-engine bombers belonging to the movement. Along with the other Cuban pilots, he had been trained by the Alabama Air National Guard before deploying to Happy Valley, an airfield in Nicaragua.

Two days prior to the invasion, Carlos had piloted one of the six planes on a bombing raid over Cuba. His target was Camp Libertad, outside Havana. The others attacked the airfield at Santiago and the Cuban air force headquarters at San Antonio de Los Banos.

Although causing widespread damage with their rockets and bombs, they paid a high price. Four of the bombers were shot down over Cuba. Of the remaining two, one, badly damaged, limped back to Florida, where it landed at Miami International Airport. Carlos' plane, running short on fuel, landed undamaged at Boca Chica Naval Air Station near Key West. Refueling, he returned to Nicaragua. After that he went on to fly two more missions before ending up being shot down and captured.

Although he was imprisoned in the same jail as Jose', they did not meet until their release, when they were on board ship returning to Miami. Afterward, they became friends, and they continued to see each other often.

Carlos listened without interruption. Once he had finished, Carlos asked, "What are you going to tell this Captain Canfield, Jose'?"

"I am still not sure of how much I should say," Ramirez replied.

"Be careful, my friend," Carlos cautioned. "There are still a lot of important people who do not want the truth to be known."

After they finished talking, Carlos arranged for Jose' to be seated at a table in a dark corner of the room, where he could see the front door and at the same time remain inconspicuous.

Settling down to wait, Jose' ordered a cup of coffee. His palms were sweaty and his hands had begun to shake. The memories of the time in prison came rushing back.

At Maria's urging, he had stopped smoking six months ago, but he now felt an overwhelming need for a cigarette. When the waitress returned with the coffee, he asked if she would bring him a pack of cigarettes. When she returned, he hurriedly opened the pack and lit one up. He inhaled deeply. The jitters slowly began to subside.

Sipping his coffee, he wondered if Captain Canfield had received his message, and if he had, would he come? He sat in the darkened room. While he waited his mind relived the events of the past.

CHAPTER 19

November 1960, The Everglades

After the meeting with Jake in Miami, Ramirez and McCormick returned to camp in the Everglades. The basic portion of the training was now nearly half over. Under the leadership of McCormick and the other drill instructors, the Brigade had begun to come together and function as a team. The physical training had hardened their bodies, and the time in the field had made them used to dealing with deprivation, whether it be that of sleep, food, or physical comfort.

Ramirez informally looked over the records, coming up with the names of five members of the brigade who had lived in the southern part of Las Villas province. Of the group, it turned out that two of them had come from the small town of Covodonga, about eight miles from Bahia de Cochinos. There they had worked in the sugar-cane fields. That evening he called them into his quarters and questioned them.

They verified the information on the charts: that there were a number of swamps located directly behind the beach proper. They also confirmed that the main roads leading to the area were paved, but during the rainy season, from September through November and again during May and June, the secondary unpaved roads were mostly impassable.

Being agricultural workers, they could provide little information about the waters offshore, although one of them recalled overhearing a group of local fisherman in a bodega mention something about reefs.

The next morning, Jose' called the Miami headquarters and passed on the information to Jake.

The vague reference to reefs made Jake nervous. He decided to put in a call to Belcher in Washington, requesting a night beach recon.

Picking up on the secure line, Belcher said, "What's up, Jake?"

"I just wanted to let you know that Ramirez, McCormick, and I have gotten together and have come up with a proposal for a landing site," Jake replied. "But before we go any further, we need to confirm some of the data contained on the chart."

"What kind of data?" Belcher asked.

"First of all, the Army maps show some swamps located behind the beach proper. This in itself shouldn't present a problem, since the maps also indicate there are paved roads crossing through them. The thing that concerns me, however, is the bottom condition close in toward shore."

"What do the charts indicate?" Belcher inquired.

"They show good water right up to the beach, but the information is based on a hydrographic survey taken over twenty years ago. The other thing that worries me is that one of the Cubans assigned to the Brigade told Ramirez he overheard a group of local fishermen talking about reefs somewhere in the area."

"That's a bit of a stretch," Belcher said. "Do they know anything for sure?"

"No, not for sure," Jake admitted. "But that's my point, Ray. We need to be sure."

"Okay, what do you have in mind?"

"I would like to have a destroyer from Gitmo pick up a Seal team from St. Johns to do a night recon of the area."

"I don't know. That sounds risky, but go ahead and give me the location of the area. I'll chop it on up the line, even though I can tell you right now I don't think they're going to go for a live recon. You've got to realize the administration is pretty gun-shy about risking another American being captured, after Gary Powers' U2 was shot down by the Russians last summer."

"I understand, Ray, but if we don't know what we are getting into, we might as well be shooting craps," Jake protested. "Look what happened at Tarawa during World War II."

"I don't have the kind of authority to approve this type of operation, and you can bet your ass the State Department is going to do their best to shoot it down once they find out." Anxious to end the conversation, he said, "Look, Jake, I've got someone on the other line. As soon as I find out something, I'll be back in touch."

Bosun Knisel poked his head in the door just as Jake hung up the phone.

"Are you busy, Lieutenant?" he asked.

Jake motioned toward a chair. "Come on in, Bosun, shut the door, and sit down. I just got off the phone with Washington. You hit it on the head when you said they should leave military operations up to professionals! What in hell ever possessed me to volunteer for this half-assed operation, I'll never know. Now I suppose you've more bad news."

"Maybe I should come back later," Knisel replied, starting to get up from his chair.

"Sit down, Bosun," Jake said. "Might as well give it to me now."

"Better hold onto your hat, Lieutenant. The freighters are a pile of shit. They look like rejects from McHale's Navy. The winches are all rusted out, and the booms look like they haven't been greased in years."

"That's all I need to hear. How about the radios?"

"Custance says they're not much better. He's checking into picking up some surplus gear, along with some portable walkie-talkies."

"Did you get a look at the LCIs yet?'

"Not yet. I plan to fly up there tomorrow."

Taking a moment to calm down, Jake said, "Okay, Bosun, thanks for the report. When you get back from Pascagoula, I want you to get together with McCormick and pick out some Cubans to train for boat crews. Right now, it looks like we'll be using Vieques."

"I'll get right on it," Knisel said, getting up out of his chair. At the doorway, he stopped and turned around.

"Just remember the old chief's saying, Lieutenant—'it all counts on twenty'."

"Thanks, Bosun," Jake replied. "I'll try to keep that in mind."

After Knisel had left, Jake decided to go over the charts one more time to make sure he hadn't missed anything. He also wanted to get his mind off the condition of the ships.

With a magnifying glass he examined every square inch of the large-scale chart of the waters off the proposed landing area. He could find no reference to coral heads or reefs.

The following Tuesday, Belcher called to inform him that his request for a live beach recon had been disapproved. Instead, they had decided to have the Air Force do a high-altitude fly-over of the area, using a U2 photo recon aircraft.

"We should have the pictures back from the photo intelligence people by the end of the week," Belcher said. "While I have you on the phone, how about giving some thought to dates for the landing?"

"What time frame?"

"Sometime in the first two weeks of January."

145

"How soon do you need them?"

"How about next week? Why don't you and Ramirez come up here? Maybe we can finalize some things then."

"Okay, I'll get right on it," Jake replied. "By the way, Ray, Knisel just got back from Nicaragua. He says the freighters are a pile of junk, just like the landing craft."

"Tell him to make up a list of what needs to be done, and I'll pass it on to Mr. Garcia."

Before he could come up with a date, Jake needed to look up some information. For one thing, he wanted to know the time of moonrise, as he would like to have some moonlight to facilitate launching and loading the landing craft, but not enough light so as to silhouette the ships against the horizon. He also had to consider the state of the tide. It was preferable to land on a rising tide. That way, if one of the boats should happen to get stuck on the beach, the tide would help float it free.

From the nautical almanac, he worked out the time for moonrise during the first two weeks of January. From this he could predict its phases. Next he determined the times for sunrise and morning twilight. Breaking out the tide tables, he looked up the times for high and low tides. Before he could go any further, he needed to find out whether it would be a night or dawn landing.

The following Tuesday Belcher called.

"Jake, we got the photos back from the intelligence people yesterday. Why don't you get hold of Ramirez and come up to Washington tomorrow?"

CHAPTER 20

The Next Day

Arriving at the terminal at Miami International around 0800, Jake checked in at the ticket counter and took a seat in the lounge. Ramirez arrived a few moments later.

On board the aircraft, the seats were only about half full. Jose' and Mike sat toward the rear, where they could talk without being overheard. After they were airborne, Ramirez asked, "Do you have a family, Jake?"

"No, not now. I was married once, but it didn't work out. We were divorced about six years ago."

"I am sorry to hear that," Jose' said. "Some day you will find the person who is right for you."

Not wishing to pursue the subject of his personal life any further, Jake said, "How about you, Jose'? What about your family?"

"I have been married to my wonderful wife, Maria, for over ten years," he replied. "We have two children: Anna, who is 8 and Luis, who just turned 6. Some day, when this is all over, I would like to have you meet them."

"I'd like that," Jake replied.

Wondering what would cause him to give up a career and family to participate in such a risky venture, Jake asked, "I hope I am not being too personal, Jose', but what caused you to volunteer for this operation?"

"You do not know what it feels like to be driven out of your own land, Jake," he replied. "It is something I owe to my countrymen who have been left behind. I still have many friends and relatives left in Cuba. But what about you? Why did you volunteer? You have nothing at stake in this."

"It's my job. It's something I've trained for," Jake replied.

They both fell silent. Ramirez was the first to speak.

"Do you think the election results will have any impact on our operation, Jake?" He was referring to the defeat of Richard Nixon by John F. Kennedy in the presidential election.

"That's a tough question, Jose', but it's probably academic anyway, since Kennedy will not take over until the middle of January. By then you and your friends should be celebrating in Havana."

Before they could continue, the flight attendant interrupted them, checking their seat belts in preparation for landing.

Arriving at the Pentagon, they took the stairway to the second floor, making their way around the ring to where Belcher's office was located. Ray was in the reception area, talking with his secretary, when they entered.

Greeting them, Belcher said, "Let's go into my office."

After they had sat down, he said, "Before we get on with business, I have some good news for you, Jake. I got word yesterday from the Naval Support Group over at Andrews that your promotion has come through." Holding out his hand, he said, "Let me be the first to congratulate you, Lieutenant Commander Barnes."

Jake had been so busy lately that he had almost forgotten about his upcoming promotion.

"Thanks, Ray," he replied.

While Jose' joined in offering his congratulations, Belcher reached into his desk and removed a box containing a pair of gold oak leaves. He handed them to Jake. "I know you won't be wearing these for a while, but at least you can take them out every so often to look at."

"Thanks again, Ray," Jake said.

"By way of celebration, what do you say I take you both out to lunch?" Belcher suggested.

Jake and Jose' quickly agreed. It had been a long time since they had had what the airlines referred to as breakfast.

"I've already made reservations at a little place over in Georgetown. Why don't you freshen up. By the time you finish, it'll be time for us to leave."

After Jose' and Jake returned from the men's room, the three of them walked out to the parking lot, where they got into Ray's car. Driving north on the Mt. Vernon Parkway, they crossed over the Key Bridge into Georgetown. Turning north on Wisconsin Avenue, Ray pulled into a parking space along the curb.

The St. Regis, in the basement of an old brick building fronting directly on the street, was one of those intimate restaurants for which Georgetown had become famous.

The owner met them at the door. From the manner in which he greeted Ray it was obvious he was one of their frequent customers.

"Good afternoon, Mr. Belcher," he said. "Your table is ready." Gesturing for them to follow, he escorted them to a table set up in front of a fireplace.

After they were seated, he presented each of them with a menu and went on to recite the specialties of the day. No sooner had he departed when a waiter appeared with a bottle of white wine, which he presented to Belcher for his approval.

"I believe this is the wine you had ordered, Mr. Belcher."

Inspecting the label, Ray repeated out loud for the others to hear, "*Antinori Tiganello*. A special wine for a special occasion."

The waiter poured a small amount into each of their glasses. After he had finished, Belcher raised his glass in toast. "Once again, congratulations, Jake." Turning toward Jose', he added, "And here's to the success of Operation Cuba Libre."

Waiting for their entree to arrive, Jake began to reassess his feelings toward Belcher. Perhaps he had been wrong. Maybe he'd been too harsh in judging him. He couldn't have gotten where he was without proving he was capable.

After lunch they went back to Belcher's office.

"Okay, gentlemen, I guess it's time we got down to work. Let's see what you have come up with, Jake."

Unfolding the charts and maps he had brought along, Jake laid them out on top of the desk. Locating the proposed landing site on the chart, he went on to brief Belcher on the factors that had been considered in making their decision.

Belcher listened without interruption. When Jake had finished his briefing, he asked, "Jake, where is it that you suspect the reefs might be located?"

"There are no reefs on the chart, Ray, but like I said earlier, you've got to remember this data is twenty years old."

"I understand what you're saying," Belcher replied. He did not wish to get into an argument.

"It looks like you guys have done your homework. I don't think I'll have any trouble selling this to the director."

"What about the photos from the fly-over?"

"Let me get them," Belcher replied.

From the file cabinet he took out a folder containing the photos and laid them down on top of the charts. Jake was impressed by their sharpness and clarity. The outline of the bay could clearly be seen, as well as the roads and airstrip. Off to the west of the proposed landing beach was a group of what appeared to be small buildings, arranged in neat rows.

Pointing to them, Jake asked, "What are these supposed to be?"

"The interpreters believe them to be beach cabanas," Belcher replied. "The larger buildings across the road are probably either restaurants or bars."

Jake noticed some dark patches in the water just offshore from the landing site. "I sure don't like the looks of this," he muttered to himself. Turning to Belcher, he asked, "What did the interpreters make of these?"

Belcher leafed through the report that accompanied the photos.

"The interpreters evaluated the dark areas offshore as either patches of seaweed or cloud shadows."

"I can see the cloud shadows," Jake replied. "They're pretty obvious, but for chrissake, I wonder how they came up with seaweed?" he said, pointing to a line of shadows close into shore. "I may not be a photo interpreter, but I just don't see how they could have arrived at such a conclusion."

Belcher was exasperated. "These people are the experts, Jake. This is what they do for a living. Besides, you said so yourself, just a moment ago—the charts don't show any reefs."

Jake shook his head. "That may be true, but if they happen to be wrong, and it turns out to be coral heads or reefs, the whole operation could turn into shit before we even get ashore. I still say we need a live recon."

Ramirez listened to the discussion going on between Belcher and Jake without comment, even though he tended to agree with Jake. It made sense to be sure.

As the argument continued, Belcher said, "You've got to get it through your head. The State Department isn't going to go along with a live recon. That's already been decided. You yourself said this is the only location which falls within everyone's parameters. The area to the west is too shoal, and the farther we move to the east, the farther we are from Havana. We can't doodle around forever. I say we go for it."

151

Belcher looked over at Ramirez for support. "Jose', what does Martinez think of the proposal?"

"It meets with his approval," Ramirez replied without additional comment. He did not wish to be drawn into the argument.

"That's it, then. End of discussion. Somebody around here has got to make a goddamn decision," Belcher said testily. "We'll go with the Bay of Cochinos, or however you say it. By the way, Jose', what the hell does Cochinos mean in English anyway?"

"It means pigs," Ramirez replied. "It's the Bay of Pigs."

Belcher looked disappointed, hoping, perhaps, for something a little more dramatic. Little did they realize at the time that the area they had decided on was one of Fidel Castro's favorite fishing spots.

By now Belcher had regained his composure. "Now that that's settled, let's get down to selecting a date." Looking over at Jake, he asked, "What have you come up with?"

"I have two recommendations, depending upon whether we go for a night landing or a landing at first light. If we land at night, say around 0300, I would recommend January 7. If we land at first light, then I would recommend January 10."

"Give me a rundown of the pros and cons," Belcher directed.

"A night landing gives us a better chance of getting ashore undetected, but it is technically more difficult. There's a risk of the boats running into each other in the dark, and the troops becoming confused and lost once they're ashore. A day landing is safer, but there's less of a chance of getting ashore undetected."

"What do you recommend?"

"Given the inexperience of the boat crews, and considering that most of the troops have never been in combat before, I think we should wait for first light," Jake replied.

"How about you, Jose'?" Belcher asked.

"Colonel Martinez and I both lean toward a night landing. We think the advantages outweigh the risks."

"What about McCormick?"

"He recommends a night landing as well," Jake replied.

"Okay, then. Let me present it to the director. I'll let you know the decision."

Getting back to the map, Jake pointed to the road junction at San Blas. "Either way we go, we need to get an advance party ashore to seize this road junction."

"What do you propose?" Belcher asked.

"The best way would be to use helicopters. Otherwise, a parachute drop, but again, a night drop is pretty risky business."

Breaking in on the conversation, Jose′ said, "I would like to be the one to lead the group."

Belcher looked at Jake. "What do you think?" he asked.

Jake thought about Jose's wife and children. Before answering, he looked over at him. "This could be extremely dangerous, Jose′."

"I know the risks," he replied.

"Okay," Belcher said. "As long as it meets with Colonel Martinez′ approval." As he folded up the charts and maps, he asked, "Any more questions?"

"Any word on how we're going to transport the LCUs to the landing area?" Jake asked.

"Not yet, Jake, but I should have an answer shortly. I'll let you know as soon as I find out. If there aren't any more questions, what do you say we wrap it up for now?"

Before they left, Belcher called Jake aside. "Look, Jake, no hard feelings. I do appreciate your concerns about the possibility of a reef. How about we ask for another fly-over, see if they can come up with something more definitive? Okay?"

"Sure, Ray, I understand. It's nothing personal, I'm only trying to do my job," Jake replied. "By the way, I do appreciate your taking me to lunch, and thanks again for the oak leaves."

"It was my pleasure, Jake. Congratulations again. You'd better hurry. I know you have a plane to catch."

CHAPTER 21

September 21, 1968, Miami

"You don't have to come along if you don't want to," Mike Canfield said.

"I don't have anything else to do," Buzz Laroque replied. "Besides, I'd like to find out what caused Ramirez to change his mind."

Getting into the rental car, they retraced their route from earlier in the day, taking the Florida Turnpike back toward Miami.

As they were driving, Laroque said, "I wonder what got into Ramirez. The last time we saw him, he was scared to death."

"Let's just hope we're not on a wild goose chase," Mike replied.

They both fell silent, each reflecting back on the events from earlier in the day, when Ramirez had seen the two CIA agents outside El Cacique.

Breaking the silence, Laroque wondered out loud, "I can't figure out how a guy like Barnes allowed himself to get tangled up in that mess."

"I think he saw it as an opportunity to put his skills to use," Mike replied. "You must remember the times, Buzz. Back in the Fifties, the Russians had us pretty much on the defensive. They were probing everywhere, trying to find soft spots, and there were plenty of them. Africa was in turmoil. The Middle East was seething with unrest. We were faced with a dilemma. We couldn't sit back and allow the Russians to gain control of most of the world's oil supply in the Middle East, let alone all those mineral deposits in Africa. We also couldn't use conventional military forces to stop them. With both the Russians and us possessing nuclear weapons, it was simply too dangerous. Besides the American people simply wouldn't tolerate going to war again after the problems we had in Korea."

"But what does that have to do with the CIA?"

"I'm getting around to it, Buzz," Mike replied. "With his hands tied when it came to using conventional military force, Eisenhower had only one alternative, covert operations, and he used them very effectively. He was successful in arranging the overthrow of the new communist government in Iran, restoring the Shah to power. He checkmated the Russians in the Congo, and prevented a communist takeover in Guatemala. He also was the one who first sent American 'advisors' to South Vietnam after the French pulled out. Along with his decision to deploy nuclear weapons in Europe, and negotiate the SEATO agreement in Southeast Asia, Eisenhower had successfully frustrated the Russians at every turn. As a result the our politicians and the American people fell in love with covert operations as the magic formula to solve all our foreign problems. Not only were they effective, but they were also cheap, compared to the use of conventional military force.

"When Castro took over in Cuba and began to make overtures to the Russians, Eisenhower turned to what had worked so well for him in the past. He asked for and received authorization from Congress to mount a covert operation to kick Castro out."

"But I thought the invasion took place during Kennedy's administration?" Laroque interrupted.

"It did, Buzz," Mike replied. "That's where Castro got lucky. When they found out about the planned upcoming invasion, Kennedy's people pressured Eisenhower to delay the landings until after they took over. Unfortunately, he went along. Had the invasion taken place in January, as originally planned, it stood a pretty good chance of being a success, but after Eisenhower cut off diplomatic relations with Cuba on January 3, Castro knew something was up.

"Getting the invasion jitters, he ordered his military police to round up anyone who was even suspected of opposing the movement. Of the tens of thousands arrested and put into prison, most were innocent victims, but he also netted a significant number of persons who were actually involved in the counter-revolutionary movement, some of whom who were also CIA informants.

"At the same time Castro was busy rounding up dissidents, the Russians stepped up their delivery of military supplies and equipment. They also were sending in advisors to train the Cubans. With our operatives in jail in Cuba, and the new Kennedy administration preoccupied with other concerns, we failed to recognize the magnitude of the Russian buildup. As a result, by the time Kennedy gave his half-hearted approval for the invasion in April, Castro's army was greatly improved over the one of a few months before. This, along with the Kennedy people insisting on making a number of key modifications to the Eisenhower plan.......

"Well, you know the rest, Buzz. The invasion was crushed. Most of the Brigade was captured and thrown into prison, where they remained until Cuban expatriates in the States raised enough money to ransom them."

"What else is new?" Laroque added. "The politicians frigg it up, and the Jake Barneses and Jose' Ramirezes of the world end up holding the shitty end of the stick, just like what's now going on in Vietnam."

"That about sums it up, Buzz, and we're still living with the consequences," Mike replied. "The Russians had won their biggest victory of the Cold War. In one fell swoop they had succeeded in invalidating the Monroe Doctrine, and to boot, they obtained a valuable base ninety miles off our coast."

By now they had arrived at La Paloma night club. As they entered the door, Jose' walked over to greet them.

"I am so glad you came," he said shaking their hands.

CHAPTER 22

December 1960, Miami

After the meeting with Belcher in Washington, the tempo of operations began to increase.

Chief Gomez called Jake on Friday to report that the work on the boats had been completed, and they were ready to go into the water. McVie was in Norfolk, working on sorting and serializing the large quantity of materials flooding into the Supply Depot. Working along with him, Chief Custance gathered up the radio equipment they would need for the operation.

From the training site in the Everglades, Sergeant McCormick reported that everything was all set for the impending deployment to Guatemala.

The following Monday, Belcher phoned Jake from Washington. "Jake, I wanted to let you know the director signed off on the landing site. Also, after considering the pros and cons, he has decided to recommend a night landing. The proposal is now on the way to the National Security Council for final approval."

"Sounds like things are moving right along," Jake replied.

"That's an understatement," Belcher said. "After the Nixon loss in the election, the Eisenhower people are really applying the pressure to get things going before he leaves office."

"How does the Kennedy staff feel about what's going on?" Jake asked.

"I'm not sure," Belcher replied. "I know they were briefed on the details last week. We'll just have to wait and see." Changing the subject, he said, "Jake, one other thing. I am getting a lot of pressure from State to move the Cubans to Guatemala as soon as possible, especially now that they have agreed to lease us the base. The engineers will arrive on site tomorrow to begin work on the runway. How about you flying down there later on next week, to check on how things are shaping up?"

"Okay," Jake replied. "But before I go, I need to get down to Guantanamo and talk to the people on the CARDIV [carrier division] staff. I also want to get up to Norfolk to talk with the destroyer types."

"Sure thing, Jake. Keep me posted, and give me a call when you get back. One other thing before I hang up. You'll be pleased to know that the Navy is not only going to allow us to use Vieques for training the boat crews, but they are also giving us the use of an LSD to ferry the boats to the landing area."

"That *is* good news, Ray," Jake replied.

Hanging up the phone with Belcher, Jake placed a call to Homestead Air Force Base to check on the availability of flights to Guantanamo. The airman on duty advised him that there was a Navy COD [carrier on board delivery] flight, with some seats still available, departing at 0830 the following morning. Jake asked him to hold a seat, while he called Guantanamo to arrange a meeting with the CARDIV staff operations officer on board the *Essex* for the following afternoon.

The following morning Jake had Chief Gunner's mate Lefebvre drive him to Homestead. On the way, he worried about the lack of defensive weapons on the freighters.

"Frenchie, I want you to round up all the 50 and 30-caliber machine guns and ammunition you can lay your hands on. I sure as hell would like to have something to defend ourselves with in case we need to."

"Aye aye, sir. I'll get right on it," Lefebvre replied.

"After you get them, have McVie make arrangements to have them mounted on the freighters."

Arriving inside the MATS terminal, Jake walked up to the counter and identified himself to the airman on duty.

"Yes sir, Mr. Barnes, you are already on the flight manifest," the airman said. "Your flight is scheduled for departure at 0830."

"What's our ETA in Guantanamo?"

"1235," he replied.

Since they had to remain at least fifty miles outside of Cuban airspace, the flight would take longer than normal.

When the flight was called, Jake boarded the C20 along with several Navy enlisted men returning from leave. There were also six Marines on board on their way to Guantanamo for duty.

Although designated a COD flight, today, since the *Essex* was in port, they would be landing on the airstrip in Guantanamo.

It was too noisy to carry on a conversation, so Jake passed the time looking out the window, watching the tiny islands of the Bahamas chain slowly drift by below, the waters offshore varying in color from pale green to deep indigo. Inside the lighter green areas, he noticed some darkly colored patches. They looked startlingly similar to the dark patches on the recon photos.

Thinking about the photos, he thought to himself, I hope to God they're not coral heads, because if they are.....He knew what coral could do. It could tear the bottom right out of the wooden-hulled LCVPs. He shuddered at the thought.

Reaching the Windward Passage, the C20 turned to the south before making a wide sweep to the west as they descended into Guantanamo airspace. A short time later the small plane touched down on the airstrip on the west side of the bay.

Exiting the aircraft, Jake stepped out into the bright Caribbean sunshine. Passing through the terminal, he hailed a base taxi.

"Where to?" the driver asked.

"Take me to the *Essex*." Jake replied.

In a few minutes the driver pulled up at the foot of the officer's brow. Walking up the gangway, Jake stopped, turned and faced aft toward the American flag flying at the stern. He started to salute, but caught himself. He remembered he was in civilian clothes.

As he stepped onto the quarterdeck, the officer of the deck came forward to greet him. "May I help you?" he asked.

Jake reached for his wallet containing his ID card. While getting it out, he said, "I'm Lieutenant Commander Barnes. I have an appointment with the staff operations officer."

The OOD carefully scrutinized his ID card. When he had finished, he stepped back and saluted, "Yes sir, Mr. Barnes. I'll have the messenger escort you to the wardroom. In the meantime, I will advise Commander Rankin that you are on board."

Turning around, he called for a young seaman wearing a guard belt.

"Messenger, please escort Commander Barnes to the wardroom."

"This way, sir," the young sailor said, leading the way aft.

In the wardroom, a couple of officers were sitting at a table at the far end of the room. Pulling out a chair at one of the vacant tables near the door, Jake sat down to wait.

It wasn't long before the door opened and a tall, thin officer with sandy-colored hair entered. He was wearing tropical khakis. Coming up to Jake, he held out his hand.

"Chuck Rankin here. Please sit down." He pulled out a chair and sat down across the table from Jake.

"How was your flight?" he asked.

"Noisy," Jake replied.

"Yeah," Rankin agreed. The C20s are not much on comfort." Pausing, he continued, "What is it we can do for you, Commander? I assume it has something to do with Operation Pluto. How about giving me a quick rundown?"

"Yes sir, it does," Jake replied, "but before I begin, I need to advise you that everything I'm about to tell you is top secret."

"Understood," Rankin replied. With that, Jake spent the next few minutes sketching in the details of the operation.

Once he had finished Rankin let out a whistle. "Well, I'll be damned! We are finally going to do it. We're going to get rid of that sonuvabitch. It's something we should have done long ago. What time frame are we looking at?"

"It looks like either January 7 or the 10th. Although this is to be primarily a Cuban operation, we will be providing training and materials, along with air and naval gunfire support."

"I guess we're to supply the air support."

"Yes sir," Jake replied. "Given the small size of the invading force, and with only a few vintage cargo planes and B26s, they're going to need all the help they can get."

"What's the skinny on Castro's air force?" Rankin asked.

"Our intelligence indicates he has about twelve planes, including two T33s, two B26s, and two Sea Furies, but we also know Russian equipment and advisors are arriving daily, so that is subject to change," Jake replied.

"How about softening up the beach prior to the landing?"

"I don't believe that will be necessary. The area is pretty remote, and we're not anticipating any opposition"

"I can't see much of a problem, then. Our fighters can certainly take care of anything Castro puts in the air, and our A4s and A6s can provide whatever close-in air support the Brigade might require. All we'll need are the usual charts, coordinates, and radio frequencies. Why don't we go on up to flag plot and get to work?"

Flag plot was on the O5 level, immediately aft of the flag bridge. Inside the plotting center, large status boards, summary plots, and radar repeaters were located strategically around the room. There was also a complete array of both internal and external communication equipment, allowing the task force commander to exercise command and control over the tactical situation.

Opening his briefcase, Jake broke out the charts of the landing area and laid them down on top of the DRT [dead reckoning tracer]. For the next several hours he and Rankin pored over them, laying down coordinates and making up overlays. Finishing that, they drew up a communication plan for the operation. It was after 1700 when they completed their work.

Straightening up, Rankin stretched his back. "Well, I guess that about does it," he said. "I can't wait 'till the pilots find out this operation's for real, instead of another Mickey Mouse training exercise."

As Jake packed up the charts, Rankin asked, "One more question, Jake. Since this is not your so-called typical operation, who's going to have overall operational control?"

"That's a good question," Jake replied. "As of now, the agency plans to retain control of the amphibious part of the operation, while all other military elements involved will be under the opcon of the task group commander, your boss, COMCARDIV Two."

"If we are going to have opcon of the military forces, we need to be cut in on all intelligence and other traffic pertaining to the operation."

"Will do," Jake replied, making a note to himself.

While he was writing, Rankin asked, "Are there any other code names for the operation other than Operation Pluto?"

"Actually there are three," Jake replied. "The Cuban part of the operation is called Operation Cuba Libre, the agency is calling their portion Operation Pluto, and the military is calling theirs Operation Bumpy Road. By compartmentalizing it that way, it makes for greater security."

"It also provides denial in case something goes wrong," Rankin added. "Covering one's ass, so to speak."

"You could say that," Jake replied.

From the beginning, Jake had been troubled with the fuzzy lines for command and control of the operation. Considering the complexity of amphibious warfare and the dissimilarity of the forces involved, it was essential that the roles for each element involved be carefully spelled out. Guidelines outlining these responsibilities had been established during World War II, and, with little change, they still constituted current doctrine.

By contrast, Operation Pluto was sort of a pseudo-military operation. Officially, the American government was not assuming responsibility for its conduct, but was acting solely in an advisory capacity. Yet, on the other hand, it had committed military forces to provide air and naval support.

Leaving the *Essex*, Jake took a water taxi across the harbor to the main side. The naval base in Guantanamo was used by the Navy mainly as a training facility. With few exceptions, all ships in the Atlantic Fleet spent three to six weeks in Gitmo for refresher training after they got out of the shipyard. Now, with relations between Castro and the United States becoming more strained by the day, the base had taken on the appearance of an armed camp. Sandbags and machine-gun emplacements were everywhere. All military dependents and non-essential personnel had been sent back to the States. Violent demonstrations along the fence separating the base from Cuban territory had become daily occurrences, and recently the situation had become even more tense after Castro threatened to shut off the base's water supply.

How different it was from the last time he was here, Jake thought. Then Cubans flooded through the gates each day to their places of work on the base, and sailors made the nightly pilgrimage in the other direction to visit the bars and whorehouses in nearby Guantanamo City.

Checking into his room at the BOQ, Jake showered and changed clothes. After he finished dressing, he walked over to the Officers Club, situated on top of a small hill with a commanding view of the harbor. In the bar, he ordered one of the club's famous rum drinks and carried it out onto the lanai, where he sat watching the sun go down in a dazzling display of colors. As the sky began to fade to black, he downed the last of his drink and went into the dining room. He ordered a T-bone steak, medium rare. While waiting for his entree to be served, he thought about his life in the Navy. Being aboard ship today made him even more conscious of how much he missed being a part of it during these past few months.

Finishing dinner, he returned to his room, where he called air operations to see if there were any flights to Norfolk posted on the board. The airman on duty informed him there was a flight scheduled for the following afternoon at 1500.

Arriving at air ops the next day, Jake checked the status board for his flight. He would be flying on a C54, which had arrived earlier in the morning with a load of cargo for the beleaguered base.

For the return trip, the plane would be flying nearly empty except for a couple of passengers. After they were airborne Jake stretched out across the jump seats and soon fell asleep. It was late when the plane touched down at the Norfolk Naval Air Station. Picking up his bag, he took a base taxi to the nearby Breezy Point BOQ, where he checked into a room for the night.

The following morning, after breakfast, he called for a base taxi to take him to the Dessub piers. The *Eaton* was tied up inboard of a nest of four destroyers. On the quarterdeck, Jake introduced himself to the chief on watch. In the wardroom, two jaygee lieutenants were seated at the far end of the table. Seeing him enter, they glanced up at him. Taking note of his civilian clothes, they gave him a quizzical look, then returned to their conversation. Jake poured a cup of coffee from the pot warming on a burner on the sideboard. Carrying his cup over to the table, he pulled out a chair and sat down at the opposite end of the table from where the jaygees were sitting. He didn't want to appear unfriendly, but at the same time he didn't feel like explaining who he was and what he was doing on board.

165

Before he had a chance to take a sip of his coffee, the door opened and a balding lieutenant commander, wearing working blues, entered.

Approaching Jake, he extended his hand. "Commander Barnes, Greg Lyman." After they shook hands, he walked over to the sideboard. "Let me get a cup of coffee before we get started." Stirring in some cream and sugar, he set his cup down on the green felt cloth covering the table and pulled out a chair. The two jaygees at the other end of the table quietly got up to leave.

Sipping his coffee, Lyman exclaimed, "Damn, this coffee is hot!" Setting the cup down, he said, "Okay, Commander, what can we do for you?"

Jake gave him a quick rundown on the reason for his visit. When he had finished, Lyman said, "Before we go any further, I would like to get the commodore in on this."

"Sure thing," Jake replied.

Getting up from the table, Lyman soon returned with Commander Blouin, the DESDIV [destroyer division] commander.

"Welcome aboard, Commander," Blouin said, upon being introduced. "Greg here says I should hear what you have to say."

While Lyman poured coffee for the commodore, Jake went on to brief him on Operation Pluto. "I don't have to warn you about the sensitivity of this matter."

"Understood," Blouin replied. "What is our role in this operation, Mister Barnes?"

"The task group is to provide both air cover and naval gunfire support," Jake replied.

"When is this operation scheduled to take place?"

"The first week of January; the exact date has not been set," Jake replied. "Whenever the plan receives final approval, Task Group 26.2 will be activated under the command of Rear Admiral Fletcher, ComCarDiv Two, embarked in the *Essex*. He will have operational control of all U.S. military forces. The Cuban Brigade will be under the command of Colonel Martinez, and the amphibious support group, consisting of seven civilian ships, will remain under control of the agency."

"Any thoughts as to how the Russians will react?" Blouin asked.

"Our biggest concern is that they will create a counter-crisis somewhere else in the world to divert our attention."

"Let them try. We can handle it. It's high time we did something to get rid of that pain in the ass, Castro, and the longer we wait the tougher it's going to be."

Pushing back his chair, he stood up to leave. "Why don't I leave you and Greg to work out the details? It's been nice meeting you, Commander. We look forward to working with you and the Cubans."

After the commodore had left, Jake continued with his briefing. "In addition to gunfire support, we are also going to need your help in escorting the invasion force to the landing zone. The merchant ships are unarmed and lack any kind of radar. Even a Cuban patrol boat would pose a major threat to them."

Jake and Lyman spent the remainder of the morning working on the gunfire support plan and plans for escorting the invasion fleet. At 1100 the stewards asked if they would clear the table so they could set up for lunch.

"How about having lunch with us?" said Lyman.

"Thanks," Jake replied.

As 1130 approached, the rest of the ship's and staff officers began to filter into the wardroom. Lyman introduced Jake around the room without explaining who he was or what he was doing on board. This resulted in a great deal of speculation as to what a Navy lieutenant commander, wearing civilian clothes, was doing on board talking with the commodore. They suspected something was up. Before long the scuttlebutt would be making the rounds of the mess decks as well.

After lunch, Jake and Lyman went up to the chart house, and continued with their work, developing a gunfire support protocol for use by the Cubans. Wrapping it up about 1500, Jake returned to the

Breezy Point BOQ. There he booked a commercial flight back to Miami for the following morning.

CHAPTER 23

December 1960, Miami

First thing after he arrived back at the Miami headquarters, Jake asked Eva to place a call to Ray Belcher in Washington.

While waiting for it to go through, he went into his office and looked over the messages lying on his desk. A minute or so later Eva called out, telling him that she had Belcher on the line.

"Thanks, Eva," Jake said, picking up on the secure phone.

"Jake, glad you're back. How did things go in Guantanamo?"

"Good," Jake replied. "I talked with Commander Rankin on the CARDIV staff, and on the way back I stopped off in Norfolk and met with the DESDIV staff."

"Good. How soon will you be ready to leave for Guatemala? It looks like the airstrip will be ready to receive traffic toward the end of next week."

"Can you give me a couple more days to put the finishing touches on the operation order," Jake replied.

"Not a problem," Belcher replied.

"By the way, Ray, Gomez called from Bayonne to say that the boats are ready to go in the water. He's waiting for instructions on what to do now."

"I've already arranged for the *San Marcos* to pick them up."

"I'll give Gomez the word," Jake replied.

"Before you go jumping to any conclusions, I want you to know that the *San Marcos* will not participate in the landing itself. They will only ferry the boats to the landing zone where the boats will be turned over to the Cubans. Then they will vacate the area. After that the Cubans will be on their own."

Displeased by the arrangement, Jake said, "Come on, Ray! That's a pretty half-assed way to go about it."

"I knew you wouldn't be happy, Jake, but that's the way it is. State doesn't want *any* Cubans on board American ships." Before Jake had a chance to object further, he quickly changed the subject. "Before you leave for Guatemala, let me know your flight schedule. I will have one of our people meet you at the airport." Jake knew there was little use arguing.

On Friday he called Belcher to pass on his flight schedule and discuss plans for the upcoming move to Guatemala.

That weekend Jake spent most of the time in his office working on the operation order. By Sunday evening he had completed a rough draft. Numbering each page with both the page number and the total number of pages, he stamped each of the pages "Top Secret" and placed them in a brown manila envelope. Marking it "Top Secret," he placed the contents inside another envelope and stamped it "To Be Hand Delivered." He then locked it in his safe and went to the hotel.

While packing his bags, he thought about calling Cindy. He picked up the phone and began to dial, but, as he had done many times before over the last couple of months, he hung up before he finished dialing the number. Somehow he couldn't bring himself to call her. He tried to convince himself that he wasn't being fair to her to ask her to wait for him, but it was more than that. While he wished desperately for a wife and family, he was afraid of making another commitment, of being hurt again. He didn't want to again have to choose between the Navy and a family, because deep inside he knew that if it came down to that the Navy would win.

Instead, he dialed the number for the front desk and left a wake-up call. Hanging up, he fell into bed exhausted, and was soon sound asleep.

After breakfast the next morning, he stopped by the office to pick up his airline tickets from Eva and to arrange for the envelope containing the op order to be sent by courier to Washington. Before leaving for the airport, he placed a quick call to Belcher to let him know it was on the way.

He was flying commercial to Guatemala City, since the airstrip at the training base was not yet operational. From there to his final destination near Puerto Barrios on the Caribbean coast, he would travel either by car or rail.

Stepping off the plane in Guatemala City, Jake was surprised to find the weather pleasantly cool as compared to Miami. At an altitude of 5,000 feet, it was often referred to as "The City of Eternal Spring."

On the tarmac, a man of about medium height, wearing a white Panama hat and blue seersucker coat, came forward to greet him. His face was nearly obscured behind dark-mirrored sunglasses.

Holding out his hand, he said, "Welcome to Guatemala, Mr. Barnes. I'm Joe Moore, the station chief here. Ray Belcher asked me to meet you."

"I don't want to appear suspicious, Mr. Moore, but if you wouldn't mind, I would like to see some identification," Jake said.

"Of course," Moore replied. Reaching his hand into his breast pocket, he removed a leather folder containing his photo ID and showed it to Jake.

Satisfying himself, Jake said, "I'm sorry, Mr. Moore. I just wanted to be sure."

"Why don't we get the hell out of this sun," Moore suggested. "Don't be misled by the cool temperatures. We are quite close to the Equator, so the sun is still very intense."

171

Inside the terminal, Moore guided Jake toward the section reserved for VIP arrivals. After clearing customs, he said, "My car's parked outside. Let's go to the embassy, where I'll fill you in on where we stand with the Guatemalan government."

The American Embassy was a large two-story dwelling in a quiet section of the city. Except for the radio antennas sprouting from its roof and the security gate out in front, it looked much like the other large buildings in the vicinity.

As they approached the gate, the Marine sentry snapped to attention, saluted, and waved them through into the compound.

Inside his office, Moore took off his coat. Gesturing in the direction of the sofa, he said, "Please make yourself at home, Mr. Barnes."

As he sat down, Jake took a look around the room. A richly carved mahogany desk sat in front of a floor-to-ceiling window. In front of it, two sofas, facing each other, sat on top of a hand-knotted Guatemalan carpet. Between the sofas was a long, low coffee table made of black and white Honduran marble. A large paddle fan whirred overhead.

On signal, a young woman, wearing a colorfully embroidered white dress, entered carrying a tray with two glasses and a pitcher filled with lemonade. Setting the tray down on the table, she quietly left the room, shutting the door behind her.

Moore sat down on the sofa opposite Jake. He poured each of them a glass of lemonade. For the next few moments they engaged in small talk while they sipped their drinks.

Draining his glass, Jake set it back on the tray.

"Mr. Moore, you said you were going to brief me on the situation here in Guatemala."

"You're right, I did. There are some things going on of which you need to be aware. Even though the Guatemalan government has generously granted us exclusive use of the base and has agreed to waive the requirement for filing flight plans in and out of the country, they have refused to allow us to mount the invasion to be launched from Guatemala."

"How come?" Jake asked.

"You have to understand their position. They are afraid of the reaction of other countries belonging to the Organization of American States, many of whom, as you well know, are sympathetic to the Castro regime. They don't want to expose themselves to criticism from their neighbors, in particular Mexico."

"Where do we go from here, then?"

"We're still working on that," Moore replied. "We're hoping that the Nicaraguan government will allow us to use Puerto Cabezas."

"The more governments that become involved, the less chance we have of surprising Castro," Jake worried aloud.

"I agree with you, Mr. Barnes, but we have to deal with reality," Moore replied. "The Guatemalan government is absolutely adamant on this condition."

Jake realized there wasn't much use in arguing. Changing the subject, he asked, "How do I get to the training base?"

"I'll have one of my people drive you there in the morning," Moore replied. "In the meantime, I have made hotel reservations for you in the city for the night. I have also arranged for a phone line to be hooked up between the embassy and the base. Until you get your own communication system set up, we'll be happy to relay messages between you and Washington."

Leaving the embassy, a driver drove Jake into the city, where he dropped him off at his hotel. That evening after dinner, Jake took a stroll through nearby Central Park before turning in for the night.

Following an early breakfast the next morning, he met his driver in the hotel lobby. Leaving the city, their route paralleled the Motagua River as it wound its way through the mountains toward the Gulf of Honduras. With high mountains rising sharply on either side of the river valley, the scenery was spectacular. For lunch, they stopped in the small town of Los Amates near the foot of the mountains. It was considerably warmer here than in Guatemala City.

Leaving Los Amates, the road remained reasonably good until the village of El Prado. There the paved road ended. It was too hot inside the car to keep the windows rolled up, but with them down the dust made breathing difficult. They stopped frequently in little villages along the way to slake their thirst. Wherever they stopped, a group of children would gather around, shyly laughing, nudging each other, while they inspected the strange-looking gringo.

Late in the afternoon, just before entering the port city of Puerto Barrios, the driver turned off the main road toward the town of Puerto Santo Tomas de Castilia. The sun was about to set when they got there. On the other side of town the road narrowed to a single lane. Ten kilometers farther on, it ended at a gate along a high chain-link fence. By now it was totally black outside.

At the gate, the driver came to a stop and dimmed his lights. A sentry, wearing green fatigues, stepped out of the shadows, his carbine at the ready. Approaching the car, he said in halting Spanish, "Please, may I see your identification?" In the dim light Jake made him out to be an American.

Reaching into their pockets, they took out their ID cards and held them out of the car window for the guard to see. Using his flashlight, he carefully examined them and shined his flashlight on each of their faces to verify their identity. After he had satisfied himself that everything was in order, he waved them through.

Following the road about a mile farther, they came upon a large quadrangle surrounded by a group of buildings. The area appeared deserted, except for some voices somewhere off in the distance. Stopping in front of a building with an American flag displayed out front, the driver came to a stop. He waited while Jake got out. Inside, except for one room with a light on, the building was dark. Latin music was coming from a radio somewhere in the distance. Outside the room with a light on, a temporary sign, marked Duty Officer, was posted on the bulkhead. Jake knocked on the door and stepped inside. A corporal was seated behind a desk. Jake introduced himself and asked if he could speak with the duty officer. Before the corporal had a chance to reply, a young, lanky first lieutenant appeared in the doorway.

Stepping forward, he said, in a slow West Texas drawl. "You must be the feller we've been expecting." Taking Jake's hand, he shook it vigorously. "Name's Liutenant Mahon, 2nd Engineering Battalion."

"Lieutenant Commander Barnes," Jake replied. "It's a pleasure to meet you, Lieutenant."

"How was your trip?" Mahon asked.

"Hot and dusty," Jake replied.

"You look kinda tired and hungry," Mahon observed. Turning to the corporal, he said, "Corporal Aikens, how about calling over to the galley and see if they can rustle up some chow for the commander here." Turning back to Jake, he continued, "While you're chowing down, I'll see to getting you a room. I can't promise much," he said, pausing to swat a mosquito on his arm. "But it does have winda screens."

"My driver will also be staying over for the night before returning to Guatemala City."

"Yes sir. We'll get him taken care of, too," Mahon replied.

Dinner consisted of Spam, which had been doctored up with brown sugar and cloves, hash-browned potatoes, and canned green beans. For dessert there was canned fruit cocktail.

The following morning after breakfast, Jake borrowed a jeep and took a tour of the base. The berthing and messing facilities were better than he had expected. He was also pleased to discover that there was plenty of space within the base proper to conduct maneuvers, with the mangrove swamps closely replicating the conditions they expected to encounter in Cuba.

At the airstrip, the engineering battalion was busy working on the runway. Parking the jeep, he got out and asked one of the soldiers where he could find the officer in charge. The soldier pointed to a captain off in the distance. Jake walked over and introduced himself.

"How can I help you?" the captain asked.

"I'm just out looking around," Jake replied. "When do you expect the runway will be ready to receive traffic?"

"We should wrap it up by Friday," the captain replied.

"We certainly appreciate the work you and your men have done. It has been a big help."

"Glad we could be of assistance, sir," the captain replied.

Returning to the jeep, Jake continued on with his tour. He was glad the captain had not asked questions, even though he imagined he had a pretty good idea it involved some sort of secret operation.

As promised, on Friday the engineers completed their work on the airstrip. That afternoon, Jake called Joe Moore at the embassy, requesting him to relay a message to Belcher in Washington. The message read, "The nest is now ready."

On Saturday the engineer battalion loaded up their equipment. In Puerto Barrios an Army ship stood by waiting to take them back to Panama. They left behind a small contingent of MPs to provide security until the Cuban Brigade arrived.

On Monday two C54 transport planes landed at the airstrip, carrying an advance party of Cubans along with McVie and McCormick.

The remainder of the brigade and their American advisors arrived on Wednesday. As the giant cargo planes pulled up on the tarmac, the Cubans swiftly deplaned and formed up smartly in battalion formation. Little did they resemble the ragtag group of civilians who had reported to camp in the Everglades a scant two months earlier. McCormick and his drill instructors had done their job well.

The following day, the advanced phase of the Brigade's training began in earnest. Things quickly came together, but with D-Day only a scant three weeks away, much was still left to be done.

Ramirez was at Fort Bragg along with a group of fellow Brigade members undergoing parachute training. Bosun Knisel and Chief Gomez were in Vieques, while Jake spent his time alternating among Guatemala, Washington, Guantanamo, and Puerto Rico, trying to keep everything on track. Morale among the members of the Brigade and training staff was high. Everyone looked forward to January 7, the date finally chosen for the invasion to take place.

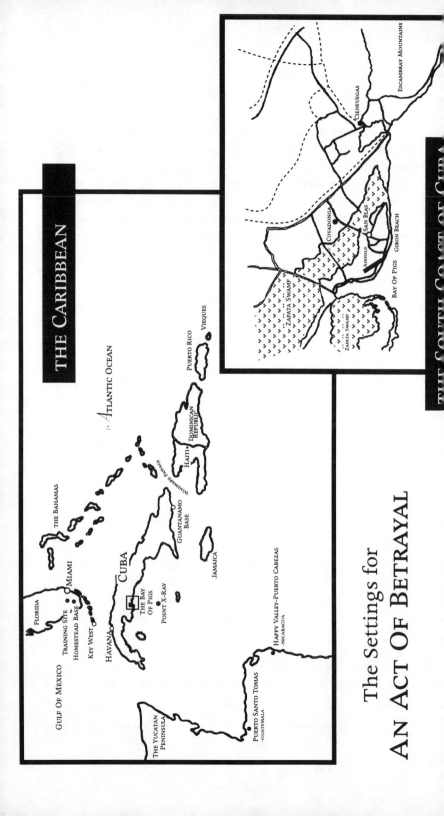

THE CARIBBEAN

THE SOUTH COAST OF CUBA

Atlantic Ocean

GULF OF MEXICO

FLORIDA

THE BAHAMAS

TRAINING SITE
HOMESTEAD BASE
KEY WEST
MIAMI

CUBA

HAVANA

THE BAY OF PIGS

POINT X-RAY

GUANTANAMO BASE

WINDWARD PASSAGE

HAITI

DOMINICAN REPUBLIC

PUERTO RICO

VIEQUES

JAMAICA

THE YUCATAN PENINSULA

PUERTO SANTO TOMAS
-GUATEMALA

HAPPY VALLEY-PUERTO CABEZAS
-NICARAGUA

CIENFUEGOS

ESCAMBRAY MOUNTAINS

COVADONGA

AIRFIELD

SAN BLAS

GIRON BEACH

ZAPATA SWAMP

ZAPATA SWAMP

BAY OF PIGS

The Settings for

AN ACT OF BETRAYAL

CHAPTER 24

Saturday, Sept. 21, 1968, La Paloma Supper Club

Jose' Ramirez came up to greet Mike Canfield and Buzz Laroque at the entrance to the club. He appeared nervous. At the table Mike noticed that the ashtray on the table was filled with cigarette butts. It struck him as odd. He hadn't remembered Ramirez smoking during their meeting at lunch. It was obvious that he was still shaken by what had occurred earlier in the day. Mike wondered what had happened to cause him to change his mind.

After they were seated, Ramirez raised his hand to call for the waitress. "Would either of you care for something to drink?" he asked. Mike and Laroque each ordered a cup of Cuban coffee. While they waited for the coffee to arrive, there was an uncomfortable lull in the conversation. Ramirez stared off into space, nervously lighting up another cigarette. Mike was beginning to wonder if he would go through with the meeting, or if it would end as the one had earlier in the afternoon. He decided not to push his luck. He would let Ramirez take his time and proceed at his own pace.

After the waitress came with their order, Ramirez started to speak in a low voice. Mike and Laroque leaned forward in their chairs. It was difficult to hear what he was saying above the noise of the band in the background. Ramirez didn't look at them, but continued to stare straight ahead as if he were watching the events in his mind unfold on a screen in front of him.

Occasionally he looked down, as if what he saw was too painful to watch. He had a determined look on his face, like someone who had been waiting a long time to tell his story, painful though it might be.

Over the next several hours Mike and Laroque sat silent in the shadows of the darkened room while Ramirez relived the events that had happened back in 1960-61. They soon became oblivious to their surroundings, people laughing and enjoying themselves at the tables nearby.

"Captain, the other day on the phone you asked if I knew Lieutenant Commander Barnes," Ramirez began. "We met for the first time in October 1960. He had come to Miami to take charge of the operation. My job was to act as liaison between his staff and the Brigade. For the following several months we worked quite closely together. From the start he impressed me as being what you Americans call a 'straight arrow.' He struggled to do the best he could, within the boundaries placed on him. As time went on, I came to consider him a good friend.

"By December, everything started to fall into place. We worked night and day practicing our assignments over and over until we could do them in our sleep.

"My group was scheduled to parachute in behind the landing zone at first light on the day of the invasion. Our task was to seize and hold a critical crossroad until the remainder of the Brigade was safely ashore...but then I am getting ahead of myself.

"After the election in November, there was a nagging concern among our leaders on what effect the Nixon defeat would have on the invasion. We knew we could count on him, but we weren't sure about Kennedy.

"In December, Premier Cardona met with President Eisenhower to express these concerns. He came away from the meeting reassured that the invasion would take place as scheduled. The president reaffirmed his promise to provide naval and air support, even implying that once we had set up a provisional government ashore he would favorably entertain a request to send in American troops. We knew Eisenhower to be a man of his word, and as long as he was president we felt secure in trusting the resolve of the American government.

"On Christmas Day, Premier Cardona visited Guatemala to wish us good luck. In an emotional farewell, he shook the hand of each man in the Brigade before getting on his plane to leave. Morale was at its peak. We were eager to return to our homeland and liberate our brothers in Cuba.

"Four days before the invasion was scheduled to take place, President Eisenhower severed diplomatic ties with Cuba. Fearing an invasion to be imminent, Castro ordered the arrest of anyone suspected of opposing the government.

"Then we received word that the invasion had been postponed. We were already embarked in the ships. Frustrated and angry, we returned to our base in Guatemala. For the next two weeks there was little word out of Washington. On good account, rumors were that Kennedy's people had convinced Eisenhower to postpone the operation until after the inauguration. Eisenhower reluctantly agreed—something he would later regret."

Ramirez paused to light up another cigarette. Inhaling deeply, he continued, "In the meantime, Castro took advantage of the confusion in Washington as the Kennedy team took over the reins of government. While the new administration dealt with what they considered to be more pressing problems around the world, the Cuban invasion was placed on the back burner. Little did they realize at the time that Castro would come back to haunt them, again and again.

"What little information we were able to get from inside Cuba over the next two months was disturbing. Russian equipment and advisors were flooding into the country, while at the same time Castro continued his crackdown on Cuban citizens.

181

"All the while, we sat in our barracks awaiting orders. Morale began to deteriorate. Fights began to break out among the troops. Disgusted and disillusioned, many were ready to give up and return home.

"Among the members of the Brigade, there was a growing distrust of the American government. With the advisors being the only Americans around, we vented our frustrations on them. Relations began to deteriorate. We tried to continue on with training, but with no guarantee that the invasion would ever take place it was difficult to generate much enthusiasm.

"By March, morale had reached its lowest point. Most of the men just sat around in the barracks, waiting for orders to return to Florida. Some of them began sneaking out at night, visiting the bars and whorehouses in the towns nearby. I remember the time when one of our officers suggested to Jake that he should hire prostitutes to live on base, in an effort to improve morale. It was one of the few times I saw Jake lose his cool. Running the individual out of his office, he let him know in no uncertain terms that there wasn't anything in his job description about him being a pimp." Recalling the incident, a slight smile crossed Ramirez' face.

"Back in Washington, Premier Cardona made numerous attempts to talk with the new president, but was unable get an appointment. Finally, in early April, he managed to meet with him. He pressed the young president for a decision.

"The rainy season was a few weeks away, but of even more concern was the fact that our supporters in Cuba were being arrested in ever-increasing numbers.

"President Kennedy promised to take up the matter with the National Security Council. Several days later we received word that the president had signed off on the operation. The date was set for Monday, April 17, with the landing scheduled for 0300."

CHAPTER 25

April 1961

After President Kennedy approved the operation, the pace of activity became frenetic. In Washington, Ray Belcher originated a message activating Operation Pluto and Bumpy Road, while in Guatemala arrangements were hurriedly made to fly the Brigade to Puerto Cabezas, where Garcia's freighters, along with the two LCIs, were standing by to receive them.

At the naval base in Norfolk in the early dawn of a beautiful spring morning, the *Eaton*, *Cony*, and *Murray* along with three other destroyers, slipped their moorings at the destroyer/submarine piers and steamed out of Hampton Roads. Of those on board, only Commodore Blouin and his staff operations officer were aware of their destination. On the *Eaton*, the visit of the lieutenant commander in civilian clothes back in December had long since faded from memory.

Clearing the sea buoy off Cape Henry, Commodore Blouin signaled for the ships to form up in column at 1,000 yards interval, and set course of 175 degrees true. This would take them outside the normal shipping lanes, well to the east of the Bahamas.

Passing through the Windward Passage separating the island of Cuba from Haiti, the small force of destroyers entered the Caribbean Sea. At this point, Commodore Blouin directed the force to darken ship and set Condition III for wartime steaming. From here on they would not even show their running lights at night. Everyone on board the destroyers now realized something big was going down.

The day before Blouin's destroyers entered the Caribbean, the carrier *Essex* sortied out of Guantanamo and took up station at Point Xray, 75 miles due south of Giron Beach.

At 0600 on April 10, one week before D-Day, the destroyer group rendezvoused with the *Essex* and chopped [changed operational control] to Commander Task Group 26.2. Assuming command of the destroyers, Admiral Fletcher directed Commodore Blouin to set up a bent line screen ahead of the carrier. While the screen was being set up, the newly formed battle group set course to rendezvous with the invasion force leaving Puerto Cabezas.

As they steamed off to the south, Fletcher scheduled a commanding officers conference for 1400 that afternoon. At 1300, two helicopters took off from the flight deck of the *Essex*. Making the rounds of the destroyers, they picked up Commodore Blouin along with his COs and brought them back to the carrier.

In the ready room they were joined by the skipper of the *Essex* and Commander Rankin. When all were assembled, the Marine orderly left to fetch the admiral.

Opening the meeting, Fletcher welcomed everyone and briefly outlined the overall objectives of their mission. Among the destroyer skippers, there were a number of surprised looks. Up until this moment, none of them had had any idea of what was going on. After he had finished, the admiral turned the meeting over to Rankin.

Walking up to the podium, Rankin continued with the briefing. "As Admiral Fletcher indicated, we are now on course to rendezvous with the invasion force off Nicaragua. Once we have them on radar, we will take up station 15 miles to their east and parallel their course, remaining out of sight over the horizon."

Walking over to a large easel off to the side, he flipped back the cover. Underneath was a large-scale chart of the landing area. On it, the landing beaches, as well as the assigned position of each ship in the invasion force, were marked. He paused to give each of them a chance to look over the chart. Continuing, he drew their attention to a red line drawn on the chart.

"Gentlemen, I want to direct your attention to this line. It marks the twelve-mile limit. Before entering inside this line, you are to report your intention to the task group commander, using the signal Code Red. Conversely, when you exit the area, signal Code Green. Is that clear?" There was a murmur of assent from around the room. Looking in the direction of the skipper of the *Essex,* he added, "This applies to all aircraft as well."

Rankin returned to the podium.

"Since the ships in the invasion fleet are not equipped with radar, we're going to have to vector them into position once we arrive at the landing area. Each destroyer will be assigned one of the invasion ships as its specific responsibility."

"Before we go on, why don't we draw lots to see who gets which ship?" Stopping for a moment, he put the names of the ships into his hat and passed it around the room. Each of the destroyer skippers drew a name. When it came his turn, the skipper of the *Eaton* put his hand into the hat and removed one of the pieces of paper. Unfolding it, he learned that the *Caribe* was to be his charge.

After they had finished with the drawing, Rankin went on with the briefing. "I'm sure you're all wondering about the rules of engagement, but before I get into that, I want to emphasize that the United States is not officially involved in the operation, and no Americans are to set foot ashore on Cuban soil. On the other hand, we are charged with providing air and naval gunfire support."

Upset with this mumbo-jumbo, the skipper of the *Essex* stood up and said, "Commander, let's quit with the gobbledy gook. Either we're involved or we're not. What if one of our pilots is shot down over Cuba? He's not going to have much choice about setting foot on

Cuban soil, and what if he does; are we going to stand by and let him be captured?"

Rankin evaded the question. "Let's hope the situation doesn't come up."

"Come on now, what the hell kind of answer is that? You can't expect me to send my pilots into combat without knowing whether we are going to back them up in case they get into trouble."

"I'm sorry, Captain, but that's the best I can do. The rules of engagement are pretty fuzzy, and they're changing by the minute."

The skipper of the *Murray* got up out of his chair. "What if we are fired on?" he asked.

"Under international law you always have the right to defend yourself," Rankin replied, "but you are not to initiate any action without permission from the task group commander."

Up until now Commodore Blouin had sat quietly by, listening in. Unable to control himself any longer, he got up from his seat. "Goddammit, Commander, how about we dispense with all this wishy-washy bullshit! The way you're describing it is like being half pregnant. If our goal is to get rid of Castro, then, by God, let's just go do it. I, for one, am tired of this pussy-footing around, going back and forth about what we can and cannot do. Just tell us what needs to be done, and let us go out and do it." With that, the room erupted in a round of applause.

Admiral Fletcher realized the situation was getting out of hand. He had to do something. Standing up, he faced Commodore Blouin.

"Commodore, although I agree with what you're saying, we also have to consider the big picture here. The president is in a pretty difficult situation with our Latin American allies. You need to consider that Castro has the support of many governments in the region, ones that we also consider our friends. We can't afford to jeopardize our relationships with them. We have our orders. We are going to have to live with them, and do the best job we can under the circumstances.

Now, if there aren't any more questions, this conference is adjourned." With that, he turned around and strode out of the room.

Getting up to leave, the destroyer skippers grumbled among themselves. None was happy with the position into which they had been placed. However, like all good naval officers, they would carry out their orders to the best of their ability.

Meanwhile, off Vieques, Bosun Knisel was busy supervising the loading of the unmarked LCUs and LCVPs on board the *San Marcos*.

With the orders stipulating that no Cubans were to be embarked on any American vessel, the Cuban boat crews had been flown out earlier to return to Guatemala. There they would embark on the freighters along with the rest of the Brigade. The *San Marcos* would ferry the Brigade's boats to the landing area, where they would be turned back over to the Cuban crews.

As he watched the boats being loaded in the well, Knisel grumbled to himself, "All this Mickey Mouse just doesn't make sense. It sure as shit would have been a helluva lot simpler for the Cuban crews to accompany their boats."

Once the loading was completed, the *San Marcos* pumped out the ballast from her tanks, got under way, and set a westerly course, passing south of the Dominican Republic and Haiti to her pre-assigned station, 25 miles north of Point Xray.

Chapter 26

In the harbor at Puerto Cabezas, the embarkation of the Cuban Brigade was well under way. Under McVie's supervision, food, ammunition, fuel, and medical and other supplies were being hoisted on board and stowed away, each pallet and piece of equipment marked with a serial number. This number would not only serve to identify the item but would also be used to establish its priority for unloading.

Before they got under way, Jose' Ramirez came on board the *Blagar* to say goodbye. He would remain behind in Nicaragua with his unit, to be parachuted in on the morning of the invasion.

On the bridge of the *Blagar*, he shook Jake's hand. "Good luck, my friend, and Godspeed."

"Thanks, Jose'," Jake replied. "You take care of yourself, you hear." At the time, both were unaware that this would be the last time they would ever see each other.

Departing Puerto Cabezas on April 12, the invasion force set course toward their destination off Giron Beach, passing to the west of the Cayman Islands. Jake looked out over the ragtag group of derelict ships. He thought about what the bosun had said about them earlier.

Once at sea, the *Blagar*, one of the converted LCIs, took up station at the head of the column. On board, besides the Cubans, were Jake, Belcher, Dick Harris, and Sergeant McCormick. The remainder of the American staff was dispersed among the other ships.

Along the way, they occasionally caught sight of one of the destroyers shadowing them over the horizon to the east. On the second morning out, a flight of four F86s from Homestead, flying low over the water, came screaming in from the north and passed directly over top of them, wagging their wings. Everyone on board took a measure of comfort from this, realizing that they were not alone. During the afternoon Jake ordered a test firing of the newly mounted machine guns.

That evening, as he leaned on the rail on the port side of the bridge watching the flying fish skim over the waves, Belcher came up to join him.

They both stood silent for a while, gazing out toward the horizon, watching the sun go down. Belcher was the first to speak. "What do you think their chances are, Jake?"

"I guess it all depends on how much support they get from the Cuban people once they're ashore," Jake replied. "Without that, not a helluva lot."

"I'm afraid you're right," Belcher said, turning to leave. It was the first time Jake had seen him concerned that things might not go off as planned.

"Well, see you in the morning. I'd better go below and check on Dick. He's been pretty sick ever since we got under way."

After Belcher had left, Jake returned to his position at the rail, trying to put the upcoming events out of his mind. By now the colors had begun to fade on the horizon, and it quickly became dark, as it does in the tropics. Soon the Southern Cross became visible, hanging low in the southern sky off the port quarter. Watching the other stars come into view, he lingered on, hating to part with the beauty of the night sky.

After a while he went below to his cabin. The slow roll of the ship soon put him to sleep.

Sometime after midnight a guerrilla radio station, somewhere in Oriente province came up on the air. All over Cuba, guerrillas tuned in on their short-wave sets. Soon the airwaves were filled with coded messages. "Chico is the Man," "Look well to the Rainbow," "The sky is blue."

On Sunday morning the Brigade's priests said mass on board the invasion ships. While they were at mass, their compatriots in Cuba swung into action. The Hershey sugar refinery was set on fire, along with a sugar-cane field in Camaguey. A bomb blew out the windows of a department store in Havana. The aqueduct supplying water to Havana was bombed, shutting off water to the city.

By 2200, the invasion force was approximately 12 miles south of the landing zone, steaming in column formation, with the *Blagar* still in the lead. Each ship was totally dark except for a small white light on the stern, making it easier for the ship behind to keep station. The *Eaton*, along with the other destroyers, was on a parallel course two miles to the east, tracking the formation on radar, relaying course and speed recommendations over the radio to their assigned charges.

By midnight the invasion force had closed to within four miles of the beach and had slowed to bare steerageway when all of a sudden, off the starboard quarter of the column, the *San Marcos* appeared out of the darkness. She was ballasted down, low in the water, with her well deck awash. Slowing, she lowered her stern gate, flooded the rest of the way down, and commenced launching her boats. Bosun Knisel and Chief Gomez were on board the first LCU to back out of the well.

Once clear, Knisel ordered the helmsman to make for the *Houston*, where they were to pick up the Cuban boat crews. Once they were aboard, the LCU made the rounds of the other boats, circling nearby delivering the crews. With a round of handshakes and hushed, murmured wishes of good luck from their American counterparts, the Cubans took over the boats. When the transfer was completed, the

American sailors were taken back to the *San Marcos*. She then steamed off, disappearing back into the black of the night, as silently as she had appeared.

After the transfer of the crews, the LCU carrying Knisel and Gomez pulled alongside the *Blagar*, to drop them off. As they climbed on board, Jake met them at the top of the ladder. "Good work, Bosun....Chief. Glad to have you back. Chief, how about checking out the outboard engine for the rubber boat. The Cubans reported they were having some trouble getting it to run properly."

"Sure thing. I'll get right on it," Gomez replied, turning to head aft toward the boat deck.

Watching him leave, Jake asked Knisel, "Care to join me on the bridge for a cup of coffee?" He was looking forward to having someone to talk to, to help ease the tension.

"Okay," Knisel replied. "I could use some coffee about now."

While the formation continued to close in on the beach, Jake and the bosun leaned on the gunwale, coffee mugs in hand, staring out into the darkness.

"You know, Bosun, I'm kinda getting used to this Cuban coffee. It's the one thing I'm going to miss the most."

"Yeah, I know what you mean. It sure beats what they serve on board our ships." Continuing to stare out into the darkness, they fell silent again, each lost in his own thoughts. Knisel was the first to speak.

"Commander, mind if I ask you a favor?"

"No, not at all, Bosun. Fire away."

"I want to go ashore with the recon group."

Jake turned to face him. "You know I can't allow you to do that. You heard the orders."

"Yes sir, I know, but I just can't let these guys go in alone. I've gotten pretty close to them in the past couple months. They're good men. They'll do their job, but this is their first time in combat. I'd just feel better if I were there with them."

Jake stopped him. "Dammit, Bosun, listen to me. There's no way. I just can't do it!"

"Okay then, don't give me permission. Just go over to the other side of the bridge for a while."

Jake was moved by the bosun's plea, by the loyalty he felt for his men. Finally, he relented.

"Okay, but, for chrissake, be careful. Just make sure you don't go ashore. You get your ass back here as soon as they land. You hear?"

"Thanks, I read you loud and clear, Commander. Now if you'll excuse me, I have things to do," Knisel said turning to leave.

In spite of his misgivings, Jake was pleased that the bosun was going to lead the recon party ashore.

At 0145 the invasion force anchored 2,000 yards off Giron Beach and began to make preparations for unloading. Conditions were ideal. A crescent moon hung low in the sky, providing some light to see by, but not enough to silhouette the ships against the horizon. A light wind blowing out of the north also helped prevent the sound of their voices from carrying to the shore.

On board the *Blagar*, a rubber boat was lowered over the side. Once it was in the water, an outboard motor, the one Chief Gomez had just finished working on, was attached to a bracket on its stern. Range lights and beacons, to be used to guide the assault waves ashore, were next loaded on board. After all the gear was stowed away, the six-man recon team, their faces darkened with soot from the charcoal burner in the ship's galley, climbed down the Jacob's ladder, their weapons slung over their shoulders. As they were about to shove off, Knisel joined them, carrying a Browning Automatic Rifle over his shoulder.

Loaded down, with the gunwales nearly awash, the boat pulled away from the side. Once they were clear Knisel took charge, directing the coxswain, to make for shore about 2,000 yards distant. As they approached the beach, the cabanas off to the left of the landing area were clearly visible, silhouetted by the light from the street lamps along the road behind them. Knisel worried about the lights. He would have preferred that it had been darker.

About 500 yards out from shore, he ordered the outboard engine shut down. From here on in they would use paddles. As they approached the landing area, music could be heard coming from somewhere behind the cabanas. A lone vehicle, appearing to be a jeep, moved slowly along the road paralleling the beach.

About fifteen yards out from shore, the bow suddenly lifted, and the boat came to an abrupt stop. "Oh, shit!!" Knisel murmured under his breath. Realizing that they had grounded out on a reef, he directed the coxswain to stay with the boat while he eased himself over the side into waist-deep water. He had to find a hole in the reef before the first wave landed.

"Okay, men this is it, this is where we get off," he whispered to the others. Holding their weapons over their heads, they made their way slowly toward the beach, when without warning the jeep turned toward the shore, freezing them like a deer in its headlights.

Flicking the safety off his B.A.R., Knisel raked the jeep with fire from his automatic weapon. He had emptied one 20-round magazine and was in the process of reloading before the others even had a chance to remove their safeties. After the initial burst, the lights on the jeep went out. By now the others had opened fire, lighting up the sky with tracers. Ordering them to cease fire, he motioned for them to follow as he cautiously made his way ashore and crept up alongside the jeep. Its windshield was shattered. Inside, two Cuban soldiers slumped over in the seat, covered with blood.

Directing two members of the team to set up the beacons on the beach, Knisel motioned for the other three to follow him as he raced down the beach toward the building where the music was coming from. He had to get there before someone had a chance to sound the alarm. Along the way he remembered he hadn't warned Jake about the reef. He tried to raise him on the radio. It wouldn't work. It had gotten wet while he was wading ashore.

The music was coming from Blanco's Bar, across the street behind the cabanas. Keeping to the shadows, the small group cautiously approached the brightly painted cinder-block building. Knisel put his ear against the door. He could hear music blaring from a radio inside. He thought he heard voices as well.

Inside the building four construction workers were sitting at the bar, talking with the bartender. They had not heard the gunfire from the beach. Either the music was too loud or they had had too much to drink.

Knisel had no way of knowing whether they were Castro sympathizers or not. He couldn't take any chances. Too much was at stake. Motioning for the others to follow, he broke through the door, firing a burst from his automatic rifle into the ceiling. Scared out of their wits, the five people in the room dived for cover. In broken Spanish, Knisel ordered them to lie down on the floor and put their hands on top their heads. They quickly complied, begging in Spanish not to be killed. Knisel looked around the room to see if there was a phone. He didn't see any. Fairly certain they had not sounded the alarm, he directed one of his men to stand guard over the prisoners. Ordering the others to check out the buildings nearby, he raced back toward the landing zone. He had to get word to Jake about the reef.

By the time he arrived back at the beach, it was too late. The first wave had already landed. Two of the LCVPs had grounded out on the reef at full throttle, tearing out their bottoms. By luck, the other two boats had passed through a break in the reef and landed on the beach proper. Fortunately, all the men were able to get ashore safely.

On board the *Blagar*, Jake saw the tracer fire light up the beach. Frantically, he tried to reach Knisel on the walkie-talkie. "Mad Dog One. This is Mad Dog," he called over and over.

At the landing area, Knisel waded out to one of the holed LCVPs and grabbed the radio from the coxswain, who was too shaken to report what had happened. Turning it on, he flipped the switch onto receive. He heard Jake's voice, "Mad Dog One, this is Mad Dog, come in." Switching to transmit, he answered, "Mad Dog, this is Mad Dog One, over."

"Bosun, thank God! What the hell's going on in there?"

"We ran up on a reef about fifteen yards offshore," the bosun replied. "Two of the VPs in the first wave grounded out, and are out of commission. We ran into a bit of a surprise on shore, but it's all taken care of for now. Recommend holding off on sending in any more boats until I have a chance to locate a passage through the reef. Once I find it, I'll set up a range light on shore. Do you read? Over."

"Read you loud and clear. Keep me posted," Jake replied. He held off asking any more questions, realizing the bosun had work to do.

Before signing off, Knisel added. "Once I get the range light up, tell the coxswains to make sure and keep them lined up on the way in. Okay?"

"Will do, Mad Dog One," Jake replied.

Seeing the tracer fire on the beach, Belcher realized something had gone wrong. He had overheard the tail end of the conversation with the bosun.

"What's up, Jake?" he asked. "What the hell's going on?"

Turning to him, Jake replied sarcastically, "Remember the seaweed on the photos, Ray? Well, two of the boats just grounded out on it and tore their goddamn bottoms out! Right now, Knisel is trying to find a hole in the reef. Until then, everything's on hold. We can't afford to lose any more boats."

Dick Harris, who until now had been in the pilot house, suspected something was up. Coming out onto the bridge, he heard Knisel's voice on the radio. When he realized the bosun was ashore, he went ballistic. "I told you there weren't to be any Americans in the boats!" he shouted at Jake. "I told you. I told you," he kept repeating. Each time he said it, his voice rose another octave.

Jake tried to ignore him, but he kept going on. Finally he couldn't bear listening to him any longer. "Stop your goddamn whin-

195

ing, Dick. I'm tired of listening to you. Right now I have more important things to think about."

With the element of surprise gone, Jake ordered the force to
lay down a blanket of suppression fire behind the beach, concentrating
on the buildings behind the cabanas. A few seconds later the sky lit up
with tracers. Inside Blanco's Bar, the guard joined his prisoners under a
table as the bullets whistled overhead.

A short time later, Knisel came up on the radio. "Mad Dog,
this is Mad Dog One."

"Go ahead, Mad Dog One," Jake answered.

"I've located the hole in the reef, and am in the process of setting up the range lights. We should be ready to resume operations in a
few minutes. Just make sure the coxswains keep the lights lined up on
the way in."

"Will do," Jake replied.

"Also, tell them to keep an eye out for me," Knisel said. "I'll
be standing by in the rubber boat outside the reef to lead them in, if
necessary, and for chrissakes tell them to go slow," he cautioned.

Everything that Jake had been afraid of happening was now
happening. Their cover had been blown. The landing had fallen way
behind schedule. Two of the boats were lost on a reef.

"What the hell else can go wrong?" he asked himself.

Luckily, after the initial problems, things began to settle down.
For the next several hours the boats shuttled back and forth through the
passage in the reef without incident. By 0630 nearly all the troops were
ashore except for a few specialized units. The landing was far from
over, however. A mountain of supplies still remained on board, waiting
to be unloaded.

CHAPTER 27

April 17, 1961, Happy Valley, Nicaragua

At 0100 on the day of the invasion, at an airfield near Puerto Cabezas, Ramirez and 160 other members of the Brigade gathered on the tarmac where four C46 transport planes stood by waiting to ferry them to their destination in Cuba.

Beneath the harsh light of the flood lamps illuminating the area, the paratroopers, dressed in combat gear with their faces blackened, knelt down on the concrete, while one of the brigade chaplains led them in prayer. After seeking God's blessing on them and their mission, he asked for a moment of silence, affording each of them an opportunity to offer up their own individual prayers. Ramirez' thoughts were with Maria, Anna, and Luis.

The brief ceremony over, the troopers picked up their parachute packs and filed solemnly up the ramp into the waiting aircraft. Inside the cavernous cargo bay, they strapped themselves into the jump seats. Grim-faced, they waited in the dim light, contemplating what fate might have in store for them.

After a last-minute check to see that everything was in order, the jump master gave the pilot a thumbs-up. One by one, the transport planes, filled with their precious cargo of human lives, lumbered down the runway into the dark of night. Once airborne, they turned and headed out to sea, setting course for Cuba, roughly 900 miles away. In the darkness of the cargo bay, the troopers sat silently with the roar of the engines in their ears.

Two hours into the flight, two Navy jets from the carrier *Essex* appeared out of nowhere and took up station, one off each wing tip of the lead aircraft. Remaining alongside for a moment, they wagged their wings in salute and disappeared back into the night sky. After that, the somber mood on board the aircraft changed. Knowing that the Americans were out there, that they were not alone, lifted everyone's spirit.

Three hours out, one of the 46s developed engine trouble and had to return to base. The other three pressed on toward Cuba. About an hour before their arrival over the jump point, Ramirez walked up and down the aisle, shaking hands, patting each of his men on the back, wishing them good luck.

At 0545 the sky began to lighten to the east, and at 0600 the coastline of Cuba appeared on the horizon dead ahead. Ramirez checked over his gear to make sure everything was in order. He remembered what the instructor at Fort Bragg had told them: "In parachute jumping, better get it right the first time, as there are no second chances."

As they approached the coast, the invasion fleet came into view. The wakes of the landing craft, shuttling back and forth to the beach, were clearly visible below. A few seconds later the standby warning light started flashing at the forward end of the cargo bay. Seeing the light come on, the jump master opened the doors on the aircraft. On signal, the troopers stood and hooked on to the trip line. Nearest to the door, Ramirez was to be the first out. A moment later the light turned green. Standing at the open door, he paused for a fraction of a second to cross himself before he stepped out into the empty void, dropping quickly out of sight The first few seconds of free fall were the worst, as he wondered if the chute was going to deploy.

Feeling the sudden jerk as the chute opened, Ramirez let out a sigh of relief. Breathing easier, he took time to look around, taking comfort from the sight of the other parachutes around him. Touching down in a cane field, he quickly collapsed his chute and worked to free himself from its harness. Others nearby were busy doing the same thing. Gathering up his carbine, he motioned for them to join him. As they gathered around, he took a moment to go over the map with his first sergeant.

Confirming their position, he said, "Okay, Miguel, have the men fan out. Let's get moving."

As they approached the small village of San Blas, everything was quiet. So far, so good, Ramirez thought. Everyone must still be asleep. Skirting around the village, he ordered a defensive line set up near the crossroads on the other side of town. While the troops were busy digging in, he reached into his pack and took out his radio.

"Mad Dog, this is Mad Dog Two, over."

"This is Mad Dog, over," Jake replied, recognizing Ramirez' voice.

"This is Mad Dog Two. The eagles have landed. We are now in our nest. Everything is quiet."

"Roger, Mad Dog Two. Welcome home!"

CHAPTER 28

April 17, 1961

At 6:30 a.m., in Havana an excited aide woke Fidel Castro to tell him that the Americans had landed at Bahia de Cochinos. Hurriedly dressing, Castro put in an urgent call to his air force aide-de-camp and his army chief of staff to give them the news. In what turned out to be a brilliant decision, he ordered his air force to ignore the landing party ashore and attack the invasion fleet itself. He reasoned that if he could prevent the landing force from being re-supplied, the invasion would quickly collapse.

After issuing orders to his commanders, he got into his sedan and ordered his driver to take him to where the landings were reportedly taking place. Arriving in the vicinity around 9:30, he set up his headquarters at the old Central Australia Sugar Mill. It contained the only telephone in the area.

Meanwhile, in the landing zone, the unloading of supplies and equipment continued without letup. Farther up the bay, the freighter *Houston* was making preparations to land her troops and equipment near Playa Larga.

It was now daylight. Scanning the skies to seaward, Jake tried to spot the combat air patrol from the *Essex*. While he was looking up at the sky, the radio in the pilot house began to squawk.

"Mad Dog, this is Cherry Tree, over."

Jake recognized Chuck Rankin's voice. Rushing into the pilot house, he picked up the handset.

"This is Mad Dog, over."

"This is Cherry Tree. Be advised, we hold incoming aircraft on the radar headed your way. Believed to be hostile. Heads up."

Jake hung up the handset and ran out onto the bridge wing. Looking toward shore, he saw a formation of six aircraft headed directly toward them. He ran back into the pilot house and grabbed the radio transmitter to alert the other ships, but by this time the others had either seen or heard them. Seconds later the sky filled with tracers as the ships opened up with their machine guns.

The *Houston*, well up inside the bay, was the closest target. Two Cuban T33 jets broke off from the formation and headed straight for her. Closing to about 500 yards, they launched their rockets. Streaking toward their target, they exploded seconds later, striking the *Houston* amidships, just above the waterline. Jake knew immediately she was finished.

Grabbing the radio transmitter, he called the task group commander. "Cherry Tree. Cherry Tree. This is Mad Dog. We are under attack. Request air cover. I say again, we are under attack! Over."

Seconds later, Rankin's voice came over the speaker. "Mad Dog, this is Cherry Tree. Jake, I have just been handed a message from Top Hand ordering us *not* to intervene. Over."

Jake reeled at the news. He couldn't believe his ears. He must have heard wrong. He asked for a repeat.

"Cherry Tree, this is Mad Dog. Say again. Do I understand air cover has been withdrawn?? Over."

The reply came back, "That's affirmative, Mad Dog. Our hands are tied. I'm sorry."

Realizing the implications of what he had just said, Rankin slowly laid the handset down. Tears of frustration and anger streamed down his face. Those around him turned away, not wishing to intrude.

On board the *Blagar*, Jake slammed the handset down. He turned to Belcher, standing nearby, and listening in. "Were you aware of this? Tell me the truth, dammit. Did you know they were going to withhold the air cover?"

"I swear to God, Jake, I didn't know. I swear. You've got to believe me," Belcher replied. From the expression on his face, Jake believed he was telling the truth.

"You know what this means, Ray. These men are going to die. Without air cover we don't stand a chance." He turned away. "My God, what have we done? It's all over. How am I going to tell them? Who's going to let the Cubans know that they've been betrayed?"

Before he had time to think about it, a B26 appeared in the sky. It was headed directly toward the *Blagar*. It was about 2,000 yards away. Running over to the 50-caliber machine gun mounted on the bridge wing, Jake removed the locking pin, swung it around, and opened fire.

From the tracers he knew he was hitting the plane, but it kept on coming.

"Goddamn this frigging BB gun," he exclaimed in frustration.

The B26 had now closed to about 500 yards, her machine guns raking the *Blagar*'s superstructure. Jake could hear the bullets ripping into the steel all around him. He braced himself for the bombs he knew were coming next. Suddenly, at the last minute, the nose of the plane lifted, causing it to stall. Spinning out of control, it burst into flames before splashing into the water off the starboard quarter. Seconds later it disappeared beneath the water. There was no evidence of any survivors.

Watching as the plane sank, Jake couldn't help but feel empathy for those on board.

"Poor bastards," he muttered to himself as he turned away. Hearing sounds coming from the pilot house, he looked inside to discover Dick Harris, his head tucked between his legs, hiding under the chart table. He was whimpering out loud like a scared puppy.

Off in the distance, the *Houston* was burning out of control. Realizing his ship was sinking, the master deliberately ran her up onto a reef, attempting to save his crew from drowning.

Witnessing the attack from his position outside the reef, Knisel hailed one of the LCUs backing off the beach. Climbing on board, he took over the helm and headed for the *Houston* at full speed.

On board the *Blagar*, Jake looked on as the flames and smoke continued to rise skyward.

"There goes the communication van and all our medical supplies," he said to Belcher, standing alongside him.

Realizing that Knisel was on the way to pick up survivors, Jake focused on other matters. He took a quick survey of the damage to the rest of the invasion force. Off the port quarter one of the LCUs was dead in the water, drifting toward shore. Calling for Gomez, who was aft, manning one of the 30-caliber machine guns, he pointed in the direction of the crippled boat.

"Chief, get on over to that LCU and see what you can do to get her back in commission."

"I'm on the way," Gomez replied, running toward the debarkation ladder. There he commandeered one of the boats alongside, directing the coxswain to drop him off at the disabled landing craft on their way back to the beach.

The attack lasted only about ten minutes. Once they had expended their weapons, the planes departed as quickly as they had appeared.

It might be over for now, but Jake knew they would be returning as soon as they had a chance to rearm and refuel. He looked around the harbor. The *Houston*, grounded on a reef, was still burning, columns of black, oily smoke rising up into the sky. The *Caribe* was listing to port after suffering a near miss from a 500-pound bomb. A seam in one of the riveted plates below the water line had opened up from the force of the explosion, causing her to take on water. Of the two remaining LCVPs, one was stranded on the beach, having been hit by machine-gun fire from one of the Sea Furies. She was a total loss. Luckily, the *Blagar* had escaped with only minor damage.

Arriving alongside the *Houston*, Knisel maneuvered the LCU close in to the stern of the burning hull. Once he was in position, the few remaining crew members and the ship's master climbed down a Jacob's ladder to safety.

Once they were on board, Knisel backed off and headed for a large group of survivors on a nearby reef, who had abandoned ship earlier to escape the flames. Nosing the landing craft up to the reef, he had the bow ramp lowered, allowing the wet and frightened men to scramble on board. Once everyone had been picked up, he radioed the *Blagar* to ask for instructions on what to do with them. Jake directed him to drop them off at the *Atlantico*, knowing she had a doctor on board.

CHAPTER 29

At the crossroads near San Blas, Ramirez watched the planes of Castro's air force pass off to the west on their way to the landing area. Shortly after, he saw the tracers streaming skyward and heard the sound from the explosions of the bombs and rockets. Soon a column of black smoke appeared over the trees and rose skyward. He knew something bad was happening.

"But where are the American planes?" he wondered out loud.

Ten minutes later he saw the Cuban planes return on their way back to Havana. He picked up his radio to call Jake.

"Mad Dog, this is Mad Dog Two. Over."

"This is Mad Dog, over."

Relieved to hear Jake's voice come up on the radio, Ramirez asked, "What has happened? What's going on?"

"We've just been clobbered by Castro's air force," Jake replied. "The *Houston* is on fire up on a reef. We also lost several boats."

"What about our air cover?" Ramirez asked.

Jake paused for a couple of seconds, not knowing how to tell him that there wasn't going to be any.

"There isn't going to be any air cover, Jose'," he finally said. "They've canceled it."

"What?" Ramirez exclaimed in disbelief. "But we were promised, Jake! How can they do this to us? Our people. Our country." His voice trailed off. "Isn't there something you can do?"

"I'm afraid not, Jose'. I'm sorry."

"What about you, Jake? What are you going to do?"

"I'm going to stay right here and continue with the unloading."

"May God be with you, my friend."

"With you too, Jose'," Jake said, slowly putting the transmitter back in its holder.

Dropping the handset, Ramirez sank to the ground. He could not believe what he had just heard. Miguel, standing nearby, knew from the look on Ramirez' face that something was terribly wrong. Looking up at him, Ramirez said, "We are finished, Miguel. It's all over. The Americans. They...they have betrayed us!"

Waiting for the inevitable return of the planes, the unloading continued, while everyone kept a watchful eye on the sky toward shore. Around noon, the radio on board the *Blagar*, started to squawk.

"Mad Dog. This is Cherry Tree, over."

Jake reached for the handset. "This is Mad Dog, over."

"This is Cherry Tree. I have a message for you from Top Hand. It reads. 'Withdraw your ships outside the 12-mile limit immediately.' I repeat, withdraw outside the 12-mile limit immediately."

Jake couldn't believe his ears. They had not only withdrawn the air support, but they were now going to abandon the Brigade as well. Reaching over, he turned off the radio and slammed the handset into its holder.

"Like hell they will," he said under his breath. "Not on my watch, they don't."

On board the *Essex*, Rankin repeated, "Mad Dog, this is Cherry Tree. Did you receive my last, over?" Not receiving a reply, he repeated, "Mad Dog, this is Cherry Tree. Please acknowledge, over."

From his position on the bridge wing, Belcher had overheard the radio message from Cherry Tree. Realizing that Jake had not answered, he went into the pilot house. "Jake, why haven't you acknowledged the message?" he asked.

"Because we're not going anywhere, Ray," Jake replied.

"What do you mean, Jake? You heard the orders."

"I said, we're not going anywhere, Ray, not until we've completed what we set out to do. I don't give a shit what they say. We're not leaving."

"Look here, Jake, I'm the one in charge of this operation, and I'm directing you to carry out your orders."

Belcher or the others might not think it was important. Maybe it didn't matter to them, but it did to him. He was not going to abandon his friends.

Turning to face him, Jake said, "Sorry, Ray, but from now on I'm the one who's giving the orders, and I say we're not leaving until we finish the unloading."

Belcher reached for the radio handset. Picking it up, he started to call the *Essex*.

"Put it down, Ray. I am warning you, goddammit, put it down."

"You can't order me around, Jake," Belcher replied. He was becoming unnerved. "Just remember who you're talking to. I'm your superior."

"Not any more you're not. As of right now, I'm taking over." Turning to Sergeant McCormick, standing nearby, and intently listening in on the conversation, he said, "Sergeant, please escort Mr. Belcher below to his cabin, and post a guard outside his door."

"Yes sir, Commander," the sergeant said, snapping to attention.

Reaching out, he grabbed Belcher by the arm. "This way, Mr. Belcher," he said, directing him toward the ladder leading below.
Belcher looked back over his shoulder. "I'll get you for this, Jake. I'll

get you. I'll have your ass court-martialed! Jake turned away, ignoring the threat.

CHAPTER 30

On the morning of the invasion, the *Essex* had taken up station about 18 miles south of the beach, in position to launch and recover aircraft. By mid-morning everyone on board was aware of the damage inflicted on the invasion fleet by Castro's air force and were chomping at the bit to intervene. The pilots were still not aware of the order for the invasion force to withdraw.

About 1300, Admiral Fletcher entered flag plot. Walking over to look at the surface summary board, he was surprised to see that the invasion force was still anchored off the beach.

"What the hell's going on here?" he asked. "Why haven't the ships gotten under way?"

"I haven't been able to get the message through to them, Admiral," Rankin replied. "I'm afraid their radio is out."

"Keep trying, and let me know as soon as you reach them. I'll be out on the bridge," he replied. Turning to leave, he said, "If they don't hurry and get out of there before Castro's planes return, they're going to be plastered."

"Yes sir, Admiral, I know," Rankin replied. Picking up the handset, he tried to raise the *Blagar* again. Still there was no answer. By now he was beginning to suspect what had happened, that Jake had turned off his receiver.

"At least someone around here has the balls to do the right thing," he said under his breath.

Earlier on in the day, high in the air over the landing zone, the fighter pilots from the *Essex* had had a bird's-eye view of the action going on below them. Watching Castro's planes bomb and strafe the ships and boats, they repeatedly asked for permission to attack, and repeatedly their request was denied. Killing off the six planes would have been duck soup for them, yet all they could do was stand by and watch.

Returning to the carrier, one of the pilots slammed his helmet against the bulkhead in disgust. Another was in tears. All were frustrated, and all were ashamed.

At 1345 Castro's planes reappeared over the landing zone. Sergeant McCormick saw them first, coming in low over the beach. Confident now that they knew the American jets were not going to interfere, they homed in for the kill. Once again the sky lit up with tracers as the ragtag force fought valiantly back.

On their first run, the *Rio Escondido* was hit by rockets from one of the T33s. The drums of gasoline she was carrying on deck exploded in a giant ball of fire. In a matter of seconds the whole ship was engulfed in flames. Crew members jumped over the side, swimming away, trying to escape. The remaining LCVP, still in commission, rushed over to pick them up.

A few seconds later the LCU, which was still dead in the water from the earlier attack, took a direct hit from a 500-pound bomb dropped by one of the B26s. In a matter of seconds she disappeared beneath the surface.

Jake watched in horror, realizing Chief Gomez was on board the LCU. Picking up the walkie-talkie, he called for Bosun Knisel. "Mad Dog One, this is Mad Dog, over."

"This is Mad Dog One, over," Knisel replied.

"Bosun, get on over to where the LCU went down, and see if there are any survivors. Chief Gomez was on board."

"Oh, God, no! Not Gomez!" the bosun exclaimed. Shoving the Cuban helmsman aside, he took over the wheel. Ramming the throttles to full, he came about and headed for the site where the boat had gone down.

Jake didn't have much time to think about Gomez as the planes kept on coming, pressing their attack, making run after run on the nearly defenseless ships. A rocket from a Sea Fury struck the *Marsopa* right at the waterline, ripping a large hole in her side. She began rapidly listing to port. The *Atlantico* was hit by a rocket, suffering major damage to her superstructure.

As with the first attack, it was over as quickly as it began. Once they had expended their weapons, the planes retreated toward Havana, the T33s doing victory rolls in the sky. This time they were totally unscathed.

On board the *Blagar*, Jake put the locking pin in the 50-caliber machine gun he had been firing. The barrel was glowing red. Turning around, he looked about him, assessing the damage. Luckily, the *Blagar* had escaped again, suffering only minor damage.

Gazing out over the landing zone, however, it was another story. The bay was strewn with the wreckage of ships and boats. Only two landing craft remained in commission—one LCU and one LCVP. The rest had either been sunk or were stranded on the beach. Off to starboard, the *Rio Escondido* was still ablaze, periodic explosions continuing to rip her apart as the ammunition she was carrying detonated from the heat of the fires. The *Marsopa* was sinking fast, and the master ordered his crew to abandon ship.

Arriving at the spot where the LCU had been sunk, Knisel slowed to steerageway and ordered the bow ramp lowered. The surface of the water was covered with diesel oil and floating debris. From the wheel house, he could see three oil-soaked bodies floating amid the wreckage. There was no sign of any survivors. He turned the wheel back over to the Cuban coxswain and went forward to assist in hoisting the bodies on board. He recognized one, as one of the Cubans assigned to the boat crew. The other two bodies were mangled beyond recognition. From the clothing they were wearing, he knew neither of them was Lefty Gomez.

Drifting downwind away from the scene, Knisel ordered the coxswain to bring her about and make one more pass through the oil slick. He hoped beyond hope that Gomez might still be alive, even though he now knew it was hopeless.

As the boat slowly made its way back through the slick, Knisel thought he saw something floating in the water. As they came closer, he saw it was a baseball hat. Snagging it with a boat hook, he brought it on board. From the name "Lefty" on the peak, he knew it belonged to Gomez. It was the one they had given to him at a staff party back in Miami. From then on he had worn it constantly.

Heading back to the *Blagar* to drop off the bodies, Knisel called Jake on the radio and relayed the bad news.

Realizing that Gomez was dead, Jake felt like he had been hit in the stomach, knowing he was the one who had ordered Gomez to be on board the doomed LCU.

Arriving alongside, Knisel climbed the ladder to the bridge. He was slouched over. He looked like he had aged a lifetime.

"What do we do now, Commander?" he asked.

"We keep going, Bosun," Jake replied. He was now more determined than ever.

"There are still supplies to unload. Let's get with it, Bosun. The planes won't be back for a couple of hours."

"Aye, aye, sir," Knisel replied, straightening up. After he'd gone, Jake ordered all the surviving ships to launch their lifeboats to assist with the unloading.

As the hot sun blazed down on them, the crews of the badly battered invasion fleet worked feverishly unloading supplies, all the while keeping a watchful eye on the sky in the direction of Havana, waiting for Castro's planes to return. The afternoon wore on, the hours ticking by, as the sun continued its relentless trek westward in the sky.

For some reason, the planes did not return. Jake wondered why. Concentrating his attention toward shore, he had failed to notice Commodore Blouin's destroyers silently taking station four miles to seaward, their 3 and 5 inch guns trained out at the ready.

The unloading continued on into the night. Around 2300 all the supplies had been put ashore.

Jake called Ramirez on the radio. "Mad Dog Two, this is Mad Dog, over."

"This is Mad Dog Two, over," Ramirez replied.

"We've finished the unloading, Jose'. I am ordering the ships to withdraw."

"Don't leave us. Please don't leave us," Ramirez pleaded.

"There is nothing more I can do right now, Jose'. I'm sorry. I will be standing by off shore."

Realizing the futility of his plea, Ramirez replied, "This is Mad Dog Two. I understand, Jake. It is not your fault, my friend." Slowly he set the radio down. He knew they were now all alone.

On board the *Blagar*, Jake gave the order for all ships to get under way and rendezvous outside the 12-mile limit.

Pulling alongside in the remaining LCU, Knisel hollered up to Jake on the bridge.

"What are we going to do with the VP?" he asked.

"Take off the crew, and then sink it," Jake replied. When you're finished, follow me on out. We'll decide what we're going to do with the LCU after that."

One after the other, the four ships remaining in commission picked up anchor, got under way, and headed out to sea. Flames from the *Rio Escondido* and *Houston* bathed the landing zone in an eerie red glow. Jake couldn't bear to look back. It was like leaving the cemetery after the funeral of a close friend, except in this case it was even worse. The fate of his friends had yet to be determined. As they were making their way out from the beach, he saw the destroyers.

213

"How long have they been there?" he asked himself. If only they had showed up a little sooner when he could have used some help.

On board the *Essex*, Admiral Fletcher stayed on the flag bridge throughout the afternoon and into the evening. He was uncommonly quiet, keeping the frustration he must have felt to himself. In flag plot, Rankin continued trying to raise Jake on the radio. When the radar showed the ships to be under way, he breathed a sigh of relief. He relayed the news to the admiral, who finally stopped his pacing back and forth.

Arriving outside the 12-mile limit, the *Blagar* rendezvoused with the other ships from the invasion fleet and stood by, awaiting orders.

Meanwhile on board the *Essex,* pilots returning from their combat air patrol were beside themselves with anger. This was not what they had been trained for. Had they been permitted to intervene, they were confident they could have made a difference. There were times during the day when Commander Rankin wished they had disobeyed their orders, as Jake had done, and attacked anyway. In the wardroom that evening, the conversations among the aviators were frequently punctuated with the phrase, "Goddamn politicians."

Earlier in the day, after they had initially escorted the ships into the landing zone, Commodore Blouin's destroyers had taken station just outside the 12-mile limit, awaiting orders from the task group commander. Their crews had been at battle stations since dawn, in anticipation of an attack from Castro's planes.

Sitting in his chair on the starboard wing of the bridge, the commodore had listened to the tactical situation unfold on the Pritac radio circuit. Hearing the message that the air cover had been withdrawn, he knew the invasion was doomed. Turning to Greg Lyman,

214

standing nearby, he said, "Those poor bastards. They're going to get slaughtered."

"From the reports of the *Essex* pilots, they already have taken quite a beating," Lyman replied.

Later, when Jake failed to acknowledge the order to withdraw, Blouin exclaimed in disbelief, "You know what, I think he's turned his radio off. You'd better alert all ships to stand by for a rescue mission."

Following the afternoon attack, Blouin couldn't take it any longer. He realized they were not going to be receiving orders to assist. He decided to take matters into his own hands. Calling out for Lyman, he said, "Send out a message, Code Red. We're going in."

"Aye, aye, sir," Lyman replied enthusiastically.

Back at the landing zone, on board the *Blagar*, with his receiver turned off, Jake was unaware of Commodore Blouin's decision to come to his aid.

Approaching the landing zone, Blouin ordered his ships to take up station four miles to seaward of the invasion force. He hoped his presence so close offshore would deter Castro's planes from further attacks on the invasion force. Secretly, he hoped to draw their fire, giving him an excuse to shoot them down. Patrolling back and forth, they waited. For whatever reason, the planes did not return. Perhaps Castro did not want to push his luck too far.

Only when the invasion force had safely retreated beyond the 12-mile limit did Commodore Blouin order his ships out of the area.

With the invasion fleet out of the picture, Castro concentrated his full force on the Cuban Brigade ashore. Now that the Americans had shown they would *not* be coming to the aid of their Cuban brothers, he was confident that victory would only be a matter of time.

The Brigade fought on valiantly, but under the onslaught of Castro's air force and recently acquired Russian tanks and artillery, they didn't stand a chance. They were steadily driven back into the swamps, where they were surrounded by Castro's army. Running out of ammunition and supplies, they finally surrendered less than seventy-two hours after they had landed. A ham radio operator in New Jersey picked up their last radio signal: "This is Radio Cuba Libre. Why will no one help us? When will help come?" After that all was silent.

The magnitude of the disaster had now begun to sink in. On Tuesday night Commodore Blouin again ordered his ships back to the landing area, this time to search for survivors.

CHAPTER 31

Saturday, September 21, 1968, Miami

In Coconut Grove, in the dim light of La Paloma supper club, Jose' Ramirez continued his story, speaking slowly in a monotone voice. His mind continued to relive the events of the past.

"The information we were receiving from our sources inside Cuba was very disturbing. Castro had become paranoid. Obsessed with the fear of invasion, he rushed to build up his forces.

"Although morale improved when we got word that the invasion was rescheduled for April, the landing unfortunately, got off to a bad start. On the very first wave two of the assault boats were lost, and from then on the landing fell farther and farther behind schedule.

"At 0620 that morning, I parachuted in along with the rest of my group. Landing without incident, we set up a defense line just outside the village of San Blas.

"Shortly after dawn, six planes appeared in the sky off to the west. At first I thought they were Americans, but when the sky lit up with tracers from the ships in the harbor, I knew they belonged to Castro. Soon afterward, I heard the explosions from the bombs and rockets, and saw the columns of smoke rising above the trees.

"After the planes had gone, I called Jake on the radio to find out what had occurred. It was then I learned that the air cover we had been promised had been withdrawn. I knew it was all over for us. It would be only a matter of time. I couldn't believe what had happened....that we had been betrayed by our American friends."

He paused to light up another cigarette. His hands had started to shake again. Taking a puff, he inhaled deeply before going on.

"For awhile, where we were, everything remained quiet. Around noontime, we heard tanks in the distance, coming up the road behind us. They were followed by a line of our troops. Joining them, we continued inland to the village of Covadonga, where the people lined the streets shouting, "Cuba Libre." Many of the men in the village volunteered to join us, and we passed out rifles and ammunition to them. On the outside of the town, we set up a defensive perimeter and dug in for the night. We knew Castro's army was on the way, but we didn't know when they would get there. We tried to get some sleep, but everyone was too tense."

"Sometime after midnight we saw the lights from many vehicles approaching from the direction of Havana. We opened fire once they got within range. The battle had now begun.

"At first, things went well for us. Our tanks destroyed several trucks loaded with troops. They also were successful in knocking out a number of their artillery pieces. But then things began to change for the worse.

"Once they were in position, Castro's forces began to bombard us with 122-millimeter howitzers, rockets, and machine-gun fire. Our men fought bravely, but our antiquated artillery and Sherman tanks were no match for Castro's recently acquired Russian equipment. All through the night they pounded us.

"Between the noise of the exploding shells, I could hear the sounds of the wounded crying for help. We provided what comfort we could, but our medical supplies were few. Most had been destroyed when the *Houston* was hit. We also lost our communications van. Now the only means we had of communicating with the rest of the Brigade, dug in at the head of the bay north of Playa Larga, was by portable radio."

Ramirez paused again in his story. Mike and Laroque sat by in silence. After a moment he continued.

"When daylight came, we realized our position was desperate. We had not slept in forty-eight hours. Our ammunition was running low. Desperate, I elected to make one more appeal for help. I tried to raise Jake on the radio, but there was no reply. I then tried to get through to Colonel Martinez, who was with the other group in Playa Larga, and finally raised him. He ordered us to fall back to San Blas, where he would attempt to join forces with us.

"Shortly after daylight Castro's planes reappeared. Now that the invasion fleet had been driven off, they concentrated their attacks on us. Under constant pounding from the tanks and artillery, and attack from the air, we were forced to retreat back into the swamps.

"Only one of our tanks remained in commission. That night the attack continued without letup. Standing in water sometimes up to our waist, we could not sleep for fear of drowning. The mosquitoes drove us crazy. By now we were almost out of ammunition.

"Some of the men tried to escape to the mountains and join up with our forces there. A few managed to make it back to the beaches, where they were rescued by two American destroyers. For the rest of us, time was running out.

"Now that there was nothing to stop them, Castro's tanks drove down the road to the beach behind us. We were now completely surrounded. Any hope of escape was lost. The next day we surrendered, but our ordeal was only beginning.

"We were loaded up on trucks for the trip to Havana, while all along the way people lined the side of the road, shaking their fists, spitting on us, calling us pigs and traitors. Once we arrived in Havana, we were paraded through the streets to the jeering of the crowds. It was not the triumphant return we had envisioned.

"After our public humiliation, we were hauled off to prison, where we were told we were criminals and would be treated accordingly. That night I was thrown into a stinking cell. All alone, I considered what fate had in store for me. The next day the interrogations and torture began."

He paused, burying his head in hands. The memories were too painful. For the first time since he had begun, Mike Canfield spoke.

"There is no need for you to go any further, Mr. Ramirez, he said. "We have heard enough."

Ramirez raised up his head. Tears were streaming down his cheeks. "No!" he objected. "I need to finally put it to rest."

The nightclub was now almost empty. The band had stopped, and most of the guests had left. In the now quiet, darkened room, Ramirez continued, speaking slowly, stopping frequently to regain control of his emotions. He went on to describe how he had been tortured, and about his false confession.

"After they obtained a confession from me, they left me alone. For the next year in that prison cell, I relived the nightmare of the invasion over and over again in my mind. How I cursed the Americans for abandoning us, for leaving us to die in that swamp! I even convinced myself that Jake had known all along that there would be no air cover. It was only after I returned to Miami that I learned how he had ignored orders to withdraw and stayed on, in the face of great danger, to unload our supplies."

When he had finished, Mike and Laroque sat silent for a moment, not knowing what to say. Finally Mike spoke. Having difficulty finding the words to express the sense of shame he felt for what his country had done, he simply said, "Mr. Ramirez, I want to thank you for talking with us. I know how difficult it was for you."

"I did it for Jake," Ramirez replied. "He was our one true friend."

Saying goodbye to Mike and Buzz, Ramirez called Maria.

When the phone rang, she rushed to pick it up. "Jose', is that you?" she said.

"Yes, it's me," he replied. "I am on the way home. It is finished. It is now over."

CHAPTER 32

April, 20, 1961, At sea off the coast of Cuba,

Once the Brigade had surrendered, Admiral Fletcher dissolved Task Group 26.2, detaching all units to return to their respective bases. Upon receipt of the message, the *Essex* departed her position fifty miles north of Point Xray and set course for Guantanamo Bay.

Delivering the Cubans to the *Blagar* that the *Eaton* and *Murray* had rescued earlier, Commodore Blouin gave the order for his destroyers to form up in column and set Condition II for peacetime steaming. They then retraced their route back to Norfolk.

The remnants of the invasion fleet received orders from Washington to return to Puerto Cabezas. Not knowing what to do with the remaining LCU, Jake ordered Bosun Knisel to scuttle it. Once this had been done, the *Blagar*, in company with what was left of the invasion force, limped back toward Nicaragua. Everyone on board was in a depressed mood, thinking about the Cuban friends they had left behind. Belcher and Dick Harris remained in their staterooms for the entire trip.

The next morning, after they departed Cuban waters, Jake was sitting at a table in the officer's mess when Knisel came in. Pouring a cup of coffee from the pot on the warmer, he asked, "Mind if I join you, Commander?"

"Sure, Bosun, sit down," Jake replied.

While drinking their coffee, they both sat in silence. Jake was not in any mood for conversation. The bosun spoke first. "Don't go blaming yourself, Commander."

Jake continued to stare morosely at the bulkhead. "What the hell went wrong, Bosun? What could I have done differently?"

"For chrissakes, you did everything you could," Knisel replied. "The whole frigging operation had 'Mickey Mouse' written all over it from the beginning! If there is anyone at fault, it's those Harvard pukes up in Washington. Once they chickened out on the air cover, that's all she wrote."

"Then how come I feel so guilty?" Jake asked.

"Face it, Commander. We all got screwed."

Arriving in Puerto Cabezas, Jake and Knisel caught a hop aboard one of the C54s returning to the States. During the flight both sat in silence. In the terminal at Homestead, Knisel held out his hand.

"Well, Commander, I guess this is where we say goodbye. It's been a pleasure knowing you. You take care now, and just remember, don't let it get to you."

"Thanks for everything, Bosun. I don't know what I would've done without you," Jake replied. "When will you be heading back to San Diego?"

"I think I'll take a couple of days leave before I head back. I thought I might go up to Brooklyn and look in on Gomez' family."

After they said goodbye, Knisel checked in with air ops to see when the next flight to McGuire Air Force Base in New Jersey was scheduled to depart, while Jake caught the base shuttle to Miami International, where he purchased a ticket for Norfolk.

While waiting for his flight to be called, he picked up a copy of the *Miami Herald* to read on the plane, and glanced at the front page. The headlines stared out at him: "Kennedy Takes Full Responsibility." Finding a seat in the lounge, he quickly read through the lead story. It began, "After steadfastly denying any American involvement in the invasion for five days, the president has finally admitted to the American people that the Cuban Brigade had been trained and supported by the CIA." Jake read on. There was no mention of his having canceled the air support promised the Cubans. Disgusted, he put the paper down and left it lying on a chair in the lounge.

He thought about calling Ramirez' wife. Going over to a phone booth, he picked up a phone book and started to look through it. Somehow he couldn't bring himself to dial the number. How could he explain what had happened?

Arriving in Norfolk, he hired a taxi to take him to the amphib base, where he checked back into his room at the BOQ.

The next morning he returned to work. After morning quarters, he stopped by Captain Ervin's office to let him know he was back. Knocking on the door, he asked to come in.

Ervin was surprised to see him. "Jake, it's good to have you back. We've missed you around here." Motioning toward a chair, he said, "Come on in and sit down."

"Believe me, it's good to be back," Jake replied, taking a seat. He wondered how much the captain knew. With all the headlines in the papers over the past week, he must have suspected something, but he didn't broach the subject, nor did any of his fellow officers.

That evening, after leaving the building, Jake stopped by the officers club. Secretly, he hoped Cindy would be working, although he didn't quite know how he was going to explain his not calling or writing. Taking a seat at the bar, he ordered a draft beer and took a look around. Another girl, whom he didn't recognize, was on duty. The bartender was new as well.

"Nursing his beer, he casually asked, "Cindy off tonight?"

"Cindy who?" the bartender replied. "There's been no Cindy here since I started, back around the first of the year. Come to think of it, I do remember one of the other girls mentioning her. As best I can recall, she quit working here around Christmas. Said she was going to sign up for some classes at Old Dominion. Seems she met a professor there, and they've been going out together. Why, did you know her?"

"We went out together a couple of times," Jake replied. "I was just curious as to whatever happened to her, that's all." At the other end of the bar, someone raised his glass, signaling for another drink.

"You'll have to excuse me, Commander, I have to go now."

Jake finished his beer, dropped a dollar bill on the bar and went back to his room.

Slowly life returned to normal. As the days passed, the events of the last six months began to recede in memory. Then it happened. One afternoon, upon returning to the office, there was a message on his desk, requesting that he stop by the captain's office before leaving for the day.

Walking down the passage, he knocked on the door to the skipper's office. "You wanted to see me, sir?" he asked.

"Come on in, Jake, and shut the door."

Ervin had a worried look on his face. Motioning to a chair, he said, "Sit down, Jake."

After he was seated, Ervin said, "I had a call from BuPers this morning. There's been a fact-finding commission convened at Fort Myer to inquire into this Bay of Pigs fiasco. You are being subpoenaed to testify. They want you in Washington first thing Monday morning."

Jake started to get up. "I was afraid of this."

"Is there anything you would like to tell me?" Ervin asked.

Jake thought about it for a moment. It was tempting to talk it over with someone, to get it off his chest. Thinking better of it, he replied, "I don't think I should say anything right now, Captain."

"I understand," Ervin replied. "Look, Jake, if there is anything I can do, please don't hesitate to ask."

"Thanks, Captain, I appreciate that."

That night Jake had a difficult time going to sleep. "What do they want from me?" he asked himself but he already knew the answer.

CHAPTER 33

May 1961, Washington

On Sunday, Jake caught the afternoon shuttle out of Norfolk, arriving at Washington's National Airport around 1730. Retrieving his bag, he exited the terminal and hailed a taxi to take him to Ft. Myer, where he checked into the BOQ.

Getting up the next morning, he put on his service dress blue uniform and had breakfast in the officers' dining room. Then he walked along the quadrangle to the headquarters building where the hearings were being conducted. Walking up the steps of the large red brick building, he entered the door and asked the corporal on duty where the Harmon Commission was meeting. The corporal directed him to the second floor.

Outside the door of the hearing room, an MP sergeant stood at parade rest. Seeing Jake approach, he came to attention and saluted. Jake introduced himself and notified him that he had been called as a witness before the commission. The sergeant motioned to a wooden bench in the passageway by the door.

"Please be seated, sir. I will advise General Harmon you are here as soon as they take a break. Right now they are in the process of interviewing another witness."

Jake took a seat on the bench. Around 1030 the door to the hearing room opened and Ray Belcher came out. Turning, he saw Jake. Jake started to say something, but Belcher turned away. Looking straight ahead, he walked briskly by without speaking. Jake's eyes followed him down the passage. From behind him, he heard the sergeant say, "Lieutenant Commander Barnes, they are ready for you now, sir."

Jake stood up and walked through the large double oak doors. The hearing room was one used by the Army to conduct general courts-martial. Directly in front of him, on a raised platform, were seven desks arranged in a row. An American flag and the Army flag flanked either side. Off to the right was a smaller desk for the reporter. Facing the platform was a single chair.

Jake marched in and stood at attention. He could feel all eyes in the room on him, staring at him. Except for General Harmon, all the other members of the commission were dressed in civilian clothes. Jake recognized several of them from their photos in the newspaper. One of those he recognized was the attorney general. Two of the others were Senator Roberts, the ranking Republican in the Senate, and Representative Jacobs, the Democratic whip in the House.

The court reporter approached, holding a Bible in his hand. Standing in front of Jake, he said, "Please raise your right hand, and place your left one on the Bible." Jake did so.

"Now repeat after me. Do you swear to answer all the questions put to you by this commission, truthfully, fully, and honestly to the best of your ability? Do you?"

"I do," Jake replied.

After he had been sworn, General Harmon said, "Please sit down, Commander." Jake sat down. "For the record, please state your full name and rank."

"Jake Edward Barnes, lieutenant commander, United States Navy," he answered.

"Before we get started with the questions, I think you should know what this hearing is all about. We have been asked by the president to conduct an inquiry into the facts and circumstances on what went wrong during Operation Pluto and to report our findings and recommendations. I must also warn you that the proceedings of this hearing are top secret. You are not to reveal the contents of your testimony, or of any of the questions asked of you, to anyone outside this room. Do you understand?"

"Yes sir, I understand," Jake replied.

"Okay, now that we have that out of the way, let's get on with it. First, would you please tell us what role you played in Operation Pluto?"

"I was responsible for training the Cuban Brigade in amphibious operations and in drafting up the plan for the assault landing," Jake replied.

"In your professional opinion, do you think the Cubans were adequately prepared to carry out their mission?"

"Considering the fact that none of them had any military training, and the time constraints placed upon us, I believe we did the best we could," Jake replied.

Before he could go on, the attorney general interrupted. "Please, let's not be evasive Commander Barnes. Either they were adequately trained or they were not. Which is it?"

"I wasn't trying to be evasive, sir. I was only trying to qualify my answer."

"Just answer the question."

"In my opinion, the training was adequate," Jake replied.

"Then how do you account for the fiasco that occurred?" the attorney general asked.

"Training was only part of it," Jake answered. "There are many factors which enter into whether an amphibious operation is successful or not."

Pressing him further, the attorney general asked, "Perhaps you could enlighten us as to what these factors might be?"

"The strength of the enemy force, planning, the element of surprise, adequate support, morale, leadership, superior equipment, timing. All enter into it, along with a lot of luck."

"Well, we sure as hell were short on the latter! Didn't you say you were also responsible for preparing the invasion plan?"

"Yes sir, I prepared the rough draft."

"It appears you didn't do your job very well in that area either," he retorted sarcastically.

General Harmon interrupted, saying, "Mr. Attorney General, please. Recriminations aren't going to get us anywhere. This is not a trial. Let us try to remember we are on a fact-finding mission. Before we go assigning any blame, we first need to ascertain what happened."

Directing his next remarks to Jake, the general said, "Perhaps, Commander Barnes, it might be helpful if you could start at the beginning and give us an account of what happened from your point of view."

For the next hour and a half Jake recounted the chain of events that led up to the invasion and beyond, from the time he arrived in Miami in October until his return to Nicaragua a few weeks previous to the hearing.

After he had finished, General Harmon glanced up at the clock on the wall. Addressing the members of the commission, he said. "Let's adjourn for lunch. What do you say we reconvene back here at 1330?" To Jake, he added, "Commander Barnes, you are excused for now, but please be back by 1330."

Jake walked to the officers club nearby. His stomach was tied in knots. He didn't feel much like eating, but he ordered a salad and bowl of soup anyway, to help get his mind off of the hearing. After lunch he went back to the headquarters building and sat down on the bench outside the door. About twenty minutes later he was recalled. Entering the hearing room, he resumed his seat at the desk in front of the panel.

After he was settled, General Harmon reopened the hearings.

229

"Commander Barnes, I want to remind you that the oath you took previously is still binding."

"Yes sir," Jake replied.

"This morning you went over with us in detail what transpired before and during the invasion. Now I would like to hear your opinion of where it went wrong."

Jake thought for a moment before replying. "Well, sir, in my opinion, there were a number of mistakes made. The equipment assigned to the operation was out of date and in poor condition. The civilian ships assigned to carry out the invasion were inadequate, and they were poorly equipped to defend themselves. There was also a breakdown in intelligence. We failed to detect the buildup of Castro's forces, and we failed to do a proper beach reconnaissance, relying solely on U2 photos. All of these were contributing factors, but the operation failed mainly because we did not execute the invasion plan as it was originally conceived. Had the operation taken place in January, before Castro had a chance to build up his forces, and had the air and naval support been provided as promised, there was a reasonable chance of its being successful."

Before he could continue, the attorney general interrupted, "Isn't it true you failed to take into account a reef directly in front of the beach? From what we've been told, it was clearly visible on the U2 photos."

Jake wondered how they knew about the reef. He then remembered. Belcher had testified before him.

"Yes sir, they did show up on the photos, but the photo interpreters had identified them as patches of seaweed."

"Come on, Commander. Obviously they could tell the difference between seaweed and coral," the attorney general said skeptically.

"As a matter of fact, I was concerned about their interpretation, and asked for a live recon of the area. However, the request was disapproved," Jake replied.

Changing the subject, the attorney general pressed on. "Why did you recommended landing in an area filled with swamps, or did you think they were seaweed too?"

"Sir, there were many factors which entered into choosing the landing site. The beach itself was firm. There were good roads leading from the area. It was reasonably close to Havana, as well as to the rebel strongholds in the mountains, and it was in a remote area, providing us a fair chance of getting ashore undetected. I might add, the swamps did not become a factor until after the mission had already failed."

"May I ask a question of the witness?" Senator Roberts, the Republican from Iowa, asked.

"Certainly, Senator," General Harmon replied.

"Something's been troubling me, Commander. We have been told by another witness that you disobeyed a direct order to withdraw the force from the landing area, resulting in the loss of a number of lives, as well as two ships. I would like to hear your side of the story."

"It's true, Senator. I did ignore an order to withdraw. At the time, the landing force was ashore, but much of their supplies remained on board, yet to be unloaded. Without this ammunition and fuel, they didn't have a chance. At the time, I also felt that I was in a better position to evaluate the situation. Besides, sir, I just couldn't abandon the Brigade. They were our allies and friends."

"Your dedication is admirable, Commander," the attorney general said. "It's too bad you didn't have the same consideration for the well-being of your crews as well."

"Sir, there are risks in any combat situation. We knew that going in. That's what we get paid for. It goes along with the territory."

"Is it not also true that you permitted one of your staff, an American, to go ashore, in direct violation of orders?"

"Yes sir, I did, but without his help in locating the reef, the landing would have failed before it had even gotten started." Jake was beginning to lose his cool. He lashed back. "If someone back here in Washington hadn't chickened out, and we had been provided the support we had been promised, maybe we wouldn't be here discussing what went wrong."

The attorney general glared back at him. Turning to General Harmon, he said, "It seems to me it is not the lack of support, but this type of renegade behavior which resulted in the mess we now find ourselves in."

General Harmon cautioned, "Mr. Attorney General, perhaps we should reserve these judgments until after the hearing is completed." Turning to Jake, he said, "Commander Barnes, please refrain from anymore outbursts."

The session continued on until late in the afternoon. Finally, General Harmon concluded the questioning, asking the panel if there were any more questions of this witness. There being none, he excused Jake, advising him that he was subject to recall, and again warned him about discussing his testimony with anyone other than those present in the hearing room.

Jake left the room in a depressed mood. He was totally drained. He walked back to the BOQ and fell across the bed. He knew his career was over. He was also certain he was going to be court-martialed.

Back inside the hearing room, the board met in closed session, with the discussion focusing on Jake's testimony and his culpability for disobeying orders.

Senator Roberts spoke in his defense. "I think we are making too much of the fact that Lieutenant Commander Barnes ignored an order. Aren't we being a bit hypocritical? We keep saying that we are seeking military leaders with a sense of loyalty and ethics, who take charge, are innovative, and exercise leadership. It would seem to me Mr. Barnes exhibited all these qualities, as well as a great deal of courage to boot. The easiest thing for him to have done was to abandon the Cubans, leaving them to be slaughtered. Instead, he saw his duty was to stay and do the job he was sent to do in the face of overwhelming odds, I might add. Perhaps we should be focusing more closely on why he was not given the support he so desperately needed." There were a couple of murmurs of assent from the other panel members.

In rebuttal, General Harmon said, "Your point is well taken, Senator, but we can't allow people to go around ignoring orders just because they happen to disagree with them. Besides, it's a moot point. It is not our job to decide on Lieutenant Commander Barnes' guilt or innocence. This is for a court-martial to decide. Our job is only to determine what occurred and pass on our findings and recommendations to the president."

The attorney general broke in, "General Harmon, I agree that we can't allow Barnes to get away with disobeying an order, but before we go recommending a court-martial there are some factors we need to consider. We can't afford to drag this matter out in public. It is imperative that we put it behind us. The president has an important summit meeting coming up with the Russians. We need to get this out of the news. We just can't have the press turning Barnes into some sort of folk hero."

When he had finished, Senator Roberts responded, "What you really mean is, there's too much dirty laundry in the closet to be aired out in public. Let's be honest here. There are a lot of others who have committed more serious offenses than Lieutenant Commander Barnes. At least he conducted himself with bravery, and has admitted his mistakes, unlike some *others* I could mention."

"Senator, I resent your innuendo," the attorney general angrily retorted.

General Harmon intervened, saying, "Gentlemen, please. Let's stop this bickering. The fact still remains that Barnes admittedly disobeyed a direct order. I still say we can't ignore that, or allow him to get away with it."

"And I say we can't afford the publicity of a court-martial," the attorney general objected. "There are other ways to punish him other than by giving him a court-martial. Instead, why don't we recommend in our report that the Navy Department flag his record, citing the find-

233

ings of this commission. That way, at least, we can ensure he will never be promoted."

After giving it some thought, General Harmon reluctantly agreed, conceding that a public court-martial would not be in the best interest of the country at this time.

Senator Roberts, however, was still not convinced. "It still doesn't address the question as to why the air cover was suddenly withdrawn, and who was responsible for making that decision. These are the people we should be going after. They are a helluva lot more responsible for this debacle than Barnes."

"You're right, Senator, General Harmon replied. "One thing at a time. Right now we're talking about Barnes. Look, gentlemen, it's getting late. Why don't we take a vote, and put this issue behind us?"

The members voted 5 to 2 to go along with the attorney general, to recommend flagging Jake's record.

CHAPTER 34

September 23, 1968, Washington

Mike Canfield arrived at the Annex at 0800. Parking his car, he entered the board room, poured a cup of coffee, and carried it over to his desk.

A short time later, Admiral Wilkerson arrived. By this time the board's work was nearly finished. All the records had been reviewed and voted on. They had only to decide on the last few selections.

At 0900, the board gathered in the tank. Twenty-three numbers remained uncommitted. Before making a final determination, the board decided to review once again all the records for individuals scoring between 65 and 75 in the voting.

While Commander Anderson, the recorder and his assistants retrieved the records and got them ready for projection, the board took a short break. Returning, they went through each record again to refresh their memory before taking another vote. Once they were satisfied, the records were projected once again, this time to be voted on. Once they had been voted on and the results tabulated, the recorder announced the results to the board. They then voted to select the twenty-three individuals who had received the highest scores.

On the way to lunch in the cafeteria, Jim Lansky came up alongside Mike. "I see our man Barnes made the cut."

"So he did," Mike replied.

"You sure as hell don't seem too excited about it."

"It may not be over yet," Mike replied.

"What do you mean by that?"

"I can't say. You'll just have to wait and see."

After lunch, Admiral Wilkerson dismissed the board for the day. There was nothing left to do until the list of selectees had been chopped through the various branches of the bureau. On the way home, Mike stopped by his office in the Pentagon to catch up on some work.

The next morning, in the board room, the members sat around, waiting for word that the list had been cleared. Around 0900, Lieutenant Commander Grieves came in to tell the recorder that he had a phone call in Selection Board Services. A few minutes later, Anderson returned and spoke briefly with the admiral. When he had finished, Wilkerson asked for everyone's attention.

"The recorder has just informed me that a representative from the performance division would like to meet with us in the tank at 0930."

On the way down the passage to the tank, Jim Lansky came up to Mike. "I wonder what the hell this is all about?"

"I guess we'll soon find out."

"Somehow, I have a feeling you already know."

In the tank, Mike settled in his chair, preparing himself for what he knew was coming up. After all the members were seated, Grieves escorted a man wearing civilian clothes into the room. He introduced him to the board as Captain Jenkins from the performance division. Leaving the room, he closed the door behind him.

Adjusting his glasses, Jenkins began, "Gentlemen, as is the procedure with all boards, my office is responsible for reviewing the list of selectees. In certain cases we possess information on an individual which is not a part of his official record, but which, nevertheless, could bear on his suitability for promotion.

"In the case of your board, there is one officer on your list who we believe to be unsuited for promotion. The individual's name is Jake Edward Barnes. We are asking that you reconsider his selection."

"So this was it," Lansky said to himself. This was why Mike had been so evasive. Before the captain had a chance to go on, he interrupted him. "Captain Jenkins, could you give us some reason why Barnes should not be promoted? Removing an officer's name from the list after he has been selected is not something to be taken lightly."

"Unfortunately, in this particular case the information we have in our possession is classified. Suffice it to say, there is something in his background which we believe makes him unsuited for promotion."

"But I thought that was our job, to determine his suitability for promotion," Jim retorted. "If there's some reason he should not be promoted, then I think we have a right to know the reason why."

"I am sorry, sir, but that is all I'm at liberty to say. However, I must advise you that if you insist on selecting him, his name will be removed from the list."

"That sounds like some sort of threat," Lansky replied. He was getting angry.

Before he could go on, Wilkerson intervened. "Thank you, Captain Jenkins. That will be all. I think we can handle it from here."

After he had left the room, Wilkerson said, "Well, gentlemen, you heard the captain. I propose we strike Barnes' name and select the next officer down on the list."

Lansky was still upset.

"With all due respect, Admiral, I disagree. The precept convening our board directs us to select those individuals we believe best fitted to perform the duties of the grade of commander. Over the past couple of weeks we've worked our asses off to do just that. Now we have someone come in here and tell us to take one of the names off the list. Then he refuses to give us a reason, other than some namby-pamby

237

about it being classified. Everyone of us in here is cleared for top secret, so what the hell are they trying to hide?"

"I agree," Don Brown interjected. When we arrived here they gave us all this stuff about how the Navy was counting on us to do our job. Now they're treating us like we're a bunch of children. I think we should take a vote." A chorus of assents could be heard around the room.

"Before we all go off half cocked, we need to think about it. They must have their reasons," Wilkerson replied. "Besides, like the captain said, if we persist, his name is going to be removed from the list anyway. What we will be doing, in effect, is denying another officer the opportunity for promotion."

"I don't think that's the issue here," Lansky responded. "We were assigned to do a job, and we've done it to the best of our ability. What happens after that is not our problem. I guess we now know the reason why Barnes was passed over before. The other board knuckled under, but dammit, based on his record he deserves to be promoted. Our voting confirmed that."

"What about that report back in 1961? No one has yet been able to explain that away," Wilkerson replied.

Until now Mike had been silent, listening to the debate going on. It was now his turn to speak.

"Admiral, I think I might be able to shed some light on that."

Wilkerson realized he was losing control of the board. He began to tap his fingers in irritation.

"Please do, Captain Canfield. Maybe then we can put this matter to rest."

Mike stood up and turned to face the board. "As you recall," he began, "I was the first reviewer on Barnes' record. You also remember the troubling fitness report when his reporting senior, a civilian, accused him, among other things, of disobeying a direct order. We were all perplexed as to why there was no disciplinary action taken, considering the seriousness of the charge."

"Make your point, Captain," Wilkerson admonished. "Please get on with it."

"Yes, sir," Mike replied.

"From early on, I suspected the report had something to do with the Bay of Pigs, so I did a little investigating on my own. To make a long story short, I flew down to Miami this past weekend and met with a Mr. Ramirez, an attorney who served with Barnes during the period in question. From him, I was able to learn what actually occurred."

"Let's move on, Captain."

"Yes sir," Mike replied. "I'm getting to the point. The morning of the invasion, while the landing was in progress, Castro's air force attacked the ships in the invasion force, causing extensive damage to them. Fearing a repeat attack, the ships were ordered to withdraw beyond the 12-mile limit, effectively leaving the landing force stranded on the beach. Realizing that without ammunition and fuel the invasion was doomed, Barnes chose to ignore the order, and in spite of repeated attacks from the air, continued with the unloading until all supplies were ashore. Only then did he order the ships to retire to safety beyond the 12-mile limit."

"But that still doesn't explain why he wasn't court-martialed for disobeying an order," Don Brown questioned.

"I don't have the answer to that, but I suspect the administration was afraid the press would get hold of it and blow it out of proportion. They didn't want the public to know how deeply we were involved, and that we had withdrawn the air cover at the last minute. It was less risky to flag his record, to keep him from getting promoted," Mike speculated.

The one thing all military personnel admired was courage in the face of danger. When Mike had finished, Chuck Diesel spoke up, "I'd say that took a lot of guts. If it were up to me, I'd have given him a medal."

"Are you finished, Captain?" Wilkerson asked.

239

"Yes sir, I am," Mike replied.

"All right then, let's put it to a vote, a straight up or down, yes or no, with the majority deciding."

The electronic score board lit up. Anderson read off the results for the record. "Eight yes, one no. The ayes have it. Barnes remains on the promotion list."

"I guess that does it, then," Wilkerson said, obviously unhappy with the outcome of the vote. "This board is now adjourned. Thank you very much, gentlemen. You are all free to leave." He got up from his chair and strode out of the room.

The rest of the members followed, returning to the board room to gather up their belongings and say their goodbyes. Before leaving, Jim Lansky approached Mike. "How about having lunch at the Flagship? I'm buying."

"In that case I'd be happy to," Mike replied.

"Captain Canfield," Admiral Wilkerson called out. "Would you mind staying on for a moment? I would like to have a word with you before you leave."

"Why don't you go on ahead, Jim. I'll meet you there."

After everyone had left Mike approached the admiral's desk. He was busy signing their detachment orders.

"You wanted to see me, Admiral?" he asked.

Admiral Wilkerson looked up from his work. "Yes, Captain, I do. I wanted to let you know I think you made a big mistake on this Barnes thing. What we have effectively done is to waste a number." He paused for a few seconds. "Now that I have said that, I also wanted to tell you I admire your dedication in following through, and doing what you believe is right. That's an admirable quality in any naval officer."

"Thank you, Admiral," Mike replied. "It has been my pleasure to have worked with you."

Wilkerson did not comment. He returned to signing orders.

Gathering up his belongings, Mike drove into the city. Exiting on Maine Avenue, he pulled into a lot across from the restaurant and parked the car. Inside, Lansky was waiting in the bar.

"What'd the admiral want to see you about?" Jim asked.

"Nothing much. Just wanted to tell me that he disagreed with me about Barnes."

"That was pretty obvious. I don't imagine he much liked what I had to say either."

Before Mike had a chance to reply, word came over the loudspeaker, "Lansky, party of two, your table is now ready."

After they were seated, Lansky asked. "How about some wine to celebrate?"

"Sounds good to me," Mike replied. "You choose."

When the waitress arrived, Lansky ordered a bottle of chardonnay. A short time later she returned with the bottle and a wine bucket. After she had left, Lansky raised his glass.

"Here's to an interesting couple of weeks."

"I'll drink to that," Mike replied.

Waiting for their entree, Lansky looked across the table at Mike. "You son of a gun, you knew all along Barnes had been flagged, didn't you? You wouldn't care to fill me in, would you?"

"Sorry, Jim. I'll admit I did know early on, but I can't tell you how. I gave my word."

"Do you actually think they'll strike his name off the list?"

"I honestly don't know," Mike replied. "We'll find out in a week or so."

After lunch Lansky and Mike said goodbye in front of the restaurant. They promised to keep in contact.

Mike decided to skip going in to the office. He drove home instead. For the first time in ages, he arrived home before Jen.

CHAPTER 35

Two weeks later

Mike had finally caught up with work in the office, and things had begun to get back to normal. Then one afternoon after lunch Buzz poked his head in the door. He held a copy of the *Navy Times* in his hand.

"The commander list is out," he said holding up the paper. "I noticed Barnes' name wasn't on it."

"Oh?" Mike replied. Laroque noticed the look of surprise on his face.

"You act like you didn't know," he said. It was now time for him to act surprised. "What the hell is going on here? You should know. For chrissakes, you were on the board."

"It's a long story, Buzz, and I am sorry I can't say anything more. Maybe someday."

Buzz look puzzled, but he didn't say anything.

That evening at dinner, Mike was quieter than normal. Jen knew something was bothering him. While they were having coffee, he told her the news. "The commander list was published today. Jake Barnes wasn't on it."

Getting up out of her chair, she came over to him. Standing behind him, she rubbed his neck and shoulders. "I'm sorry, Mike. I know how much you believed in him."

"It's not only about Barnes, Jen. It's more than that. It's about fairness and trust. Remember when you were a kid and believed in Santa Claus, and how you felt when you discovered it was all a hoax? It was a long time before you trusted anyone again."

Epilogue

Three years later

After he finished his tour of duty at OPNAV, Mike received orders to command the cruiser Newport News. He and Jen moved to Virginia Beach, where they moved into a new home at Witch Duck Point.

Completing his assignment at OPNAV, Buzz Laroque was transferred to duty as air operations officer at NAVAIRLANT. He and Mike remained good friends and visited each other often when the Newport News was in port.

Ray Belcher continued on as an assistant Director in the CIA. He aspired to head the agency one day.

Dick Harris was promoted to head the Latin Affairs Division in the State Department.

Jose' Ramirez continued to practice law in Miami.

Bosun Knisel retired from the Navy and went to work as a customs agent in San Diego.

Jake Barnes retired from the Navy with twenty years and moved into a two-room furnished apartment in Virginia Beach. A year later he was found dead, after a neighbor called the police when she noticed his newspapers had not been picked up for several days. The obituary did not list the cause of death.

HISTORICAL NOTE

In the days immediately following the Bay of Pigs invasion, after it became apparent that it was doomed to failure, President Kennedy met separately with former President Eisenhower and former Vice President Richard Nixon at Camp David to seek their advice. Both advised him to send in American troops to get rid of Castro once and for all.

Afraid of adverse reaction among our friends in Central and South America, as well as the Third World countries in the United Nations, Kennedy decided against the use of American forces. Instead, five days after the initial landings he made a radio address to the American people accepting full responsibility for the operation, without disclosing any of the details.

In the aftermath of the debacle, the president established a commission, headed by General Maxwell Taylor, to conduct an investigation into the matter. Although the findings of the commission was not made public, one of its members, Admiral Arleigh Burke, leaked information to the press that it was the president himself who had made the decision to withdraw the air cover at the last moment.

The report of the Taylor Commission is still classified.